For M.D.

I, A Child

Claire Hamilton

Solidus Press

Published by Solidus Press

For further information regarding this book,
see www.clairehamilton.com.

Typeset by Paul Manning

Printed in Poland by Totem

Art direction | alison@designandpurpose.com

ISBN 978 1 5272 3667 7

Josie

Having seen her, all I want to do is catch her. There is only one way. I must do it in Winsor and Newton hues. I must do it before the dream fades.

I run to my studio, reach for my palette and squeeze out orbs of colour. Pale chrome yellow and flake white with a touch of alizarin red for the skin – for she is pale, so pale. As for her eyes, the eyes that looked through, beyond me, those eyes will be cobalt blue muted with olive green, the pupils umber.

I position my canvas, dab at the pools of pigment and begin. I have to work fast. I must get the pallor of her skin, suggest the intensity of the eyes, their unearthliness. I caught something of that in the opening flurry. But it was only an impression. I glance at my watch. I can steal another hour and still make it to the clinic in time for the appointment. But first I must bring her to life. Turning back to the canvas, I press a drop of cadmium red onto my palette.

As the hour of the appointment approaches, I am stroking out her hair in yellow ochre. Faintly I hear my mobile blurt twice, three times. But I cannot be sure. The sun moves round and comes through the window. Momentarily closing my eyes, I see across the reddish lining of my lids the child, still bright as in my dream. Dimly registering that I have missed the appointment – knowing the cost of it, Will's pain, his bitterness, in the half-state between art and waking, I labour to bring her into being.

As evening falls, the remembered vision of her is already scattering into fragments. Hair, eyes, cheeks, all blowing out of reach like autumn leaves. But by now I have caught it; its fleeting image is settling on my canvas, remade in glistening oils.

Locking my studio, I cross the courtyard towards the house and go into the kitchen. The lightness I feel having finished the work, my weightlessness, makes the fridge door heavy to pull, the chair to move, the kettle to lift. Floating across the floor, trying to weight myself with coffee, it occurs to me that, however unreasonable I might appear, I have on this day – this most momentous day of all days in my still-young adult life – accepted some kind of fate.

Hearing Will's key in the door, I slip down from the kitchen stool I am sitting on. 'Hi!' I call into the silence.

There is the clap of keys falling into the pot, the breath of a coat flung across the banister, but no returned greeting. I go into the hall. He is waiting for me, his mouth thinned to a line. I plant a kiss, a perfect O, on his cheek.

'Why didn't you turn up at the clinic?'

I move quickly away down the hall. 'Let's have a drink.'

'But you didn't even ring, you didn't …'

I lead him into the living room. It's a room I painted in colours of almost tangible harmony; walls a muted sage green, woodwork oyster. At a time like this, I'm hoping they might help.

'Can you imagine how embarrassing it was for me, waiting for you ...?'

'Sit down, Will, and I'll get us a drink.'

He sits upright on the sofa, framed by a terracotta throw that does nothing to mitigate his darkness. In the kitchen I lift down two glasses, pour two shots of clear liquid and cloud each with a spurt of soda. I want him softened, imprecise. I drop four ice cubes in the drinks and carry them back. As I cross the room the cubes nudge against the rims. I place them on the coffee table, then sit on an easy chair at an angle from him.

Will takes a slow sip, then puts his glass down. He turns to me. His tone is careful. 'So why didn't you come? Have you gone off the idea?'

As I search for an answer, I can feel him battling his frustration.

'You want to go ahead, don't you? I mean, we talked about it. We agreed, didn't we?'

'Yes we did.'

'Then why cut the appointment?'

'Because …' I leave the word hanging.

'Because what, Josie? Are you still hoping it'll just happen? Is that it? Because if so, the danger is we'll get used to it – to just hoping. We won't take any steps until it's too late.'

'I know.'

He's regarding me intently. 'You do want a child, don't you?'

'Yes, of course.'

'Then why miss the appointment?'

It's that question again.

'Because … because I … Because it's not the right way.'

'But what other way is there!' He gets up, spreads his hands in exasperation. 'For God's sake, tell me! What other way is there?'

I get up too now, fuelled by a different frustration – one he won't understand. We stand for a few moments, confronting each other. Will gives a martyr's sigh, then shrugs. I can sense him searching for familiar ground. When he speaks again his voice is conciliatory.

'Perhaps the idea of it, the whole effort of it, scares you?'

I hang my head. 'No, not really.'

He turns to me with resignation and repeats his earlier question as if I haven't understood it. 'So why not come for the appointment?'

Because she stopped me. I can't say this. The inability to say it makes me angry. He sees the blaze in my eyes and retreats to the sofa. For a long moment I remain silent, staring at the floor. How can I explain to him? I try again:

'Will, it's … it's not just about the end result; it's about, about how I …' As I speak I feel a tightness within me, a desperate need to be understood. I bend towards him and touch his hand. 'Will, it's a sense ... it's more than that. Will, I've had a dream … I've seen … I've been trying to paint …' The sentence falters, the words suddenly impossible.

'Painting! Is that what you were doing? When all the time I was sitting there, waiting …'

'It wasn't like that. It wasn't …'

His face is closed. It's become a wall. Will's wall. The wall of one man that somehow presents a unity of reason, an assurance of his being right. I know there is no gap in it, not even a thread-thin inlet that can let in my strange experience. And so the moment – assuming there had ever been one – flees from us.

I retreat to my chair. When I speak again, my voice is someone else's – thin, submissive. 'Can we wait a little longer?'

He gets up and comes over to me, treading warily as if I might flinch from him like an injured animal. He's doing his best to control his anger. He bends and kisses me above the eyes, his face forced full of patient understanding. 'As long as we don't leave it too long.'

He walks out of the room. I hear his footsteps running up and then down the stairs again as he fetches his gym kit and, after that, the thud of the front door as he pulls it shut behind him.

The next day I cross the courtyard towards my studio, my throat closing against a thrust of grief. I unlock the door.

This is my artist's shrine, my temple. I scan the room through a lens of tears. The straw flooring stretches away like spilled sand, lassoing potted plants, burrowing beneath stacks of canvases hunched against the wall. I watch its blurry progress with a painter's eye, blink and let the definitions settle into place. Half-finished works await my attention: close studies, still lifes, landscapes. But today there's only one that draws me.

The portrait is on my easel in the middle of the room. The child stares at me as I approach. I want to get past the eyes, go near enough to examine the brush strokes. Close to, the face splinters into landscape. The cheeks become heaped wheat – titanium with chrome yellow; the nostrils and eye-sockets strokes and swirls of olive, umber and cerulean blue; a drip of flake white drifts in the pool of each pupil like a tiny sailboat. A few steps back and the stubbled landscape fuses into flesh again, the nostrils flare, the sailboats light the eyes, the eyes once more regard me.

The detritus of the previous day is still strewn across the bench beside the easel – twisted tubes, rags splotched with colour, clutches of brushes in jars. I push them to one side and lay a sheet of primed paper across the table. I pick up a stick of charcoal and begin dribbling it across the surface.

A tendril unfolds across the paper.

As I draw, the questions come. What if I'd told Will, risked being honest with him, said what had happened, how I really felt? I begin looping out leaves. The largest leaf becomes an eye.

But I tried didn't I? 'Will, I've had a dream ...'

I'm adding hairs. The hairs are tiny shafts. They make a wheel of spokes around the eye.

How can I explain to him, make him understand? But if it's so hard for me to believe these mute impulses, how can I expect it of him?

The eye is uncoiling in a spiral of fine lines.

The trouble is, I know what he thinks. He thinks I'm afraid. And if I try to explain, if I show him the painting, he'll say I'm acting like a child, fearful of responsibility, hoping instead for some saving miracle.

I take the pattern to the edges of the paper. There *is* fear in me. But not for the reasons he suspects. I turn the paper and start to draw more spokes.

I'm drawing a web with an eye caught in the middle of it. I pinch in the pupil a little above the centre and thicken its base. Then I stand back and look at it. The web is hanging from a leaf – a slender filigree that will barely hold against the wind.

I know now what the fear is. If I break the fragile strands of the thing, if I tell Will, his scepticism could shake my faith and prevent it from happening.

Will

'Can I claim for Morgana's cat food?'

Will looked at his new client, a Miss Katy MacLaren, dressed in black, and curled like a cat herself on the chair beyond his desk, and felt a flicker of irritation. After all, he thought, they had gone through quite a list already, enough for him to risk making a fool of himself with HMRC.

'I think that to push it any further might provoke a raised eyebrow at the very least – even an investigation. And I don't think we want that!' To his surprise, he saw his client's lips were trembling.

'It was only because you asked if Morgana was black!'

She barely got through the sentence before the laughter burst out of her, making her silver earrings shake at her neck. Will found he couldn't help laughing with her. The tension between them eased. He cleared his throat.

'Now,' he said, 'let's recap on all the areas we've covered. As far as what you can claim is concerned, there is, of course, a proportion of heating, lighting and other domestic costs. Then there's the use of your car for meetings and psychic fairs, I think you said. Perhaps you could keep your petrol receipts for these occasions. Also your food and accommodation if you have to stay away from home – although we can only claim so much for that. Then there are the tools of your trade ...'

He looked up and once more caught a hint of suppressed laughter quivering in her mouth. He cleared his throat again.

'Look, I'm sorry, but you are serious about your business, aren't you? I mean, if it's really just a hobby ...'

'Oh no, I am! It's just hearing you lay it all out like that.' She let out another burst of laughter, teeth luminous against a stretch of lip.

Will shifted in his chair. 'The tools of your trade,' he repeated. 'These being your packs of cards, your travelling table, your velvet cloth, your colour chart and ribbons ...' He cleared his throat, hating the words he was about to say: 'your glass wand, and your crystal ball.' He sat back. 'I think I have the picture now.'

Again the stretch of lip, the gleam within. But this time all she gave him was a smile.

Will laughed politely. 'Then there are printing and stationery costs, not forgetting your advertising expenses.' He stood up and extended a hand. 'If you could let me have all the necessary receipts.'

She stood, too, lifting a bright purple bag dotted with yellow moons that had been draped over the back of her chair and slinging it over her shoulder. She took his hand and, for a moment, held it as if it were an extension of herself. Was that how she held her wand? When she let go, he looked down at his sheet of notes, pretending to check the calculations as she slipped from the room.

At six o'clock, Will was still sitting at his desk reviewing his day. Since Katy MacLaren, a succession of clients, mostly regulars, had visited him and he had gone through the motions. It was easy enough in a job like his. Nobody expected him to use his imagination, even though there was the inevitable joke about creative accountancy, which usually masked the expectation that he would oblige. But Will was a straight-down-the-line man, known and respected for it. Most of his clients were businessmen, successful enough to have a whiff of the corporate about them but not yet in the Fat Cat league. He was considered too 'small time' for that. And, besides, having a practice in a market town rather curtailed his prospects.

He had never resented this constriction. It had been a joint decision, mostly based on Josie's love of nature, her painting, and the need for a garden for her to transform. And, in any case, he liked the border country. Living in the Welsh Marches suited him. Not too expensive and yet not too far from civilisation. It was a good place to settle down and start a family.

Start a family. The thought kicked him painfully. He wondered yet again what was going on with Josie, why she wouldn't come to the clinic. Perhaps she really was scared of the procedure, but felt unable to admit it. That would make sense. But of course he didn't want her to risk her health – that was the last thing he wanted. Yet the desire to have a child was so strong in him – to see his own little boy calling from the garden, running towards him in muddy trainers with arms outstretched ... the vision was so powerful he felt at times he would sacrifice anything for it.

Time to go, before he got too maudlin. In a few minutes he was in his Fiesta, joining a fish-tail of traffic leaving town, rear lights glittering in the dusk. A current affairs programme on the radio: the Bank of England was lowering interest rates. Well, at least it would help with the mortgage.

Dusk was descending as he turned into the drive of the house he shared with Josie. It was lit with solar lamps which threw shadows against the hedge. Ahead he could see the bulk of Josie's studio. Her lights were on, but all the windows in the house were black – so she hadn't yet gone in. He felt resentful. Nowadays she was never there to greet him; she was always in her studio. She was treating that sprawling untidy barn of a room as a place of retreat. He wondered what she was painting in there now. It was somewhere he rarely invaded: he felt unwanted there.

He went into the kitchen, took out a bottle of lager from the fridge, and cut himself a slice of cheddar. As he ate the cheese he looked up idly at the wall, his gaze resting on his own portrait.

There was only the one drawing of him, sketched soon after they'd first met. It had been hanging in the kitchen for so long, he barely noticed it now. She'd wanted to draw him in those early days. But he'd found it difficult to sit passively while she stood at her easel, squinting at him with her thumb against a stub of pencil, marking the angles and contours of his face. He remembered he'd been struck by her professionalism, half-hating the experience while at the same time feeling a certain admiration. It was only a charcoal piece, yet he thought she'd caught the look of him quite cleverly, and in some ways he was pleased. But there was something penetrative about it that made him uncomfortable. Perhaps that was why he'd never wanted to sit for her again. Like so many things, this had somehow been tacitly agreed between them. He had a vague suspicion that she'd found it hurtful, though she'd never said as much. It was just another layer of distance between them.

He thought that, on the whole, he preferred the brief sketches she made of children as they ran in the garden, or her pictures of flowers. These were the ones she displayed at her annual exhibitions. For a few weeks each summer, she would open the garden, clear out her studio and transform it into a viewing space, hoping to tempt visitors to buy her art. Then he was allowed to wander around like any of the other punters.

He sighed. Whether or not he understood her artistic skill, he certainly admired her courage in pursuing it. She'd stood up to a father who'd opposed her, and had got herself into Camberwell Art College. She'd also earned enough to get by, drawing portraits and tutoring A-level students. But all that was before she met him – before he offered to support her, release her to do her art.

Of course, he knew he should be grateful that she still made some sort of contribution with her garden and her paintings, yet he felt resentful. He thought bitterly that perhaps she'd never really loved him – that theirs was a marriage of convenience, and all along it was art she loved, not him. And though she cooked with him and walked through the fields with him and made love with him, her heart was in a different dream.

As he sat there, the gloom of evening thickened and the silence and emptiness of the house became more palpable. Whatever was she doing, still closeted in her studio? Surely she'd heard his car, could by now see the kitchen lights shining across the courtyard? He finished his beer and set the glass back on the table.

He was still sitting there with the empty glass in front of him when Josie at last came in, fingers smudged with black crayon, her hair escaping from a schoolchild's hair-band. He could see the dent of her knees in her canvas trousers. She looked fragile and he wanted to hold her. Instead he remained sitting.

'I'm sorry,' she said. 'I was so engrossed, I forgot the time.' She began to say more, but then shut it down with a small wave of the hand.

'Never mind.' He got up. 'I'll help cook.'

'Thanks.'

'I'll chop some salad.'

He took a sharp knife from the block. Josie had brought some lambs lettuce from the greenhouse and some early herbs – parsley, chives and sage. He laid them across the chopping board and began scissoring them with the heel of the knife. While tousling the sliced herbs and lettuce in a bowl, he dripped vinegar and oil into the leaves. Josie was stirring chicken pieces in a wok, mixing them with browned, semi-opaque half-moons of onion. Strips of red pepper and a heap of sliced mushrooms lay beside her. Potatoes were coming to the boil.

They ate at the kitchen table; a junk-shop find, with a broken drawer and green-painted legs beginning to peel. The noise of their forks on the pottery plates was loud.

'Did you have any new clients today?'

Will looked up guiltily, disturbed from a reverie he'd thought was private.

'Yes,' he said, 'as a matter of fact, I had two.' He put half a potato in his mouth.

'One', he said, when he could speak again, 'was a property developer. Good percentage there.' He smiled.

'And the other?'

He crushed some lettuce onto his fork. 'Oh, the other was really wacky. A Tarot card reader who does all sorts of odds and sods. Colour-readings, spell-casting, scrying – you name it!'

'I hope you treated her with your usual professionalism.'

'Of course! Though I don't expect she makes much money with a business like that.'

'Why not?'

'Well, it's hardly mainstream, is it? Just a bit of *hocus pocus* when all's said and done. It isn't even as if it really benefits anyone.'

'I think you're being a bit harsh.' She looked directly at him. 'Whatever you believe, people like her can offer hope.'

'And how does she do that?'

‘By helping people to explore possible scenarios.’

‘Like what?’ He spoke with an edge of belligerence.

‘They study the cards together and try to work out some meaning, some clue to a way forward in their lives. That can be quite a catalyst for change.’

Will felt irritated. Josie was, as usual, making too much of things. He pushed his plate away and got up.

‘I’ll put the kettle on.’ He turned on the tap with a flick of his hand, letting the water burst in a fat spray across the edge of the sink.

Josie

In the spare bedroom, I pull the blind against the morning sun. In the filtered light, I sit at my computer. I'm on a quest, scrying the screen like a clairvoyant, seeking an answer to the most profound question ever asked. I want to know how to create life.

And, as expected, Google gives answers:

ART

As in 'artificially'?

No.

As in 'artfully', 'artistically'?

As in 'Assisted Reproductive Technology'.

I open my notebook and jot down the information: *Assisted Reproductive Technology (ART). ART procedures usually involve IVF. IVF involves taking fertility drugs.*

Scrolling further down the screen, I learn that fertility drugs can cause OHSS – ovarian hyperstimulation syndrome. There's a list of side-effects. I write them down. If this treatment fails to produce a pregnancy, there are more complicated procedures. I find them under the heading: Other Types of ART. There's ZIFT – fertilised embryo (zygote) inserted into the fallopian tube; or GIFT – Gamete Intrafalopian Transfer. The technical words roll past in plain black font. Nothing stands out. There are differences between these methods and I have to read the paragraphs several times before I realise that some involve fallopian rather than uterine implants.

Despite the spring sunshine beating on the blind, it's cold in the room. I switch on the halogen heater and scroll down the screen looking again for something less clinical that I can relate to. And, all at once, there it is, standing out in such simplicity that I read it aloud: 'Your doctor will combine your eggs with your partner's sperm in a laboratory dish.' I stare at the words, flicking the pen between my third and index fingers. Then I draw a pestle and mortar, marbling it with threadlike lines. Underneath I write: *The Combining.*

I scan the site again seeking further elucidation. 'Assisted hatching', 'retrieval', 'embryo culture', the medical terms sprinkled throughout the text present themselves to me one after the other in a colourless procession. Among them are some Latin and Greek phrases that offer more pleasing sounds. One in particular – *Zona pellucida* – rolls so sweetly off the screen it almost bursts on my tongue. 'The *zona pellucida* supports communication between *oocytes* and follicle cells during *oogenesis*.'

The halogen fire glares raw sienna against my leg. I reach down and set it to rotate left and right. 'Females that produce eggs that lack a *zona pellucida* are infertile …' *Needles, probes, scans* ... the words are falling in rhythm with the drone of the heater. *Agonists, antagonists, oocytes, oogenesis* – each is a liquid exhalation.

Limbs of heat are climbing my body. My eyes close and now I'm floating in space. I'm scanning the darkness looking for her, when suddenly there she is, rushing towards me, face looming, cobalt eyes and yellow ochre hair – *close, so close!* Then, as swiftly as she comes, she recedes, sucked back into the dark; her pale face splintering into glittering fractals.

The vision gone, I open my eyes. The heater is still droning, the computer screen still offering its monochrome explanations. But now the alien terms have fled my mind and only two words remain. I switch off the fire and go downstairs. In the kitchen I pick out a red marker from a clutch of pens in a tin. In my notebook I write ART and GIFT in bold letters, circling the words in thick vermilion lines like lipstick.

When Will comes home I am making an effort, tidying up the house. He kisses me on the cheek.

'I thought we could go out for a meal tonight,' he suggests.

I freeze. I know what this means. He wants to have a 'proper talk' somewhere where I can't make a scene.

'Oh,' I counter quickly, 'I was just about to start cooking.'

'Too late for that. I've booked us a table at The Yellow Freesia.

It's a new place on the edge of town. Quite smart. I thought we might try it out.'

Widening my eyes to apply mascara, I'm hoping the ritual preparation will help transform my mood. I scan my wardrobe and pull out an ivory blouse and pewter trousers. Tonight I will be neat and boundaried, not colourful and flowing.

Apart from the yellow freesias on each table, the place is as bland as my outfit. Seated in the centre of the restaurant, I can't help thinking of other meals we've had together, ones I looked forward to – tables in pub corners where Will held my wrist between wine glasses; where candlelight glazed him in transparent gold ochre. Now, as we sit in the chandeliered glare and he leans towards me, his eyes are like prisms, the pupils contracted to small black points.

'I love you, Josie. The last thing I want to do is hurt you.'

'I know.'

'I hate this distance between us. I wish we could talk.'

I raise my glass and press my lips to its thin, cold rim.

'I wish you would tell me what you feel.'

Something in me wants to burst out: *I feel caught in a vice!'* Then T. S. Eliot's phrase 'etherised upon a table' swims into my mind unasked, and all of a sudden I find myself hating the starched white table cloth and the silver implements laid on it.

'I feel etherised by wine.'

Will looks puzzled, then angry. 'Why do you do this? Deliberately speak in a language I won't understand.'

That's the trouble, I think. He can't possibly understand.

'I'm sorry,' I say.

He lets go of his anger with an effort and lays his hand across the table in invitation. Instead of taking it, I lift my glass again.

A waiter appears, dressed in piano-key black and white, takes our orders, and departs.

'The way I see it,' Will begins, looking down at the table and trying to sound reasonable, 'there's no other option, is there?' He looks up in time to acknowledge my nod. 'I wish there were, Josie, I really do.'

He picks up a bread roll, takes a mouthful and eats slowly, allowing time for the remark to sink in. He tries again.

'After all, we both want children, don't we?'

He looks at me expectantly.

I nod again.

'And we've drawn a blank.'

There's no denying the simple logic of his argument. I can only nod once more.

Will is getting into full flow. 'Not so long ago that would have been it. We'd have had to have given up. But we're lucky enough to live in a time when remedies are possible.'

'Are we?'

My voice is petulant. I've been spoken to like a child. Now I sound like a child – a child who wants to go on believing in the gift-bearing fairy.

Will looks at me sceptically.

'But,' I begin.

The waiter appears bearing two food sculptures on oval plates – a square of salmon latticed with lemongrass mayonnaise and a tower of pressed peppers, tomato and goats' cheese. He lays them on the table with a flourish. Will looks unseeing at the crafted food. I take a mouthful and swallow without taste.

'But what?'

It's always this way. When Will musters the forces of reason to back his argument, I can't find what's left to say.

'But, is it right to force life like that? It doesn't seem natural.' I know the remark is lame. I'm playing for time, trying to put my thoughts together. Will's lower lip pushes up, anticipating his response.

'But, Josie, you could apply that argument to any medical procedure.'

'I know.'

'If it's the health risks, I do understand. But, as I said before, we need to find out more about it. We need to go for that appointment. What I can't understand is why you won't even do that.'

Because she … I can't say it so I reach instead for the first thing that comes.

'Because I don't want to be implanted with a zygote!'

The Greek word pierces the air between us. Does Will know what a zygote is? He flinches, taken off-guard. I press my point.

'It's easy for you. It's not you who has to be the host – who has to risk your health!'

'What do you mean? What risks are there?'

Suddenly I have a definite target. He hasn't stopped to think about it properly, hasn't considered the drugs' effects. In fact – I realise with a shock – he hasn't imagined what it would be like for me at all.

'What do I mean!' My morning's research returns with unexpected clarity. I begin counting off on my fingers: 'Bloating, weight-gain, shortness of breath, dizziness, pelvic pain, nausea, vomiting, swollen ovaries, ectopic pregnancy – oh, and did I mention it might cause death?'

'But that's what we were going to find out. That's what we were going to discuss.'

'Yes, with experts, with professionals – with *men,* men who can only theorise, weigh up the risks statistically, men with no real feeling about it, because none of them have to actually *undergo* it!'

'Is everything all right, sir?' The two-tone figure of the waiter hovers beside our table like a snatch of melody.

'Yes, lovely, thank you,' Will says.

We eat in silence for a while, then Will lays down his fork.

'I'm sorry if it seems a lot to ask of you and I understand that you might be a bit frightened about the procedure. All I'm suggesting at this stage is that we find out a bit more about it.' He picks up his fork again and resumes eating, as if there's nothing more to be said.

But once we start, I think, I can imagine what will happen. I'll get overtaken by the logic of it, the reasonableness of it all. We'll get to know the medical staff involved, we'll have their reassurances. That's when it'll happen. She'll fall back into the void again. Despite the painting, the dreams and visions, I'll lose sight of her. Worse still, I'll lose sight of the thread that connects me to her.

I look directly at Will. 'I'm not afraid of the procedure.'

My denial comes out strongly, and for a moment I feel empowered. It's true, I'm not afraid. But as soon as the words leave my mouth I realise what I've done. My statement was unguarded. At one stroke I've ruined my only defence.

Will pauses, his last forkful of salmon poised mid-air. 'You're not? Then what on earth ...?'

'You mean what's my objection?'

Will nods, mouth full.

'Of course I want a child. You know that. More than that, I've dreamed of her.' I break off. I realise I've made the same mistake again.

Will swallows his mouthful. 'So you've dreamed of a child. Our child?' He's waiting for my acquiescent nod. I keep my head still.

'Then surely we should press forward.'

I look at him and slowly shake my head. 'I don't think it'll happen that way.'

Will stares back at me. When he speaks again his tone is long-suffering. 'Is it that you want a child so much you fear raising our hopes, risking the pain of failure. Is that it? Because if it is, Josie, I do understand. But fearing failure isn't going to get us anywhere.'

His attempt at empathy is impressive, but it's not the real issue.

'It's not that.'

'Then, for God's sake, what?'

I can see his patience is nearing exhaustion. I know what he's thinking: 'What is the matter with you, woman? Why can't you express yourself properly?' All I can do in response is try another logical argument.

'But is it right? Is it right to force another life into being when there are so many unwanted children?'

'You mean you think it's selfish? Selfish of us to want our own child – the most natural desire of nearly every couple in the world?'

In truth I don't think it's selfish at all. But Will is now pushing the argument.

'You think we should adopt? Is that it? You think it's somehow our duty to take on someone else's rejected child?'

But you haven't seen her. She hasn't come to you. You haven't fallen under her spell.

'I don't think it's wrong to want your own child.' I'm speaking hotly now. 'I don't think it's wrong at all. But it's perfectly possible to love a child that already exists.' I stop. I realise I've inadvertently taken us into unknown territory. In attempting to avoid the issue, I've entered an area we've never even contemplated.

'I see,' Will says. 'I didn't know this was your attitude. I knew you had a social conscience, but I didn't know it would extend to this. More particularly, I didn't know you'd put it before me – before my feelings, before my perfectly reasonable desire to create our own child.'

He lays down his knife and fork. Adroitly, he's turned my rejection of his argument into a rejection of himself. He regards me for a while without speaking, then gives an exaggerated shrug and returns to the remains of his herbed salmon.

The rest of the evening is uncomfortable. Reaching at moments to try and express myself, I know there's no way to put my case. There's no language that will do – none that he would understand.

As we drive home in the darkness of the car, I can sense him beside me, tense and silent. When we get inside the door, he helps me take off my coat and then begins undoing my dress. Feeling me flinch, he says angrily: 'So you don't want to do it naturally, either!' He flings his coat over the banister and goes up to the bedroom.

That night we lie back to back, a composite Janus figure, each staring into separate darknesses. In vain I try to summon the child. '*Art*' I think, '*Gift*' I think. But the words break in my head and sway uselessly above a great abyss.

Josie

Early next morning, my mind still tight with useless arguments, I ease myself out of bed, pull on some trousers and one of Will's old jerseys and creep downstairs. A faint light glazes the cobbles as I cross the courtyard towards my studio. The canvas is a dim square in the middle of the room. The child locks eyes with me, her face indistinct, her skin a pale blur. The window behind her is a silver rectangle. I go past her and stand, looking out across the garden, exhaling small clouds on the cold glass, searching for the mountains. The Sugar Loaf is the most elusive, its peak ready to disappear in smoke behind the slope of the Skirrid. To its west lies the heavy bulk of the Blorenge, visible in low winter light as a hunched shadow. But today all three are bleared into the sky. Dawn is rising in blotches of rose gold, thinning to pale ochre. Its colours hold promise. Perhaps it will finger the mountains into being, conjure their shapes on the horizon. But after its first frail showing, the light turns lemon, then gathers in on itself, and soon the glass is smeared with tiny spears of rain. I look down at the garden, to where it crouches wetly – a dark bowl of somnolent life awaiting revival.

I leave the window and examine the portrait. In the early light her eyes are black sockets, her skin still ghost-pale. She needs more warmth – perhaps a mix of flesh tint with a touch of alizarin. I pick up my palette, squeeze out the colours and load my brush. As I approach the canvas the child's face shrinks from me, the flecks of white in the eyes seeming to halo them with fear. I stop, the loaded brush poised mid-air. But the portrait is unfinished, isn't it? Surely it needs more work. As I lower the brush I sense the child's relief. I put the palette down. When I look again her cheeks seem more alive, less chalky. I watch as her face slowly eases into definition, animated by the growing light. Maybe, I think, she doesn't need touching-up after all. I stand, staring at her. She returns my gaze. After a while I decide to move her. The paint is still wet enough to smudge so I take her down carefully, keeping my thumbs on the edges of the canvas. She feels weightless in my arms. Like a dancing partner, I swing her towards the back of the studio and place her on a spare easel beside the window. There I steady her briefly before going back to my bench. Although she is now angled in the corner, her eyes shift focus, slanting towards me as I lift another canvas.

While she watches I mix some purple and squeeze out a slick of cadmium yellow. Soon sharp indigo and yellow blooms appear on rising spokes. Trust. Friendship. That's what freesias are supposed to represent. Do we still have that, Will and I? I paint fast, resisting an urge to break away, run into the rain, escape the torment of relationship. I mix indigo with purple madder, twisting the sharp little branches into billowy fingers raised against a blackening sky.

The rain has stopped but the light is still hollow.

Will

When Katy MacLaren entered the room she did it unobtrusively, slipping round the door like a shadow. Even so, Will could feel her vibrancy. A smile was already playing on her lips before she sat down. She looked across the desk at him, her eyes sparkling with barely concealed humour.

'Good morning, Miss MacLaren!' he said. 'As you know, I've gone through your receipts. Now I need to run through some of these expenses with you.'

She shifted herself sideways in the chair and crossed her legs.

'You didn't expect me to do it all so quickly, did you?' she said, like a child expecting praise. 'I thought if I didn't do it straight away I might forget all the extras!'

'Extras?'

'Yes, the little things. You know, the odd packet of herbs or joss sticks, that sort of thing. I mean, it's good that I can claim for everything like that. It's just that keeping track of it all is quite an effort. And I never thought of myself as a businesswoman before. In fact, I never used to charge for any of it at all.'

'But now you realise you can make a living ...' Will broke in.

'Exactly. Though I still feel a bit guilty about it. Specially since I didn't even have to study for it or anything.'

'Didn't you?' Will's voice was polite. He wondered what there could possibly be to study.

'Of course not! I've always been able to do this kind of stuff. It's sort of second nature.'

She leaned towards him and said conspiratorially. 'You see, I'm not like you. I haven't had to fill my head with figures, go to college. Nothing like that.'

She leaned back again, adding with a flourish, 'Although I do have figures in my head, you know?' She laughed. 'That surprises you doesn't it?' It was a leading question.

'Yes,' he admitted.

'Aren't you even a bit curious?'

There was that laugh again, a kind of twittering. She looked at him expectantly.

'All right,' he said, reluctantly. 'Tell me.'

This time she wasn't looking at him. 'It's like,' she said, 'it's like. Oh, perhaps it's easier to say what it's not like. It's not like dull dry figures on a page, not like making calculations. It's something completely different.' She searched the air. 'It's something like a dance. A dance with coloured numbers.' She smiled at the thought.

'I expect it's different with you,' she continued. 'With your quick brain, you've got all the times tables speeded up – the ones you learned at school, all up there in your head.'

'I do have a calculator,' Will said drily, hoping to move on.

'I know, but still you must know them quite well, mustn't you? I mean as you're working with them all the time, they must become a bit like friends.'

'Working with what exactly?'

'Numbers, of course! Or do you call them figures?'

She sat back, half-releasing him from the interrogation, uncrossing her legs.

'Actually,' she said, 'people like me call it numerology.' She leant forward again and spoke almost in a whisper. 'But really, it's a form of magic!'

Afterwards Will could not remember why he had let her go so far. She had managed to wheedle out of him his date of birth, which she then reduced to a personality number, whatever that meant. The trouble was he knew only too well what it meant. It meant he was dull, stubborn and unimaginative, as she had delighted in telling him. And, of course, he had to endure more laughter. Yet, curiously, she seemed to like his stolidity. She kept telling him four was a good number; after all, it was the number of matter – whatever that implied. But he had to admit that material things were important to him. He also quite liked the idea that he was loyal and tenacious. Then it occurred to him that perhaps it was traits such as these that were keeping him locked in his marriage when things were so extraordinarily difficult.

Josie

We are crossing each other like shadows, slowly easing away from each other, altering our routines so we no longer coincide. This morning Will got up early and left me sleeping. Even before I opened my eyes I sensed the hollow beside me. Despair threatens to drag me into its slough of despond. I need to ground myself.

I get out of bed, cross to the window and look out at the rural vista. The fields pour in cadmium greens and yellow ochres towards the horizon, where they flow into an empty sky. The mountains are still whited out, but I know they're there. Despite the haze that obscures them, the weather seems good enough to make a start on the garden.

Knowing I'll have heavy work ahead, I force myself to eat some breakfast, then pull on a jacket and climb down the terraced steps into the little vista below.

The morning sun is weak, the grass patchy with frost. My boots punch out heel and toe marks as I cross it. Ahead of me the lawn spreads towards an old brick wall held together by sinews of Virginia creeper. Last summer I tacked a mirrored trellis to the crumbling bricks and already the stems are nicely obscuring the edges. At the far end the lawn curves inwards between fan-shaped flower beds. In the mirror it begins again, spreading backwards in an elongated oval, making the view endless.

I reach the right-hand bed and pause. Bamboo stakes stand in a row against the wall. I visualise a backdrop of hollyhocks – single blooms, white-edged with bruised haloes around a yellow eye. Here, every year, inspired by childhood memories, I scatter seeds. Last summer, a cloud of peppermint-candy phlox sprang up, fringed by a mix of purple-swirl lupins, sky-blue delphiniums and a patch of pinks. But now, save for a lacing of early weeds, the earth lies bare.

I cross to its sister bed and walk carefully between the early shoots of camellia, acanthus, hostas and fatsia. Behind them, latticed against the wall, a fig tree's pea-like growths are little beads of hope. Despite the lingering cold, I can feel spring twisting in the air.

As I retrace my steps across the grass, a shaft of weak sunlight flashes on the glass panels of the greenhouse. Behind it, half-obscured, is the garden shed, webbed with ivy. I open the door, releasing a smell of damp wood and grass clippings. Tools hang on hooks, and packs of seeds are stacked in neat envelopes on narrow shelves, their names still visible on faded photographs – Violets, Sweet William, Canterbury Bells ... My shoulder brushes against a garden fork and sets it swinging. I lift it down, carry it up the garden and thrust it into the ground in front of the bamboo stakes.

The compacted earth is damp and yields easily. The tines of the fork pricking the ground bring scent and colour crawling out in lines of ochre. I fetch a bag of compost from the shed. After half an hour's work I step back to admire my efforts. The turned soil is transformed to burnt sienna. I stand a while gazing at it, planning my summer show. This year I need to attract more bees, and this is the bed to do it.

I replace the fork and tour the garden to see what else needs doing. The oval pool is silted with leaves, the arches in the hedge like wild eyebrows. But in spite of its untidy state, the design of my garden still thrills me. At one time this was an unpromising patch at the base of a slope. Redesigning it was like sculpting – another texture to feel and play with. And so I dug out features, shaping and squeezing and coaxing them to fit with each other. Then I used mirrors and paint effects to suggest vistas I could not physically create. Now the garden offers far more than I could have imagined.

I go through an archway to where a narrow walkway runs behind the lawn, obscured by the hedge. Some arches open onto it, others lead instead to seated bowers. I designed these as places of intrigue or refuge and it's easy to get lost. Even Will never seems to remember which is which. I weave my way through the various twists and turns. Carefully positioned in hidden alcoves are statues of brightly painted animals on metal plinths. The first one I come to is the stag. Its painted wooden antlers are a tangle of bistre and bismuth orange, speckled with bird droppings. Beyond it I can spot the eagle in fierce manganese blue glinting through the woven branches. The blue is faded but the beak and talons are still strong. I take my time examining them before returning through another arch. Here, part-obscuring the rest of the garden, is my favourite – a leaping salmon – a fish-tailed half-moon in bright cadmium yellow. And – like the others – it's a triumph of *trompe l'oeil.* I can't help feeling a thrill of pride whenever I see it. I sit down on a wooden bench fretted with moss. The whole garden being something of an optical illusion, it's important to keep surveying the space from different viewpoints, to keep a check on the sight-lines.

As I contemplate my achievement, the mossy damp seeps into my jeans, but I hardly notice it. I'm trying to remember how small the garden actually is. I designed it to evoke the scope and grandeur of a larger plot, and now I'm beginning to be convinced by it myself. I look around me. Even though it's overgrown, I can see how to bring it up again. I turn my thoughts back to last summer. It was a bold stroke, throwing it open to the public, but I'm glad I did it. When visitors came, I could see how the garden teased them, offering its mix of earthy promise and illusion. I noticed how each element claimed their attention: the pond, the statues, the little bowers. Softly, subtly, they beckoned the visitor into hidden places.

Afterwards some of them wanted to know how I'd achieved my effects. I told them it was just a question of imagination. Some of them still looked at me in awe as if I had some special gift. Now as I look around me, I can see why they were impressed. But all I've really done is tease out virtue from deficiency, proving that, however unpromising the space, there's room for everything: a pond, a spreading lawn, small trees and flower beds together with unexpected features – grottoes and statues, secret passages with twists and turns, dead ends.

I shift on the stone seat, the damp beginning to cramp my legs.

I know the visitors come for my garden and not my art, but then they wander into the studio searching for souvenirs. And this is where they find them – my flower paintings, my little betrayals.

An errant gust of wind lifts my hair. I shake my head in an effort to clear my thoughts, then get up stiffly. If I want the garden ready for this summer, it's time to plant some seeds. I return to the shed and flick through the faded packets. I'll begin with the phlox seeds. Sow them in a cloud of candy pink, like last year. Once again, in hope, I'll plant my nursery.

Josie

Hypertufa. The long 'u', as in 'truth', makes it sound sophisticated. 'Hyper-tougher' would be more accurate. I'm making a trough for the patio. Holding the cardboard boxes in position, gravel biting my knees, I finish loading sand in the top box and cram the tufa mix – a blend of peat moss, sand and cement – between the two. I now have a box within a box. Worms of wet cement dribble between them. I smooth them off and tuck a sheet of plastic round my creation. Wiping my rubber gloves on my jeans, I stand up, pleased with my effort. I can already picture its rough edges brimming with blue violas, white daisies and the tattered flags of spent nasturtiums.

'Hell-o-oh!'

The call, stretched to three syllables, intrudes into the silence. It's coming from the top of the drive. I turn my head expectantly.

'I'm sorry to burst in on you like this,' says a woman's voice.

Approaching me is a slim young woman in black denim jeans and a pale polo-neck sweater. She has mahogany-coloured hair carved tight to her cheeks and a turquoise scarf splattered with tangerine and lemon in a loose twist around her neck.

'I've broken down. I managed to pull into your drive but I couldn't call the AA because I can't get a signal.'

As she speaks she smiles and inclines her head to one side.

'I'm so sorry to bother you but is there any chance I could use your phone?'

I can hardly refuse, but I know there's a protocol involved in these situations. Keep the stranger outside the house – that's it.

'Of course,' I say, smiling back at her. 'I know some networks are out of range round here. Wait there a minute.'

I fetch the phone. As she keys in the number, I'm wondering what to do with her while she waits.

'Thanks. They'll be here within the hour.' She looks round the little courtyard, then at the house. 'Mind if I use your loo?'

What can I say? I lead the way through the hallway and point to a door beneath the staircase. Then, for something to do, I retreat to the kitchen and fill the kettle. By the time she comes out, it's already boiling. I offer her a coffee.

'That's very kind. I'd love one. But if you want me to get out of your hair, I'll take it out to the car.'

'No, it's OK. I needed a break anyway.'

'In that case, why don't I introduce myself. My name's Esme. Esme Lightfoot.'

'I'm Josie – Josie Jones.'

'Cool name.'

'Is it?' I wave a hand. 'Have a seat.'

'Thanks.'

Esme pulls out a chair and sits at the table. Strewn across it is a selection of dirty mugs, used plates and unprepared vegetables. She's taking everything in, looking round the walls, appraising the room. 'I like your kitchen,' she says.

'I'm afraid it's rather ...'

'Bohemian?'

'I suppose you could say that – if you were being kind!'

We both laugh awkwardly.

'It makes mine look rather clinical.'

I think of her tight denims and flat pumps hidden beneath the table.

'It's a bit minimalist. Not a thing out of place. I'm not sure I like it entirely.'

She fiddles with a patch of biscuit crumbs, scouring out a circle with her finger, then looks up again. Her gaze settles on the clutch of pens and pastels in the pottery mug.

'You're an artist, aren't you?'

'How do you know?'

She sweeps her arm in an arc around the room.

'Can my kitchen tell you that much?'

'Possibly, but I'm afraid I cheated. I peered through your studio window while you were getting the phone.'

I pour boiling water over the coffee granules. 'Milk?'

'Please.'

I hand her the coffee and put the milk carton on the table. 'But in any case,' she says, 'there's something about the way you look at things that gives you away.'

'Oh?' I sit down opposite her.

'Yes. The way you half-screw up your eyes as if constantly measuring distances. I reckon even an amateur could tell.'

'You mean you're – what – a professional occupation-guesser?'

'Partly.' She smiles. 'I'm a psychologist.'

This was unexpected. 'Freelance?'

'Not entirely. Half the time I'm attached to a hospital.'

'But not today.'

'Fortunately not today.'

While I'm wondering what, if anything, one can ask a psychologist, Esme glances up at the wall then looks across the table.

'Are you married?'

I nod.

'I thought so. And is that a drawing of your husband?' Her eyes flick to the charcoal sketch.

'Yes. He hated sitting for it, though.'

'That's a shame.'

I share her examination of my sketch even though I know every line and smudge of it.

'And are you?' I ask.

'What?'

'Married?'

'Not exactly. I live with someone.' She gives a short laugh. 'Nathan. He's a university lecturer. And now I think about it, he would love posing while I sketched him – if I had the ability, that is!'

'Well, that's the only one I've done of Will. He wouldn't sit for me again.'

I'm aware of the faint timbre of complaint in my voice. If she's any good at her job, she'll have noticed it.

'It's because you're too good,' she says.

'You think so?'

'Yes. You captured more than he bargained for.'

I'm looking at her with new interest. 'Is that your professional opinion?'

'It's what I suspect. Art as good as yours can be very revealing.'

I swallow my coffee too quickly, which leads to a burst of coughing.

'But, of course, you knew that.'

I nod, though I can't quite think why. Just then my phone rings. Esme picks it up.

'They'll be here in five minutes,' she says. She gets up. 'That was quick! I'd better get back to the car. Thanks so much for the coffee.' She holds out her hand. 'It's so nice to meet a free spirit!'

I follow her outside and watch until she reaches the top of the drive, where she turns and looks back.

'And good luck with your painting,' she calls. She's waving an arm, her voice just audible from beside her car. Seconds later I hear the pulse of an engine as a wasp-coloured van comes into view.

I leave her to it.

In the warmth of the kitchen I rinse out the coffee cups and make myself a sandwich. I eat it slowly, looking up at my sketch of Will. It must be six years since I did it, and in that time he hasn't changed much. At least not physically. Sitting for me might have made him uncomfortable but there was a spark between us. In those days he was still awed by my art. In those days our differences kept us together.

When I've finished I make a half-hearted attempt at clearing the table, but leave the heap of vegetables to sort later. As I cross the hall, I spot a card that has skittered across the wooden floor. My name is written across the top of it in neat handwriting which breaks into a flourish on the tails of the Js. On it are two lines:

Really enjoyed my breakdown at yours. And thanks for the coffee – it was just what I needed! Call me if you fancy a drink sometime.

A phone number is scribbled across the bottom together with a signature – Esme. Her name glows on the card in an aura of yellow ochre.

Will

At the end of the day, Will was reluctant to leave the office and go home. He pulled a stack of papers towards him and began idly scanning the columns of figures. But, as often now, he was finding it difficult to concentrate.

His marriage. *Debits and credits.* Weighing it all up seemed an endless task. In the left-hand column was everything he had to lose. *Assets, shares, investments*, everything he'd put into the relationship – *shares* being the most ironic: they barely shared the same bed nowadays, let alone anything else. As for *investments*, what on earth should he do? Pull out now and cut his losses, or reinvest? Whichever he chose was risky.

With a sigh, he packed up his briefcase, walked slowly to the car park and put it in his car. Instead of setting off straight away, he walked to the main street and stopped at a florist, pleased that he'd managed to catch them before they closed. He returned to the car armed with a bunch of pink lilies. A last-ditch reinvestment, trembling on the seat beside him.

At the roundabout he decided to take the back way home. It might be a slower route, but it was usually traffic-free. As he drove, he glanced in the rear mirror. Behind him the lone breast of the Sugar Loaf raised a taut nipple against the evening sky. So, the spring weather had finally brought out the mountains. Suddenly desolate, he turned off the road and pulled up outside The Crown and Anchor.

The place exuded an air of comfortable expectancy, spindle-backed chairs tucked beneath old pine tables. He'd hoped he might find Andy there, or some other colleague he could share a drink with. But the bar was empty, so he ordered a pint and sat at a corner table by himself.

Lifting the glass towards his lips, it occurred to him that he should have bought two bunches of lilies, one for Josie, the other for his mother. She would have appreciated that. Or perhaps chrysanthemums might have been more the thing. In any case, it would have given him an excuse to go round and present them without having to stay too long. He didn't want to risk an interrogation. If his mother knew there was friction in his marriage, she might take too keen an interest. She'd disliked Josie from the moment he'd first brought her home. 'That one's no good for you,' she'd said. 'Far too fond of her arty nonsense.' To date, he'd always stoutly defended his choice of wife. But now, peering through the amber liquid, he couldn't help wondering whether his mother had been right after all. This was a track he could ill afford to go down. He looked at his watch: 6.15. It was already dark outside. If he was going to capitalise on the flowers, he'd better get home soon. He drained his glass and left.

He got out of the car in the glare of Josie's studio lights and lifted out the lilies, their podded heads lolling from the green cellophane. He was tempted to knock on her door and hand them to her there and then, but thought better of it. He began doubting the whole gesture. The Yellow Freesia idea hadn't worked, so why should anything else? He let himself into the house and jammed the bunch, still wrapped, in a jug of water.

While waiting, he could, of course, make a start on dinner. He picked out a red onion and a green pepper and laid them on the wooden board. He began slicing the onion, then put the pieces into a frying pan. Just as he was tipping the sliced pepper into the pan, Josie came in.

'Hi!' she said brightly.

'I've been home a while,' Will said. 'Didn't you hear the car?'

'Oh, sorry, no.' She moved towards him and picked up a knife.

'Or notice the lights come on in the house?'

Josie dropped the knife on the table and put her hands on her hips.

'Look, Will. I didn't expect you home this early so I was in full flow.' She turned away. 'Anyway, it's not as if you race home to see me.'

The last words were muttered but loud enough for him to hear. As she'd turned she'd seen the lilies stuffed into the jug. She spotted them a beat too late. The muttered comment lay across the space between them.

'Nothing I do is any use, is it? Coming home early, bringing you flowers! None of it!'

He went over to the sink. As he pulled the lilies roughly from the jug, two buds broke off. He brandished the rest in front of her aggressively.

'Stop, Will! You'll break them.' She took them from him, avoiding his fingers, then filled a vase with water and swiftly arranged the blooms, placing them in the middle of the table.

They finished preparing the meal without speaking. As they ate, the vase of lilies stood between them, their saffron tongues eloquent in the silence.

After she had cleared their plates away, Josie placed a bowl of fruit on the table. Will picked up an apple and began quartering it. In an attempt to relieve the tension, Josie said: 'Someone broke down outside our house today.'

'Oh?' Will looked up briefly.

'She seemed quite nice, actually. I gave her a coffee while she waited for the AA.'

Will bit into the apple and considered his reply.

'You should be careful, inviting strangers into the house. It could have been some kind of scam.'

'I know. But I'm sure she was genuine. She told me she was a psychologist.'

'One of those people who mess with your brain? Oh, you can't trust *them*!'

He chuckled at his little joke, but Josie only looked away in exasperation.

Josie

Walking to the end of my studio, I catch my foot on the leg of the easel, sending a tremor through the painting of the child and making her cheeks quiver. Her eyes look at me obliquely. She's slightly dislodged, one corner of the canvas threatening to slip off the easel. I straighten her, then turn to the window and scan the horizon.

Today I plan to paint a clutch of trees and buildings hanging in reflection and then reverse the painting. As with the garden, it excites me to tease the eye into seeing the reflection as reality.

An hour later I'm painting well, the composition coming together so easily it no longer absorbs my full attention. My thoughts stray to Will. We're so distant now, we're hardly able to speak to each other. If we can no longer communicate, I reflect miserably, then what's left between us?

In an effort to distract myself I let my thoughts drift to the painting school I ran last year. Some older women came, I remember, with grey eyes and messy artists' hair. They were the kind of women who knitted or crocheted or – more adventurously – teased out wool on spinning wheels lovingly restored by husbands, and wove their own cloth. Wearing their own creations, these women presented a rag-bag of colour that I found heartening. They were women who tended their creativity, refused to fade into the twilight with age.

Next to them the young man, Tom, appeared sombre in his faded black jeans and charcoal T-shirt. Good-looking and the only male, he should have been the darling of the group, but all his energy was transmitted to the movements of his brush. While the women chatted and fretted over a smudged eye or lengthened eyebrow, blotting and blotching and endlessly repainting their work, Tom kept going, doggedly measuring and marking with his thin thumb on the stem of his brush. He was ensuring that no hair stray from its allotted space, no shadow stretch too wide, no lip or eye become too bold, too vibrant. Seeing him like a crouched crow among the gaudy women, there were times when I longed to seize my brush and patchwork his jeans in emerald green and alizarin crimson.

One morning he arrived early and helped me set up the easels. He looked at the pile of plastic palettes and the twisted tubes of paint I provided – a host of extra colours not included in the starter packs – and pulled his lips together disapprovingly.

'You shouldn't help them so much,' he said gruffly. 'You should make them mix their own.'

I was taken aback at his criticism but knew that, however clumsily he spoke, he meant well.

'Possibly that is a weakness of mine,' I said, 'my passion for colour.'

I saw him flinch at the remark and I didn't know why. Was it about the provision of so many hues, or had something else made him uncomfortable? Could it be the mention of passion? Whatever it was had brought a touch of colour to his cheeks. Was he embarrassed for me? I knew how I must appear to him – the errant teacher indulging her obsession for the established shades. Clearly he'd expected more of me, needed, perhaps, to admire me. But how could I explain to him what they meant to me, had meant for as long as I could remember?

I look down at my palette with its blots of squeezed paint. How old was I when they first whispered to me? I must have been six or seven, the age when children discover the excitement of hobbies. Some children in my class collected stamps, or caterpillars, or football cards. I collected paints. I saved my pocket money every week, desperate to own the whole spectrum – a tube of every Winsor and Newton hue. I felt there was power, not only in the colours, but in the names themselves. I remember lying sleepless in the night, chanting their names, pasting the darkness with their tinted litany – burnt umber, alizarin crimson, cobalt blue, titanium white, rose madder, cadmium red, raw sienna, yellow ochre. To me, each name worked a cryptic spell that could call into being a specific pigment and speak its essence.

Of course, I could not explain this to Tom.

Josie

I wake with a feeling of foreboding. I'm only too aware of its source. The planned Sunday lunch has been a black mark on the calendar for weeks and there's no avoiding it. Will, by contrast, seems in a better mood. Already up and out of bed, he's deposited a cup of tea beside me before disappearing into the bathroom. I can hear the shower running, his deep voice humming through the spray. With an effort, I climb out of bed.

We arrive at the restaurant at exactly one o'clock but there's no sign of the others. As usual Will has chosen the venue. The interior is large and pulpy with soft furnishings. Sprigged violets dot the walls. Heavy curtains framing the bay window are swept back, their stiff folds crumpling on a royal blue carpet. The room is filled with rectangular wooden tables covered in ivory tablecloths.

We are shown to our table. While we wait, I'm mentally stripping the room, tearing down the curtains and replacing them with slatted wooden blinds, throwing crimson cloths at right angles across the tables, painting the walls Naples yellow and lining them with metal racks displaying necks and rumps of wine bottles.

I've barely finished transforming it before the two sets of parents arrive. We go through the usual greeting ceremony.

'This is nice!' declares Frieda, looking around appreciatively.

She settles herself in the chair opposite me. I glance down at the folded napkin slumped over the top of my glass.

As my mother-in-law fiddles with her own napkin, I regard her with half-closed eyes as if I'm about to paint her. Frieda's nose neatly divides her face, the shadowed half dioxazine purple, the other cadmium orange. Thick coral frames encircle her eyes. The magnifying lenses give her pupils an unnervingly large dimension.

Suddenly she swoops forward, picks up a knife and scrutinises her lips in its silver blade. The image quivers in reflection for a moment, like a segment of tangerine.

'It's blemished!'

It's not clear whether she means her lipstick or the knife. She nudges her husband.

'Brian, ask that waiter to get me a clean knife.'

Brian sighs, takes the knife from her and swaps it with his own.

'You should have called the waiter!' Turning away from him she addresses the table. 'That's typical of standards nowadays.'

There's a consenting murmur. Beside me I can feel Will unfolding his napkin across his knees.

On the opposite side my own mother is sitting tensely, her cheeks pinched as if to suppress unwelcome remarks. Her face is a perfect ovoid, her cropped hair carved in arches above her ears. As I look at her, I imagine the flattened circle of a hat haloing her face in pale white straw. The image takes me to a childhood scene. A rare seaside holiday with just the two of us, my mother and me – pale sand squashed between our toes, small white triangles like cut sandwiches bobbing and dipping across the sea. In my memory she seems softer somehow, transformed by the hat.

'All right, Josie love? Things going OK?'

I give her a reassuring smile. 'Fine.'

She turns away relieved, while I fiddle with my fork. I wish she would wear a hat more often. She needs the softening effect. Her features are sharp and angular like her name: Ja-net. I watch her as she carefully opens the large folded menu, scanning the choices with nervy movements of her head like a pecking chicken. It's as if she can never sit still, never inhabit her own universe with any sense of calm.

'Well, are we having starters, then?' My father's voice rumbles beside me disturbing the general quiet.

'Whatever you like, Hugh,' says Brian, regarding him briefly across the table as if seeking a moment of male solidarity.

'The duck à l'orange sounds good,' my mother offers brightly.

'Oh, you know me, I don't bother with all that fancy stuff,' Frieda says.

'How about we all share some pâté and toast for starters, then?' Will says. 'That's all I want, anyway.' He looks at Frieda, 'What about you, Mother?'

'Fine by me,' Frieda replies, devouring the menu. 'And, as for the main course – well, I'm happy with the roast lamb. That'll do me!'

'How about the smoked salmon and prawn platter or, even, the home-made lasagne?' puts in Hugh, eyeing her across the table. 'I always think the tried and tested dishes are the best. Can't be doing with all this newfangled gourmet stuff!' He gives her a wink.

'Oh!' she laughs. 'Lasagne!'

'You hate Italian,' says Brian.

'Well, normally,' Frieda lowers her head, scanning the menu once more through her glasses.

'It's in the bottom right-hand corner.' Will's voice rings out helpfully beside me.

'Let me have another look ...' Without lifting her eyes, she adds: 'And what are you having, Josie, dear?'

'I think I'll have the fish.'

She holds the menu closer. After a moment she raises her head and gives me a strangely triumphant look. 'Well!' she announces, 'I must confess I'm tempted by Grandma's Ravioli. In fact, that sounds just the ticket!' She flashes a conspiratorial smile in Janet's direction. Receiving no response, she grabs her glass. Noticing too late that it's already empty she raises it anyway.

'Here's to Mother's Day!'

'Mother's Day,' they all echo.

'Now pour me some more wine, Brian!' she says impatiently. 'And where's that waiter. It's time we ordered!'

By the time the food arrives, Frieda's face is sprinkled with minute vermilion spots, her make-up slippery beneath the coral lenses. My father, as ever, is perfectly at ease with her. He likes her no-nonsense outlook. In his words: 'Frieda's a good sort. Says what she thinks and no messing around. You know where you are with her!'

'How're things with you, Janet?' Brian's trying to engage my mother in conversation, but forced to hold it in fits and starts over Frieda's head. 'Still living in the same house?'

'Yes,' my mother replies, 'but we're thinking of ...'

Her plans for a conservatory are drowned by a shriek of laughter from Frieda. My mother gives up and, instead, gazes across the restaurant, her eyes far away.

After fielding a few pleasantries from my father-in-law, I withdraw from the general conversation and let my mind wander to my mother again. I'm wondering why I haven't thought of it before, that pecking chicken image. It's so appropriate. All through her marriage my mother was cooped up. We both were. And I suppose we must have felt safe when I was small, sheltered by the great rock of my father. The trouble was, as I grew up, it became oppressive.

I feel Will's elbow digging me in the ribs. I think at first it's a shared moment, but he's just spreading his napkin out across his lap. At the same time he's laughing at one of his mother's jokes before catching my father's eye over her head. As I lift a piece of fish to my lips, a glob of white sauce falls onto the cloth. I move my plate to cover the mark before Frieda can see it. As I do so, I inadvertently brush against my father's arm. He's sitting beside me, a huge bulwark, but he's not protecting me at all, certainly not from Frieda. I glance up at him. So far he's barely spoken to me. I'm wondering what to say to him, but he's looking away, intent on joining in the general affability. Then my mother's high laugh rings out from the far corner. After a few sips of wine, she's beginning to relax. She beams round the table.

'Well, isn't this nice, all of us together for once!'

Again, there's a general rumble of agreement.

'Yes. It reminds me of when Will was little. I always used to enjoy our family occasions. I remember when ...'

'And how's your painting going, Josie?' Brian asks.

'Oh, fine! I'm busy getting ready for my summer show.' I know he's not really interested, but it's good of him to ask. He makes the effort every time we meet and I'm grateful for it. He takes an interest in the garden too, and we chat for a while across the table while Frieda rolls out her memories of Will's childhood to anyone who will listen.

As I watch my parents genially playing the family game with Hugh and Frieda, I find it hard to remember how cold they were when I left home. Unable to understand why I should waste my time studying something as impractical as art, they hardly spoke to me during my student days at Camberwell. That is, until I met Will.

Sensing his sudden discomfort beside me, I return my attention to the table and discover that Frieda, having pushed her half-eaten ravioli to one side, is now reminiscing in earnest.

'Of course, at that time, we all thought Angie was going to be the one. Will was so devoted. But we did worry a bit. I mean, she was such a scrap of a thing. And no hips at all – well, at least nothing you could call remotely child-bearing!' She gives a girlish laugh, a strange high giggle. As she makes her dreadful statement, I'm wondering if it's wine-induced, or if she's been preparing for this moment. 'But then, Will does seem to go for the thin ones. Still, with Josie. Well, we live in hope – of course.'

'And, after all, it is Mother's Day!'

I turn in shock as the phrase darts out of my own mother's mouth. Is she tipsy, too? Will takes my hand as all faces turn enquiringly towards us.

'So, when are you going to make me a proud grandmother, then, Will?' Frieda asks. 'After all, I can't wait for ever!'

The remark is followed by appreciative murmurs. I choke on a mouthful of fish and try to extract my hand.

'Well, as to that,' I hear Will say. 'I think we might have some encouraging news to report.'

I listen open-mouthed as Will confidently begins taking charge of the table.

As soon as we get home, I turn on him. 'How could you do that?'

Will shrugs. 'What else was I supposed to do?' His voice is calm, reasonable. 'They have a right to know.'

'No, they don't! And, besides that, we haven't agreed on anything yet!'

'I thought we had,' Will says coolly. 'I was just waiting for you to come round.'

'For me to …'

'Yes, after an initial panic – which is quite natural, I suppose.'

'But you haven't let me.'

'If you mean I haven't let you explain, I've given you plenty of opportunities. I've been waiting patiently. But it's all to no avail. It's you who won't talk to me.'

I snatch up a pen and twist it in my hands, stifling an impulse to throw it at him.

'So, you think it's all a fait accompli and you dared – you dared to tell our parents I'd failed to conceive and we were going to do something about it.'

'Yes. I'm sorry my mother grilled you a bit on the procedure, but she was only trying to be supportive.'

'Supportive! She was *gloating* – she was gloating because, just like that Angie I too was obviously unable to deliver the goods. It had to be my fault.'

'Don't be silly!'

'*Don't be silly!* Didn't you hear her? I haven't got the hips!'

Will is turning away, walking towards the kitchen. 'If you're going to over-react, when that comment was a harmless bit of humour …'

'Harmless! Will, I don't think you know the first thing about your mother. You've never been able to see straight where she's concerned. She's a manipulative –'

'You leave my mother out of it!' he snaps, turning on me as I follow him through the door. 'In any case, your own mother was just as bad, so why not blame her!'

I'm about to protest when I realise it's true. My mother *did* join in the interrogation but, of course, she was encouraged by Frieda.

Well?' Will is taunting me now.

'She would never have said anything if your wretched mother hadn't …'

'Don't call my mother wretched!'

'Oh, Will, stop it! Stop it!' I'm close to tears. 'If we can't be onside about this …'

'Then what?' Will comes up to me. 'Say it, Josie!' he demands. 'Just say it!'

'What is there to say?'

'That we might as well split up!'

Pain shafts through my breast and for a moment I'm unable to breathe. 'Will ... No! Will ... Stop!'

'Stop!' Will echoes. 'Stop what? It's you who's doing all the stopping! We can't go forward, can't make plans, can't have a child. Can't do anything! You've put a bloody full stop to it all.' He glares at me. 'Don't you realise – you're ruining everything!'

'I'm not, Will! Truly I'm not. I'm just worried that ...'

'No, you're not. You're just throwing it all away. Everything we agreed, everything we planned.'

I make a last attempt: 'That's not how I feel, Will.'

Will raises his arms in a gesture of despair, then drops them. 'How can you be so bloody selfish!'

He's rejected my effort. Yet again he's failed to hear me. I can feel my anger return, swelling towards explosion. I'm unable to control it. 'But it's not just me, is it? Look at how you treat me! You don't care, you don't listen. Everything is control with you. Everything has to be ordered, measured, planned. And that's how you'd have this pregnancy. Calculated and controlled, like you. Can't you see? You're like a machine! You don't live, you don't feel, you don't allow anything in that might rock your boat. And you expect me to go along with what *you* want. That's all that counts isn't it – what you want – because it's all so sensible your safe ideas, your set ways. No, Will. It's *you*, you who keeps spoiling everything!'

Will steps back, shock showing on his face. I've never spoken to him like this before and for a moment I think my words have hit home.

'*I* keep spoiling everything?' His voice is thin with disbelief. 'No, it's *you*, Josie. It's *you* who's bloody ruining it all, and it's *you* who's wrecking our marriage!' He's backing away, crossing the kitchen, making towards the hall. 'Until you come to your senses,' he's pointing his finger at me, 'until you become halfway reasonable about this, there's nothing more to be said.' He pulls his jacket from the peg. 'I'm going for a drink!' he calls out, slamming the front door behind him.

Several hours go by before he comes home again. He creeps into the house as though trying not to rouse me, though all the while I'm lying on our bed wide awake listening to every noise he makes. The last sound I hear is Will opening the door to the spare room and shutting it again.

The following evening neither of us mentions the previous day's drama. Instead we maintain a careful distance. It feels as if we've reached a point of no return, a point where, if either of us speaks the wrong words, the last vestige of balance between us will slip away and our fragile world will topple irretrievably.

Josie

The following day I wake to find Will has gone out early but left a cup of coffee for me beside the bed. It's still warm enough to enjoy. I realise he's trying to keep the lines of communication open. If we're unable to speak without descending into argument, at least we can make some reconciling gestures.

In my studio I'm feeling lighter than usual. I've no idea why. It's contrary to what I should be feeling. Perhaps we've let off some of our destructive energy, and now the emotional field between us is less heavy. Whatever it is, I want to make the most of my strange optimism.

I pick out a large prepared canvas, move my easel closer to the window and place the canvas on it. I like my window. I use it to frame a view, as a way of seeing. Sometimes I amuse myself by deliberately misting the glass, blurring the landscape so that its forms are stripped of detail, trees reduced to line, grass to stippled powder. Today I breathe on the glass, then look down at my garden, screwing up my eyes until I'm unable to see detail anywhere, and can only make out vague patterns – the arches in the hedge, a patch of shrubs, the outline of the little pool. In my imagination I can extend the vista, turn the shrubs into a clutch of untamed undergrowth, widen the pool into a sweep of water reflecting peaks and slopes from the mountains above.

I'm so close to the window that for once the child stares away from me. I've been afraid to touch her with a paintbrush ever since she shrank from it. But now, before I begin my project, I hold her up and let the light shine through, revealing the uncovered streaks of canvas. Her face isn't too bad but the background is sketchy, a mix of pthalo blue and raw sienna stretched too thinly. Surely it wouldn't hurt to fill that in? I put her back on the easel, mix the colours on my palette and begin to paint carefully around her hair. As long as I avoid her face, I think she'll let me do it. The canvas yields as I apply my brush, making her move and breathe.

This time the oils enrich her. As I rub and spread the paint across the canvas I feel a shared rhythm grow between us. This is the child's medium, her essence, as it is my own. The mix of it, the textured feel, the boldness of the palette knife scraping across the canvas, these are my substances, my tools, my work. The pigments are in every fibre of my body. To me they are viscous as flesh.

I think of the space between canvas and brush and what it brings: *creation* – the act of art. Is it through such summoning that the child will come?

Will

Will was sitting in his office, documents in support of a client's hopelessly optimistic tax repayment claim spread out before him. When the phone rang, he picked it up irritably, knowing the interruption would oblige him to go back over the paperwork again. But the soft tones of a female voice relaxed his frown.

'I'm so sorry if I'm interrupting something important,' said Katy, 'but I absolutely had to ring you. Are you very busy, or is this an OK time to speak?'

'No, no, it's fine,' Will heard himself reply. 'I don't have a client for at least an hour.'

'Good,' said Katy, and then paused.

'Well, it's just that I've been feeling a bit bad about labelling you. Saying you were four-square and all that.'

'I see,' said Will non-committally.

'I mean, I thought what we uncovered was really good and I don't want you thinking I'm totally crazy.'

She laughed unconvincingly. Will sensed her insecurity but didn't know if it was about him, her work or the situation between them. He decided to leave her in her awkwardness and see what happened.

'The thing is, I know it was a bit much me trying to take you so far so quickly but, it came to me there might be some things about it you could understand.'

'Like what?' Will's mind was still partly on his client's affairs.

Her voice sounded almost timid. Where was the confident vamp he had last encountered? Her respectful tone was unexpected, awkward. It threatened to wrong-foot him.

'Well, it's about the number four and why it's so important. You see it's all about the underlying substance, you know, the basic matter that's holding up our reality.'

'Oh,' said Will. This only confirmed his solidity, his dullness.

He wished she wouldn't keep saying it. He was a four-square sort of guy.

As if she could hear his thoughts, she continued: 'And that's why your work, your job is so important. You're helping to hold the material world together. That's actually what you're manifesting.'

There was another silence while Will struggled to understand her meaning.

'That's probably why I'm drawn to you,' she said. Her voice was confessional, intimate, almost a whisper.

Will put his pencil down and glanced at his spreadsheet. One number seemed to stand out: 4,482. He decided to break the moment.

'Well,' he said, 'this is all very interesting, and it was kind of you to ring, but I'm afraid duty calls. I must get on with constructing more reality!'

He was pleased with his little joke. It kept things light between them while acknowledging her ideas.

Katy had stopped speaking but he could hear her breath in his ear.

'Look, I'm sorry if I sound a bit peremptory,' Will said. 'I do appreciate your trying to get me to understand all this, and it's very flattering to know my personality is so fundamentally important, but I don't see where it gets me.'

'Oh, you'd be surprised,' breathed Katy, ending the phone call.

As the phone went dead, Will felt unexpectedly bereft. The sound of her breathing had been strangely comforting. He could have suggested having a drink with her. That would have been better than going straight home after work. The thought of returning home felt like a kind of death, a shrinking back to the world of the mundane, as if he had been cut off from some vital lifestream.

Josie

The child gave me a shock when I first came in. Painting the background has altered her more than I expected. I mixed the pthalo blue and raw sienna with olive green and now she appears to be coming out of a rich darkness. Although her eyes are more dense, her hair has taken on a strange luminosity. She's like some ethereal creature tumbling from a cave of brush strokes.

I walk to the middle of the studio. From this distance it's as if she's trying to struggle out and come towards me. I wish she wasn't locked in oils. I wish I could lift her free. But all I can do is return her gaze and let her watch me while I'm painting.

With an effort I turn away and decide to finish a close study, a botanical piece I began a few weeks ago.

I hold it up and look at it critically. Having put it aside I can assess it more clearly. My efforts were better than I thought. I was painting an artichoke – lapped layers of leaves with that strange orchid-like shape and the deft spike. Their roughness, which seems to hold the light, made it easier to give them depth. I was trying to achieve a particular delicacy and precision my pupil Tom would approve of. But I want my artichokes to explode from the canvas – unlike Tom's passionless work.

I position the canvas on the easel and squeeze out my paint colours. Hooker's green is the perfect colour for the knobbed leaves. Three hundred years ago William Hooker created the pigment for his botanical paintings, and it's still the best medium for the job. Besides that, the name gives it a certain frisson. As I work, I can almost taste my artichoke, the soft flesh held inside, that delicious pulp gathered by the teeth, unfolding on the tongue.

I smile, finding myself thinking of Freud's artichoke. When he was a boy his father gave him a book containing coloured plates of Persian scenes, with the strange intention that he and his younger sister should have fun destroying it by tearing out the pages. Freud likened the action to tearing an artichoke leaf by leaf. I begin wondering what it would feel like to pull such exotic pieces from their bindings. Already I'm conjuring images of golden temples, palaces with domes and minarets, hanging gardens with fountains and shaded colonnades, ice-blue mountains, red-cloaked kings and silk-robed caliphs riding elephants with gaudy orange canopies. Two children ripping out the stuff of childhood dreams.

As I think of this and paint, each thistled lobe becomes a leaf of Persian fantasy: a curled slipper, a snake's head, a lotus flower or a paisley teardrop.

The work is flowing, taking hold. I'm not just tasting the leaves now, I'm inside them. Behind them lies the heart. It's a hard thing, palpable. I begin conjuring with the name: *Arty choke*. The word is provocative. When you prepare the bulb for cooking, you dig out the choke and throw it away, the immature heart too bitter to eat. But what if it was left unchoked, allowed to grow unhindered?

I remember once putting them on the windowsill – two artichoke plants in pots, and leaving them out to blossom. I can still see the burst of them – a violent force of Persian pink and cobalt violet.

I glance across at the portrait, at the child escaping the darkness. What if she could emerge like that, realise her full force and burst out of the canvas?

Josie

I spend half the morning consumed by my work. Mid-morning I decide to break off for a coffee. Still in my painting trance, I go into the kitchen and catch sight of Esme's card pinned to the noticeboard. It's been there for a couple of weeks now. I know if I leave it there much longer the moment will pass. On an impulse I pick up my phone and text her: 'Hi, it's Josie. Thanks for the card. And the invite. Sorry I haven't got back sooner but I'd love to meet up again.'

A few minutes later Esme calls me. The sound of her voice pulls me from my trance. 'Hi! As it happens, I'm going into town right now. Could meet you for lunch if you're up for it. What do you say?'

'Fine. Why not?'

'Where would you like to go?'

'How about Artco?'

I dress in a yellow top and white linen trousers, then twist one of my hand-painted silk scarves round my neck.

As I drive along the dual carriageway, the pointed cone of the Sugar Loaf disappears, dramatically reappearing as the road swings in a great arc towards the town.

I drive into the car park just off the main street. Here the Blorenge bulks shockingly close. I turn my back on its huge shoulder and walk through to the main street.

As I push Artco's door open to its chrome and glass interior, I can see Esme is already there, seated at one of the round metal tables. She stands up as I approach and we embrace.

'God, you look like a painting,' Esme says, eyeing my scarf.

'You don't look so bad yourself,' I say. She's wearing a black bolero jacket over an olive dress.

'I'm glad you suggested this place. It wakes the old town up a bit.'

Tom comes over to us, a wide smile on his face. I'd forgotten he worked here. It's interesting to see him away from the class. He seems more relaxed.

'Josie!' he says. 'Fantastic. Haven't seen you for ages. I've missed you.'

'Hi, Tom!' I'm wondering how to greet him now he's no longer my student. I kiss his cheek. He puts his arm round me and gives me a brief squeeze.

'And who's this?'

'My friend Esme.'

'Pleased to meet you.' Tom gives another of his smiles. 'Now, what can I get you ladies?'

'I'll have a latté.' I turn to Esme. 'What about you?'

'A cappuccino.'

'We haven't looked at the menu properly yet, Tom,' I say, 'but we'll make a start with those.'

'Right you are.'

As soon as he's gone, Esme clears her throat conspiratorially.

'Not bad!'

I purse my lips in response.

'Is that why you suggested this place?'

'He's an old student of mine. I'd forgotten he worked here.'

'Good choice, anyway,' Esme says.

After Tom has brought our coffees, she leans across the table.

'I'd say he's got the hots for you, Josie!'

I laugh, suddenly feeling as if my world has lightened.

'And is that your professional opinion too?'

Esme waves her hand dismissively. She picks up the large menu.

'Oh God, I can never make up my mind.'

'Neither can I!'

'I suppose I'll have a chicken wrap, as usual. I always end up with that.'

'Try something more daring for once!'

'OK, what do you recommend?'

'Tom!' I hail him across the room and he comes over immediately. 'What's the most exciting thing on the menu?'

He scratches the side of his head. 'Well, some of it's quite spicy, if that's what you mean.'

'No, a new taste is what we're after,' Esme says. 'Something a bit experimental.'

'Well, you could try our new chef's latest dish: Artichoke Ragout with Saffron and Olives.'

'Perfect.'

We order two portions.

'I've got a thing about artichokes,' I say. 'At least, I have now I'm painting some.'

'I suppose it must be like that,' Esme says. 'If you address something in your painting, it has an effect on you.'

'That's possible. But I don't know how profound an effect. It might just be because you have to examine it more closely. In any case I'm finding it quite sensual, I think it's rather Freudian.' I laugh. 'But now I expect I'm getting into your territory.'

'Not really. You might think anyone who studies psychology would know about Freud but he's rather outdated now. 'Father of', and all that, but the field has moved on a long way.

'What about Jung?'

'Same thing really, though I would say he's also a bit too esoteric.'

'More of a layman's interest?'

'Yup, but it doesn't mean I'm not open to what he has to say. It's just that he doesn't exactly feature on mainstream psychology courses.'

'Does Freud ever?'

'Some. But even so.'

'A bit too sexual?'

'Can one be?'

I laugh again. At this moment Tom brings our lunches, identically displayed on slate slabs.

'Looks promising.'

I take a mouthful and chew quietly, contemplating. 'Not bad.'

'Just think,' Esme says, 'if my car hadn't broken down when it did, I'd never have met you.'

'I know. Strange that.'

We eat in companionable silence for a while. Then Esme says: 'I know it's a cliché, but I feel like I've known you for years.'

'Ditto.'

'Weirdly, with you, I feel I don't have to make any great effort. We can just hang out.'

'God – I don't think anyone's said that to me in a long time!'

'I used to say it all the time.'

'So did I.'

The phrase takes me straight back to art college, to days when I hung out in cafés chattering and laughing with other students; when I walked loose-limbed, flicking my hair, eyeing up the men.

'I can see I've sent you spinning back in time,' Esme says.

'Sorry, yes. I was remembering how carefree I was at college.' I'm trying to remember what happened to all that. There was no sudden shift, no moment of crisis. It was all so slow – barely noticeable, like aging. Until one day you wake up and realise the bare legs and the laughter have stopped being easy.

Esme is looking at me quizzically.

'Sorry. I was just thinking how positive it all was, how bright the future looked then.' I let out a sigh. 'Of course, it probably wasn't like that. I expect there were all kinds of anxieties I've forgotten about.'

'Youth's like that. Agonising at the time but golden in retrospect.'

'You say that, but what about all the hope we had then? The whole world lay before us: career, love, parenthood, all beckoning – full of promises.'

'And now?'

'Now they just seem to bring a new set of problems.'

'Nothing is ever as good as its promise,' Esme says.

'Is that another aphorism?'

We laugh and the mood lightens.

As soon as we've finished our meals, Esme says: 'Why don't we go and check out the main gallery?'

'If the so-called art on the walls is representative, I'd rather not!'

'From a distance, I thought it was rather good.'

I raise my eyes to a ceiling that's hidden somewhere above a pattern of iron grids.

'What's wrong with these paintings, then?' Esme's voice is challenging.

'You really want to know?'

'Of course!'

'OK then.'

I wave my arm, indicating three canvases of varying sizes on the far wall. 'They're derivative. The painter's trying to be surreal. He's aping Max Ernst. Only he's got no flow or subtlety. These are nothing but cheap imitations. They're not saying anything.'

'Does art have to say something?'

'Oh, Christ, Esme, don't give me that. It's like being back at college!'

'But does it?' Esme persists.

'I think you can usually tell if something's just surface effect or comes from a deeper experience.'

'Sure, if you're a painter yourself. But what about someone like me?'

'If you saw the two artists' works side by side, you'd immediately be able to tell the difference.'

'How so?'

'Well you're a psychologist, for a start, so you can recognise an interior landscape when you see it. And, in essence, all Ernst's work is an exploration of that inner reality.'

'Doves, hordes, forests, towns and visions,' added Esme.

I look at her in astonishment. 'So you know about Ernst? You bloody sneak!'

Esme laughs. 'I don't know that much – just that the childhood trauma of losing his sister along with the family parrot probably inspired all his bird paintings. It's something I came across in a magazine. It intrigued me, so I checked him out.'

'Then you do know the difference! You know this guy's just playing. You were just testing me!'

Esme gives me a delighted smile which holds just long enough to embrace Tom as he comes towards us with the bill.

Will

When Will left his office for lunch, well after his usual one o'clock, he was slightly rattled. He prided himself on being able to bring his interviews with clients to a swift ending, thus maintaining some regular order to the day. His last client, however, a musician, had insisted on telling him about his gigs. He was evidently very excited by them – not that the guy made any money to speak of. Will had to stop himself from making the curt comment that anecdotes about the other band members were of no interest to him. Instead he had answered in monosyllables and drummed his fingers on the edge of his desk, hoping the young man would take the hint. Eventually, he had stood up and looked at his watch.

'Well, I'm afraid I have other clients. Thank you for giving me your accounts. I think I've got the picture now.'

A quick nod and the young man had finally left. Now, with his lunch hour curtailed, Will wondered which way to head. He had a two o'clock client, so he decided on the café next door. That was a shame: he'd been looking forward to a decent lunch, and the restaurant round the corner was so much nicer. Will felt an unfamiliar surge of self-pity. There was so little joy to be had at home, he wondered if his little daily pleasures were beginning to count too much.

Sighing, he turned towards the nearby café, then froze. Sitting in the window was Katy MacLaren. She was alone. Too late! She'd seen him. How could she miss him, sitting where she was? A broad smile, a red slit, those white teeth. She beckoned him in.

Squeezing himself onto the bench opposite, he saw she had an empty coffee cup in front of her.

'I was just going to order another,' she said. 'Shall we order two?'

'Er – yes,' said Will.

‘I was thinking of just having sandwiches, but a full round’s a bit much. Must watch my figure!’ She wriggled prettily and patted her stomach. ‘But I don’t mind sharing with you.’

The waitress came over and took their order: two cappuccinos and a plate of mixed sandwiches.

‘You know,’ said Katy leaning back and looking appraisingly at him, ‘I can’t stop thinking about our last meeting.’

‘It’s kind of you to say so.’

Will felt flattered. The irritation of the morning began to ebb away. He cradled the wide cup in his hands and took a sip. He was aware that flecks of foam had left a tide-mark on his upper lip. Languidly Katy swept her tongue over her own lip to indicate that he should do the same. He took another sip and then extended his tongue. Deliberately, exaggeratedly, he licked his upper lip. They both laughed.

‘For a Number Four Man, that was unexpected!’

The naming of him had apparently delighted her.

‘And I’m not counting lovers!’ She was teasing him with her eyes – her eyes were like mirrors. He knew she was inviting him to look, to see himself as she saw him – an exciting challenge up for the chase.

He looked down and fingered the coffee spoon. He stirred it through the pale fluid, gathering up the floating blotches of chocolate.

‘And what do you think of *me*, Mister Number Four Man?’ The question was direct, flirtatious.

‘I’ve certainly never had such an unusual client,’ Will answered carefully.

He was relieved when, at that moment, the sandwiches arrived. They took one each and bit into them.

‘I hope I didn’t offend you,’ Katy said, a piece of rocket curling from her mouth. He suppressed the urge to reach out and pull it from her. It was the kind of thing he would do with Josie. He missed such little familiarities. He missed brushing back her hair to kiss her neck. He missed …

Katy was saying something else.

‘I suppose it’s all right. I mean it’s not like you’re a doctor or anything, is it? So it's OK for you to have lunch with one of your clients.'

He cleared his throat. 'There are no boundary issues, if that's what you mean. At least, not of the professional sort.'

So far he could not fault his own behaviour. He just wanted to enjoy the encounter for what it was but give nothing of himself away.

Katy gestured towards the plate of sandwiches. 'I'm full,' she said. 'How about you finish the last one?'

'All right!' He took it with a smile and allowed himself to meet her eyes briefly once more. The gleam was gone. She was suddenly grave.

'Actually,' she said, 'it's been really amazing coming to you. You've made me feel like I might have a real profession after all; I might even make proper money.'

'Well, of course you can,' he said.

'When you're someone like me, it's not easy getting people to take you seriously.'

As he took the last mouthful of his sandwich, she leaned forward and added conspiratorially, 'Some people hate me, you know.'

Will looked up enquiringly. 'Why's that?'

'Because of what I do?'

'But you help people,' he said, remembering Josie's comments. 'You give them hope.'

'That's what I tell myself. But I still get hate mail, you know, although it's more hate email nowadays.'

He frowned in puzzlement. 'Who on earth from?' he asked.

'Mainly from Christians. They think I'm doing the devil's work!'

'Oh. Well, I suppose it's possible some still think like that. But not so much in this day and age, surely? I mean, the days of witch-hunts must be well and truly ...'

He was interrupted by the waitress. 'Would you like to order anything else?'

'N-no thanks!' He looked at his watch. 'Oh, heavens, I need to get going! I've got a client.' He took out his wallet and put a twenty-pound note on the table.

'Look Katy,' he said. 'I'm terribly sorry. Can you pay for us out of that? I haven't got time to wait for the change and I'm afraid I haven't got anything smaller.'

As he swept his coat away from the table, she called after him: 'Thanks, Will – thanks a lot!'

When he reached the door he heard her add: 'Is it all right if I call you Will?'

Josie

I've placed a cylindrical vase on the windowsill, twisting it so the Chinese calligraphy runs down the front. The effort is unnecessary, but it pleases me. Especially as I have to keep looking at it. I'm playing with perspective, shutting one eye to assess the distance between the vase and the window's edge, then opening both eyes and watching the lines jump. I've read about the double vision that looking with both eyes causes round a single focus and I'm trying to see beyond my focus of the vase. I know it will take practice. It's like seeing through a 3D picture. I remember the first time I attempted that, seeing only the image as if printed on the outside of a veil, then staring at the thing with increasing frustration, willing the veil to thin. At last, when my patience was almost exhausted, my eye slid through and there was the holographic object hovering in a void beyond.

While playing with the vase, I'm aware of the mountains in the distance. All winter they've framed my view, the sharp point of the Sugar Loaf erect above the dark slope of the Skirrid – the so-called Holy Mountain. I remember climbing it, reaching the trig point where the last remains of St Michael's Church lie: two stones of a vanished gateway. Skirrid. The word a mix of bistre and ivory white. It means a shivering, a shaking of its mountain head, a holy tremor.

All the while I'm experimenting with perspectives, I'm aware of the child. When our eyes meet I find her unsettling. She's not just watching me anymore, she's commanding. Commanding me to free her, to rip her from the canvas. And I feel powerless – as if I've given her life, yet trapped her in some kind of limbo. A limbo in which she's forever emerging. For, after all, what is she? A wish-fulfilment, an idea I've raised up through my art, given some sort of fleshing out, only to find she's ultimately unrealisable. Looking at her, I can't help wondering about art. About the use of it. Has it the power to change the world or is it just a storehouse of dreams?

The oils have dried now, so I can touch her. I run my finger down her cheek, feeling the coarseness of the canvas, the strokes and knots of paint. There's no softness there. She's nothing but a trick, a lie. Suddenly I can't bear to look at her. I take her down and turn her to face the wall, propping her against a stack of other paintings. The back of her canvas, loosely stretched within the frame, flexes briefly then stills.

Will

Will was sitting in his office trying to work. Ever since the conversation he'd had with Katy about numbers, he seemed to be uncomfortably aware of their effect on him. He looked down at his calculator and made out a series of curves: 969,099. There were too many 9s. He disliked the number 9. For him it was a number of exposure. It reminded him all too painfully of the time he and Josie had first met – a time it still shamed him to remember. Nevertheless he found himself going over the experience again, reliving each agonising moment, picking at the memory like a scab that would be better left alone.

He winced as the picture came unbidden to mind. For a start, he had been naked – but it was not how a naked man likes to think he appears to the eyes of a woman on first sight. He was a student then and short of money. The casual job offered by the art college, though embarrassing, offered a good hourly wage, so he thought it wouldn't hurt to try it out.

He remembered how he'd sat there, naked and unmoving, with only his thoughts to distract him, semi-hypnotised by the soporific chafe of charcoal on untreated paper. When the break came it was a huge relief. Grabbing his robe and covering himself up, he went round the easels, and found he was unprepared for what he saw: his body presented from nine different viewpoints like phases of the moon. He was shocked by the rigid geometry of it all: the ovoid hollow beneath his arm, the curve of his buttocks, the square steps of his vertebrae.

But – as if that wasn't shameful enough – worse still was his face. Surely this was a mistake? He stood back peering at the canvases in disbelief. In every drawing, the line of his nose formed the limit of reflected light, the far side darkened with charcoal shading. But, on each canvas, caught in the shadowed side, was a fish-tailed, drooping eye. It was something he'd never noticed before.

So this was how Josie first perceived him, he thought wryly, like a cubist drawing, his arms extended rods, his manhood a tiny cone against a triangular blackened groin. And yet, despite this inauspicious start, she'd agreed to meet him for a drink.

She'd arrived at the pub swathed in trailing scarf-ends licking round her like coloured tongues. She was exotic, exciting. He remembered how desperate he'd been to win her, how he'd planned his campaign over the following months – laying his devotion and dependability before her like some rare offering. But all the time he'd felt a fraud who could only win her under false pretences.

He sighed and picked up his calculator again. He wanted to do a few more additions, if only to get rid of all the 9s. But he found it difficult to concentrate. He was thinking of the first time he and Josie had made love. He was remembering how, when he'd finally loosened her twists of clothing, he'd gazed at her pale freckled body with a sense of awe. Her limbs were long and lean and she'd clung to him, her breasts tight against his chest, her fingers wreathed around his neck. Now he wondered miserably if they would ever make love again.

Then his mind turned unbidden to Katy. Katy breathing in his ear, Katy teasing him with her mouth, smoothing her stomach, playing with her loose black hair. He could stand it no longer. The uncertainty of everything was killing him. He needed to reach solid ground, he needed to know what was going to happen with Josie. Then he had an idea. It was ridiculous, of course. The method was unreliable, foolhardy. But perhaps it couldn't hurt to give it a try. He toyed with some papers, drummed his fingers on his desk, then picked up his mobile and called Katy's number.

'Hi,' he said, trying to sound professional. 'It's Will. I'd like to book a reading with you.'

Will

Will was watching her hands, her fingers working deftly, cutting and sorting, cutting and slipping the cards together, her bangles jangling like soft alarm bells. There was something hypnotic in the practised dance of card and finger.

'Look, maybe this was a bad idea,' he said, half-rising.

'Don't be silly!' She slapped the cards down on the table once more. 'It's the least I can do, after all your help.'

She looked across at him and a hair from her fringe caught the tip of her eyelash. 'Besides,' she said with finality, 'it's my pleasure. Now take the cards.'

They were laid before him neatly, face-down, backed with an innocent pattern of blue and white tartan. But he'd seen glimpses as she'd flicked and sorted, worrying sights of disturbing images. What was he doing here?

He surveyed the room again. If he had expected a fairground booth swathed in red silks, with a crystal ball as centrepiece, he was disappointed. The room in which she practised her 'craft' – he thought that was what she called it – was plain. Maple shelves lined one wall, there were white linen curtains at the window and, beneath it, a small side-table covered with a green cloth. Shapes in the cloth told him there was a collection of objects beneath. He was glad they were covered up. Both the wooden table and the folding chair he sat on were simple and pleasant. Only in one corner could he spot anything unusual. There was a collection of glittering objects; mostly an assortment of crystals, but amongst them was a small pyramid. On the window sill was a statuette of a winged goddess.

'Take the cards, Will!'

He picked them up.

'Now shuffle them.'

He felt the edges of the cards against his palm. As he fumbled with them, several fell out. Expertly, she scooped them up and returned them to his hand.

'Now cut the pack.'

He looked at her, frowning.

'Like this.' She lifted half the deck away and placed the remaining pile face down on the table. She pushed the pile towards him. 'Let them feel your energy.'

Will put his hand on them reluctantly. He felt only fear and awkwardness. But there was something else. An unpleasant prick of excitement. He cut the pack and held out his chosen stack. Her fingers stroked them lightly as she put them down. A simple cross made of cards lay before him, with one on top of the other in its centre. She turned the top one over.

'This is the Querent. It represents you. The King of Pentacles.'

The card showed a man sitting awkwardly on a throne, swathed in a ridiculous costume of vine leaves and bunches of red grapes, holding a knob-headed wand in one hand and a yellow circle with a pentacle on it in the other.

'Analytical, logical, professional,' she said. 'Rather controlled.'

She turned over the next card.

'The crossing card. Four of Wands. This is harmony in the home, romance.'

She looked up at him, her eyes like little moons. 'Here is your conflict.'

Will flicked his own eyes away. Damn, he thought.

Reaching to the top of the cross, Katy turned the next card over. 'And now the Crowning card.'

Will found the image unattractive. It showed a man sneaking away with five swords in his arms. Another two swords were stuck in the ground behind him.

'Seven of Swords. Your Present Situation.' She flashed him a look. 'You're trying to achieve what you want through guile.' Her teeth gleamed as she closed her mouth on the word. 'Sometimes necessary in this life.'

Will felt an involuntary quivering at the corner of his eye.

'And now the Base of the Matter.' She turned the card at the bottom of the cross. It showed a robed woman standing in a garden with strange symbolic circles clustered around her.

'Nine of Pentacles. This is your hidden longing – hidden even to yourself.'

He battled a strong urge to sweep the cards off the table and put an end to the game. They were giving this woman power over him, allowing her to probe his secret thoughts. Guesswork or not, she was building on them, using them to reach into him.

'Self-satisfaction. Usually a good card, but in this case, I would say …' She hesitated. 'Possibly too sure, too moral. All in all, too sure of your own opinion to see the need for change.' She let the information hang while she prepared to turn the next card.

Will was not looking at the cards; he was watching the tip of her tongue run along her lips. She turned the left-hand card. He looked down again. The card showed a youth sitting beneath a tree with three cups in front of him, a fourth held by a floating hand.

'This is the immediate future.' She sighed. 'Depression, dissatisfaction, boredom. It's Cups, so that means emotion. I'm guessing it's to do with your relationship again.'

Will squirmed. Was this really just guesswork?

'There's an element here of feeling cheated,' she said. 'Though actually,' she added, tapping the card, 'it's often the querent himself who does the cheating.'

Her fingers touched the bottom line of four cards that flanked the cross. As she began turning them, Will was conscious of an unwelcome quickening of his pulse. When she came to the last but one she paused, her fingers on the back of the card.

'The ninth card. Hopes and Fears.' She looked across at him. 'Before I turn it, Will, you need to know about the nature of Tarot. Hopes and fears, though they might seem like opposites, can both be in one card, one image'.

For the first time he felt she was no longer playing a game with him.

'This is where we stop being logical; and the impossible – if you like, the conflict of reality – comes in.'

This is what she truly believes, he thought. And this is the difference between us. A great gulf.

She turned the card.

Will could not help but recoil at its strangeness. He felt adrift amidst uncomfortable mysteries. A woman sat blindfolded, arms crossed over her chest, a sword in each hand, the sea stretching behind, a new moon overhead.

'The Two of Swords.' She breathed the words, and again Will wanted to stand up and run out of the room.

'A state of paralysis.' There was a new mastery in her voice. 'Refusal to face what's happening. Desire to cling at all costs to the safety of what you know.' She looked at him searchingly. 'Does this have meaning for you, Will?'

A new emotion was spreading over him. It was dangerous yet inviting. He struggled against the feeling that he was being understood, seen deeply for what he was, for what he was suffering.

'Yes.' He had not spoken for some time, and the word sounded hoarse.

She nodded her head. The movement was slight, signalling professional acknowledgement.

'And now the Outcome.'

The last card revealed a Pope seated on a throne flanked by two pillars.

'The Hierophant.' She arched a slender eyebrow. 'That's interesting.' She picked up the card, holding it lightly with thumb and finger, and rocked it from side to side. 'A spiritual teacher, but of a more orthodox type.' She paused, looking up at him, then added emphatically: 'And what you seek will come. Though maybe through a new relationship.' She placed the card back in position. The spread lay before them in its pictorial glory. 'Well, that's it!' she said. 'Do you have any questions?'

'No, thank you.'

Will was trying to rise. His legs were stiff. He leaned heavily on the little table as he got to his feet. The cards shifted towards each other.

'Cup of tea?' She was up before him, already at the kitchen door.

'No. No thank you.'

'You should at least have a glass of water after all that work.' She swept her hair over her left shoulder. 'And it is work, you know.'

Josie

'Now tell me,' Esme says. 'What's it like being an artist?'

We're sitting at the bench in my studio, a bottle of Pinot Noir and two glasses in front of us, looking at one of Dali's prints pinned to my noticeboard.

'Well, I don't know really.'

'Because you've never known anything else? Don't give me that! You must know you're a bit different. Less ordinary, if you like.'

'But so are you. I don't think it's just the so-called artists who are unusual. It's anyone who …'

'Anyone who what?'

'Well, *you* know.' I wave my glass, searching the air for the right words.

'What?'

'Sees things differently.'

'You mean thinks for themselves.'

'Not just that.'

Esme looks at me steadily. 'You mean who follows their dream.'

'Something like that. It's difficult to explain.' I take another sip then put my glass down again. 'People think if you do that you're a bit mad. But, of course, really the artist isn't mad. However strange some paintings are, they're just an expression of a different way of seeing.'

'Art is certainly a different way of seeing,' Esme agrees.

'I suppose you could say some of my pictures are a bit strange.'

I can see Esme's not convinced. The paintings on display are mostly of flowers – jugs with flowers, fruit with flowers, and clumps of flowers in windows. There's nothing strange about them. But Esme's caught sight of my charcoal drawing. The edge of it is protruding from a stack on the table, showing the pencilled web and the corner of an eye caught in it.

'Ah!' I say, following her gaze, 'you've picked out my real work.' I pull out the paper so Esme can see the whole eye revealed. The pupil is like a spider with trailing strands of web.

'Actually I'm a bit ashamed of the still life paintings,' I say quietly. 'They're what I paint to sell to garden visitors. That's how I buy time for painting these.' I pull out a canvas from a stack leaning against the wall. On it is a tangle of blooms with a small child's fingers raised defiantly against the sky. I pull out another one and prop it up. It shows a pale-fleshed couple embracing on a couch. The woman's body is turned towards the viewer, her pubic hair a vibrant triangle of red. Behind her, a bra hangs in fleshy Daliesque strings from the knob of a wardrobe door. A spent condom drips from the bed. I watch as Esme takes it in.

'From what I can see,' Esme says after a while, 'your work seems to have a Blakean influence.'

This surprises me.

'I don't mean William,' Esme says. 'Peter.'

'Could be.' I sit down again.

'You know where Peter Blake's old set used to hang out?'

'You mean the Ruralists?' I shake my head.

'Some quirky tea-rooms near Bath.'

'Really?'

'Yep. My mother used to take us there when we were young.'

'What was it like?'

'A crazy, romantic place with odd objects lying about and swings for the children, twisty tree-branches, smoothed-off tree stumps – you know the kind of thing. And junk-shop tables dotted here and there with faded cloths draped over them, and mismatched garden chairs – a real fantasy land. We loved it. The Ruralists used to celebrate their birthdays there.'

'I'd love to see it.'

'Well, if it still exists, let's go.'

'Did you ever meet Peter?' I ask her.

'No, but I did meet some of the others. They were quite gentle people, as far as I remember. Real ruralists. I think Peter was the hard nut.'

'His work's more challenging.'

'Ah! Then, tell me, why's he the influence?'

'I don't know. I like his nudes, I suppose.' I glance at the triangle of scarlet pubic hair in my painting. 'They always seem a bit confined. Straight-jacketed.'

'And is that how you feel?'

'Oh,' I say, laughing. 'I'm not one of your clients!'

'Fair enough, I'll lay off the analysis! But, seriously, about your paintings. Do you know what I think?'

I raise an eyebrow but I've already guessed what Esme's going to say.

'I think you should ditch the flowers and concentrate on your real work.'

After she's gone, I sit looking at my painting of the nude. I'm considering the vibrancy of the scarlet triangle against the woman's cloudy skin, the soft give of her thighs. Passion and delicacy held in tension, the vamp and the yielding girl. If I showed Will the painting, I wonder which he'd see.

I slide my hand inside the waistband of my jeans and reach a finger inside. Slowly I caress myself until the feeling wells and overflows. Afterwards, the loneliness of the impulse – an act for sharing – brings a quiet ease of tears.

Josie

Despite what Esme thinks of them, I need another flower painting for my open studio event. I decide to paint some phlox. I'll use the patch of Peppermint Twist I sketched in the garden last summer but never finished. Working quickly I watch the blooms burst indulgently from the canvas in a bold mix of cadmium red, alizarin crimson, flake white and pthalo blue.

While I paint, I feel restless. The leisurely feel of oils, the slow drying time that allows for contemplative change, the moving from one half-finished canvas to another – all are at odds with my new urge for rapidly completing images. For a wild moment, I even consider using acrylics in a bid to speed things up. The thought is ridiculous, but I know why I feel the need to rush. I need more stock for my open studio sales. All too soon, the summer will come upon me, and before then there is so much to do – the garden, the paintings. I don't know what will happen between Will and me, but for now I need to get ahead. Compelled by the fierce life of my blooms, I work hard all day and find it difficult to break away when Will comes home.

After another tense meal together in which neither of us offers much conversation, I leave him sitting in front of the TV and go back to my studio, drawn by the phlox. There's something intimate about painting in the late evening, I think. I flesh the blooms out further, pricking the flower heads with deep magenta, as if pulling colour from the night sky.

By the time I've finished work, locked up my studio and returned to the house, Will has already gone to bed. One dim lamp still glows beside the bed, left on for me. I slip quietly beneath the duvet and lie beside him, my mind overwhelmed with tones of brilliant rose. Unable to sleep, I pick up a slim volume beside the bed and read a short poem by Yeats, making out the words carefully in the subdued light. 'Tread softly because you tread on my dreams.' I take comfort from this last line. It seems to vindicate my position. This is the last thing I think before drifting off to sleep.

Hours later, I wake in blackness, my heart jumping against my chest. The child has woken me. This time she appeared as a plume of wailing whiteness, a desperate phantom calling across a blank abyss.

When my pulse has calmed, I go downstairs. The Rayburn, with its heavy plates and chipped black enamel, feels like a human presence. I sit, drinking a cup of tea, watching the sky yielding a faint silver powder as dawn breaks. I go back to bed, easing myself in quietly. I lie there unmoving, listening to Will's steady breathing and trying to conjure again the child of the night. As the light spills across the sky I feel the unaccustomed longing like a thickening pain swelling first one breast and then the other. This is what it must feel like to lose a child, I think, and have the milk still coming.

When I return to my studio later that morning my eyes feel heavy, as if they're not fully open. I push the key in the lock and hear the reassuring click of its withdrawing tongue. Now I can enter sanctuary. I lock the door behind me and briefly scan the room.

My eyes light on the easel with its strong pink blooms. I catch my breath and gaze at the painting, my chest sharp. The pricks of deep magenta between the tiny flower heads form eyes, a shadow outlines the nose. Slowly I approach the painting. As I draw nearer, the small face scatters, blurring into petals. I take a step back. It's disappeared. I retrace my steps towards the door, but no matter where I stand, the flesh-coloured blooms flare innocently on the canvas. The child has gone.

But the child was there. For a fleeting moment, she reappeared through oils. I banished her only to find her in another painting, peering through nursery plants like the unknown children who run about my garden on open days.

Josie

A life of avoidance: that's all we have now. We spend our time evading each other's eyes, passing without touching, leaving margins round each other. Even at night, though still sharing a bed, we're not touching. Spring is coming, and with it, lust, desire. Sometimes Will reaches out for me in his sleep. But we're so far apart I can't respond. I'm unable to feel, unable to think, and worst of all, unable to paint. Every day I go to my studio but, instead of painting, I lie sprawled on the couch, too heavy to move. Although she appeared among the phlox, I've still got the child's portrait turned against the wall. If she can somehow sense the pain she's causing, she's offering no help. And tonight I can't stand it any longer. I'm prepared to give up anything – the child, my whole dream, to lie comfortably in Will's arms again.

I can hear his car arrive. He's earlier tonight, almost like old times. I'm already in the house, so today I'll greet him with a hug. I'll be affectionate to him. But as the front door flies open and I see his face, the greeting falls back in my throat. I retreat to the kitchen, shrink against the chrome rail of the cooker. I can hear him in the hall putting down his briefcase, taking off his coat. I fill the kettle and set it on the hob. I leave the kitchen and go into the sitting room. I glance at the sofa covered by the brave colours of the throw, my few pictures on the wall, all looking so normal, but there's nothing here to help me. If I can raise something in myself, find some courage – that might stop it. But already he's coming through the doorway, his face distorted with anger.

'Why?' he demands. 'Why has it come to this?'

I look at him. I've no idea what to say.

'Why do you refuse me love?'

The phrase coming out of his mouth is so formal that, for a moment, I wonder if he's rehearsed it.

'I – I don't!' My voice is meek. 'At least, I don't mean …'

I know my submissiveness is infuriating. But it's too late, our hated roles have slammed into place. We have no choice but to act out our drama. With logic deserting me I scrabble for clarity.

'God knows, I feather this nest enough for you, don't I? You can do what you want in that studio of yours. Spend the day how you like. But when I come home, there's nothing left for me, is there? Nothing!'

'That's not fair, Will. I do work. You know I do.'

I attempt to change the script.

'I'm sorry,' I say, 'I know I must seem distant to you. I don't want to be. It's only for a while, until I work a few things out.'

'Yeah, sure!' His tone is scornful. 'But you don't have any trouble with your new friend, do you? You've got time for her, haven't you?'

'You mean Esme? I've only just met her.'

'All the same, you've got plenty of time for *her*!'

'Will, she's only been round a couple of times!'

He's swaying unsteadily. Has he been drinking?

He comes towards me.

'I heard you talk with *her*, laugh with *her*, the two of you hidden in your private little den!'

'When?'

When do you think? The other night. When I came home and she was still with you! So, of course, I kept away. I don't know what you get up to in there. Because *I'm* not allowed inside! *I'm* never invited in, am I?'

The kettle's screaming. He's close now, too close, his breath infused with whisky, his face a force of anger. 'If you're available for her, why do you run away from me? Why do you flinch when I want you, turn away when I reach for you? It's more than a man can stand!'

'Will. It's not like that. I ...'

His sudden boy's voice breaks the spell. 'For God's sake, I don't want pity, I just want a wife! Is that so hard for you?' He lunges towards me, his face level with mine. 'And', his voice is angry again, 'I want a child.'

'Will, so do I. You know I do.'

'Then why treat me like this? Why?'

I shake my head miserably. I have no answer.

'You don't even know, do you? That's how pathetic you are! You don't even know!'

He turns abruptly and walks out of the house. I hear his car door slam and the engine accelerate as he drives away.

Josie

Will hasn't come home. I lie alone in our bed, the patchwork quilt heaped over me, trying to recover a sense of equilibrium.

The moon is full, the thin drapes that serve as curtains barely holding back its light. Will's dressing gown is hanging on the door – by day a warm brown, in the filtered light a tapered lamp-black shroud. The way it hangs, I can half believe he's standing there in silent reproach. The silhouettes around me have become fantastic emanations in the moonlight. The dressing-table mirror glitters, the pots and trinkets throw shapes across the floor. Discarded clothes on a chair become a huddled form, the bedstead a cage of black spikes against the gloom. I shut my eyes but in the dark behind my lids the same stern shadowland appears.

I give up trying to sleep, slide out of bed and lift my dressing gown from the chair heap. Moonlight accompanies me down the wooden staircase, the door latch clattering as I let myself out.

The spring night air is not as cold as I expected. There's even something welcoming about my garden in this light. The tree branches – bone-black boles across the sky, seem less threatening than the objects indoors. The grass slips under my feet as I run down to the pond. Here the moon's face is spread, its perfect circle skittered by the twitch of the water. The tranquil busyness of it is somehow calming. I sit in the silence, soothed by the moon's light-play. I feel my mind emptying as I watch, the silence broken only by the soft clap of a bird's wings, the breath of branches shaking in a passing breeze.

Such natural noises after the quiet of the bedroom are reassuring. But now I hear rustling from the hedge beyond. The sound doesn't belong; it isn't made by natural creatures going about their business. I hold my breath. There it is again – distinct, though faint. A predatory note disturbing the tranquillity. I get up, my heartbeat painful in my ears. Resisting the temptation to cut quickly across the lawn, I walk back slowly, fearing that if I hurry I might draw chase. Only when I reach the steps do I make a last dash towards the house.

By the time I close the front door behind me, I can hardly breathe. My chest is squeezed with adrenalin. I lean my back against the door, waiting for the pain to subside, then go into the kitchen and fill the kettle, my mind spilling with questions.

I know there was someone there. I registered a presence with every small hair on my body. But how could they have got in? The lower garden is bounded by the walkway between the hedge and outside fence. The fence is tall, difficult to scale. The only entry to the garden is through the top of the drive. So, whoever it is must have come down the drive, crept past the house while I was in bed, and been hiding there, waiting.

I make myself a coffee with an unsteady hand. In place of milk I add brandy. Should I ring the police? But what would I say? I have nothing concrete to report. A handful of cracking noises, and a feeling. I need some kind of evidence. I sit in the rocking chair leaning my head against its high back, rocking myself as questions chase through my mind. Who was hiding there, and why choose this night, of all nights? Then a new thought presents itself. Is this the first time, or has someone been here before – listening, watching, waiting for me to be alone?

My hand is still shaking as I raise the mug to my lips. The liquid is hot enough to scald my throat but I barely feel it. If I can't ring the police, could I ring Will? While I drink I consider his reaction. He'd think it was a ploy to get him back. He'd blame my over-active imagination. Either way it would simply increase his contempt. No, I can't tell him. Resolving to keep the experience to myself, I realise that in some ways I need this new fear, if only to divert me from the other, deeper one – the fear of losing Will.

For the remainder of the night I sit in the wicker chair, rocking it to and fro as the clock ticks through the hours before dawn and the fragile light begins its crawl across the kitchen.

Josie

'I don't suppose it was anything more than my fevered imagination. I couldn't sleep and I felt so restless.'

Sitting next to Esme on a bar-stool in Snapper's wine bar, I'm wondering if I did the right thing calling her. Nevertheless, I can't stop myself pouring it all out.

'And then, of course, I haven't slept on my own without Will for so long now, I'm not used to paying much attention to extraneous noises.'

'I suppose not. But look, if you're worried, you could always stay at ours for a couple of nights. Just until Will comes back.'

'That's really kind. But I'm sure it will all blow over soon enough. And in any case, I can't allow myself to start being frightened in my own home.'

Although her offer is generous, I don't really want that kind of help. What I want is to talk about my relationship. The trouble is it's a subject I've studiously avoided for fear of trespassing on her professional work. Now I realise I've avoided it almost to the point where it's unnatural between friends. It also means I know very little about Esme's own relationship. But that can wait. Right now I desperately need to talk about my problems with Will, and perhaps, after all, this is the time to risk it. I drink some more wine and put my glass down decisively.

'When Will and I started out, we had such high hopes. But then I expect everyone does.'

It's a tentative beginning but it appears she hasn't heard me. After waiting for some sort of reply, I decide despite being a therapist, or perhaps because of it, Esme isn't making it easy. Nevertheless I decide to try again.

'We were never very alike – opposites in many ways, like most couples, I suppose.' I leave the sentence hanging.

Esme says quietly: 'But maybe that's the journey of it, the

accommodating of the other person who is, in many ways, such a stranger.'

Her voice is so hushed, I wonder if she's talking about herself. But now, with Esme's quiet prompting, I can feel the words inside me welling up. Before I can stop myself, I burst out:

'I know. And at first you love them for it, but then it gets more difficult. Much more difficult.' Esme's listening presence propels me on. 'And now we've had the worst row ever. Will's left, and I don't know where he is.' I pinch the stem of my glass hard. 'He was so angry – we were both –' I break off, unable to continue.

'People get very emotional', Esme says quietly, 'when a lot is at stake.'

'But we're so far apart we can't seem to get back!'

Esme inclines her head a little to one side. I imagine it's a gesture she uses with her clients.

'But we can't sort it out. We can't just sit down and talk about it. We've always been different, but at least we've always been able to talk. That's been the thing. That's been …'

'And now you're retreating from one other. Unpicking the bond. Unravelling.'

'But it's not what a relationship should do.' There's an unwelcome desperation in my voice.

'Sometimes, it's just what a relationship should do.'

'It feels dangerous.'

'It can be if you leave it too long.'

I look down at the bar. I'm aware that I haven't told her what's at the heart of it, what's causing all the pain and dissention.

As if she can read my thoughts, Esme asks: 'What's at the bottom of it? Is it a clash of views?'

'Yes ... I don't know,' I say miserably. 'We both want the same thing; it's just the way to go about it. There's the way that's obvious, and then there's the other …' I put my face in my hands. Next to me I can hear Esme quietly sipping her drink.

'It's all about the baby,' I say at last, speaking through my fingers.

'Baby?'

I lift my face again. 'The one we haven't got.' I squeeze the stem of my glass until it hurts. 'I'm sorry, I've no right to burden you with my problems, especially when you have to deal with these things every day.'

'No, no, it's all right. Besides, it's much better to confide in someone before it's too late.' Esme leans her elbows on the bar. 'I'm guessing you're having trouble conceiving. Either that, or one of you doesn't want children at all.'

I let out my breath in relief. 'You're right. We do want a baby, both of us, and yes, we've got problems. We've been trying for ages but it's not happening. Will wants us to go for IVF. It's the obvious answer, but somehow I can't make myself go along with it. I just can't. I don't know exactly why.'

It's all coming out so quickly I worry that I'm saying too much.

Esme's nodding her head. 'New developments are not always as miraculous and helpful as they might seem.'

I wait for her to say more but instead, she begins tapping her fingers on the edge of the bar. She stops as if she's reached a decision then turns to me and says abruptly:

'As it happens, I do have some experience of this.'

'You do?'

'Not personally. But in my work.'

'Oh.'

'But I –'

'You have to be careful, is that it?'

'Oh, I can manage the confidentiality bit. It's ...'

'What?'

'It's not my job to influence you.'

'I can see that. But what can you do?'

'I can give you a different viewpoint from Will and your consultant.'

I push my glass to one side and lean my elbow on the bar. 'Shoot,' I say.

'Are you quite sure? Because if –'

'I'm quite sure.'

She takes a breath. 'OK then, Josie. What you're talking about – IVF: it's huge.'

'I know.'

'No, you don't. No one really does.'

'But *you* do?'

'I've counselled women. I've seen what it costs.'

'A lot of money. I know. Enough to bankrupt some people if you go through it several times. But you could argue anything's worth it.'

'I don't just mean financially.'

'There are physical risks too.'

She nods. 'But that's not all.'

'What else is there?'

Esme sips her drink.

'Josie, do you know the statistics – the success rate?'

'Isn't it about fifty–fifty?'

'Is that what Will's told you?'

'What is it then?'

'For women in their mid thirties it's roughly thirty per cent.'

'So less than a third of the women who undergo it get pregnant?'

'That's right.'

'I thought it was better than that.'

'And what do you think happens to the other two-thirds, the ones who fail?'

'I suppose they're the ones you counsel.'

'I've only seen two couples who've been through it, but I've seen several women who've come to me on their own.'

'And?'

'For all of them it's pretty much post-trauma stuff. But then, as you probably know, it takes quite a lot of guts to do it in the first place.'

'I know you have to inject yourself.'

'Some women find that very difficult. They have to inject their stomach every day, which is painful. But it's not just that. It's the effect of the injections.'

'The hormones?'

'Yes. It's like a massive reboot. First you have to shut the ovaries down, then you have to wake them up with a huge boost of hormone. It plays havoc with the woman's emotional stability. And that, of course, affects her relationship.'

'But surely they're in it together?'

'Just think about it for a minute, will you, Josie?'

'So what effects does it have then?'

'Well, for a start, sex stops being spontaneous and the husband can't always do it to order; then the wife feels let down as if she's doing more than her share. But, in any case, she can't maintain a balanced state of mind about it. How can she when she's being chemically manipulated?' Esme shakes her head. 'A couple's relationship has to be very strong to withstand the emotional turmoil. When it fails, it's as if the whole heroic effort was for nothing. It's too much for most people. A lot of couples split up afterwards.'

For a moment I feel vindicated by this information. Esme has given me a way out, a psychological rationale built on statistics. I could present it to Will and leave it there. I might well do that.

'I didn't know all that,' I say. 'And in some ways it's reassuring because the fact is I don't want to let Will down and I do want a child. But I don't want to do it like that, and I can't get him to understand.'

I'm aware I've shifted the conversation – made it entirely personal.

'Look, Josie,' Esme says, 'it's not for me to advise you. I can only present you with what I know.'

I can't help it; I have to push her.

'I need your take on it, though, as a friend. What do you think I should do?'

She shakes her head.

'Please, Esme! You can drop the professional bit. I just want to know what you would do.'

She sighs. 'Well, OK, as long as you realise this is just what I think as a friend.'

'Of course.'

'In that case, from my perspective, I would have to say that it's primarily your decision. Quite apart from the emotional trauma, it's your body that's affected, not his. It's a woman's choice whether or not to have an abortion, so I think it should also be her choice when it comes to IVF.'

This is a good, clear point, I think. I could just agree with her and leave it at that. But Esme's my friend. I want to tell her the truth. I want to outline the real issue as I see it. It's a risk, I know. But I need to find out what she thinks.

'Thank you,' I keep my voice measured. 'Everything you say is valid and I can see that it's powerful stuff. Except, in my case, the simple decision of whether to go for IVF or not isn't the problem. It's not a question of weighing up the risks or fearing the procedure. I've tried that. It's something different. A gut feeling. A feeling that it's not the right way.'

I pause. Esme won't think I'm crazy but, like Will, she may think it's an excuse, and that the real issue is fear of the process. I look at her directly. 'What I'm trying to say is that I can't make myself do it. I can't explain why. All I know is I can't do it because it doesn't feel right.'

Esme returns my gaze. I realise she's considering her reply, deciding how to speak her truth without letting me down. Whatever it is, I suddenly know I can trust her judgement. Esme will mean what she says. And what she says will be insightful. I wait for her to find the right words.

'Gut feelings are important.'

She makes her pronouncement as though it's sufficient justification in itself.

'Do you mean ...?'

'Yes. One should always listen to gut feelings.'

'But –'

'What else is there to go on?'

'Can they really be trusted?'

'Ah! Well that's another question entirely, isn't it?'

'What do you mean?'

'I mean if you listen correctly, if you get it right, then you should definitely obey your instincts.'

'So it's all about being sure you're picking up the right message.'

'Yes. Every time a woman comes to me with a problem I try

to uncover her gut feeling about it. I've never known anything get solved if she goes against that.'

'Really? That sounds almost too easy.'

'On the contrary. Accessing your intuition is extremely difficult.'

'So how do you do it?'

'You have to be very aware of yourself, able to cut through your fears and prejudices, and instead recognise your deepest promptings, your inner voice.'

I nod enthusiastically.

'But, even if you're convinced it's telling you something,' Esme continues, 'that's only half the battle. It can be very hard to obey.'

'Yes.' The relief of feeling understood is making me tearful.

'Yet it seems you're doing just that.'

'I am?' I pull a tissue from my shoulder bag and blot the corners of my eyes. I decide it's time to confess a bit more. 'Perhaps, if it was just the feeling, I wouldn't be brave enough to act on it. Only I've had dreams as well.'

'Dreams? Now you're walking right into my territory!'

'So you don't think I'm –?'

'Crazy? Far from it. Dreams are the gateway to the unconscious, as the great man once said.'

I raise an eyebrow.

'Your friend Jung. And he'd have found this fascinating.' She pushes her glass forward and climbs down from the stool. 'But first I vote we order some more wine and retire to those leather seats in the corner.'

When we've resettled ourselves, she turns to me. 'So,' she says – and this time there's no doubting the professional authority in her voice, 'tell me about your dreams.'

Josie

By the time I push open my front door it is dark, but I feel light inside, lighter than I've felt in a long time. The house is empty. If Will was intending to come back he would surely have been home by now. I'm wondering if he too is spilling out his troubles over a row of drinks. Whatever conversation he might be having, it could never be as extraordinary as the one I've just had. In a haze of euphoria, I make myself some tea as an antidote to the wine I've drunk. Perhaps he'll come in later.

But as time ticks by and Will still doesn't appear, rather than agonising about our relationship, I turn my attention to the night visitor. If I'm to sleep alone again, I need to think what to do.

In the end I take some bedding into my studio and pile it on the couch. The decision is not a rational one. The building is, if anything, less secure than the house, but it feels safer because it's my sanctuary.

I wrap myself in the duvet and lay my head on an old velvet cushion. Comforted by the array of paint tubes and pastels, by midnight I'm becoming drowsy. I am just closing my eyes when I glimpse a pile of bills and invoices on a table in the corner. It's enough to send a shot of adrenalin through me. Even though Will usually does the final calculations, I always dread what I have to do in preparation – recording the sums, setting out the receipts in order. Every year I have to steel myself to do it. For the few days it takes me, I feel as if I've entered the monochrome world of early cinema. I can never inhabit it for long and am always relieved when I've done my bit and it's time to hand over to Will. But will he help me this time? Perhaps not. The thought makes me shiver. Sleep will probably elude me now – at least for a while.

I close my eyes but instead of sleeping I think of the strings of numbers Will holds in his head. They seem to me like black marks on a canvas, dense as a flock of birds yet tightly columned, bounded, lacking colour, vibrancy or splattered pattern. What if they were rainbow-coloured – 1 indigo, 2 violet, 3 blue, 4 green, 5 yellow, 6 sizzling orange, and 7 red? Could they be played with? Will deals with them all the time. He obviously feels comfortable in their presence. Perhaps numbers give him a reassuring sense of order. Yet I find it hard to imagine they've ever really called to him; that he ever woke as a child and saw their shining forms hanging in the air.

Although we're so different, Will and I, in a way, we complement each other. He's dependable – at least he has been until now, and that's something I've valued. But is that enough? I begin wondering if the qualities of one man are spread too thinly for a woman. Perhaps what a woman needs is the full range of hues with all their corresponding passions – the security of sable through to the vibrancy of alizarin red and yellow ochre.

I open my eyes. I realise I've been thinking of Will as separate from myself, weighing him up as an appropriate partner. Is he doing the same with me? The thought is unsettling.

It's then I hear it. A noise like a key being dragged along the brick wall of the studio. I tense under my duvet, holding my breath against the banging of my heart. Letting my breath out, I slip from under the duvet and make myself walk to the door. I listen for a while, then unlock it, pull it open cautiously and look out. There's no one to be seen. Feeling bolder, I step outside. The garden lies around and below me in the moonlight, peaceful and still. Should I check round the side of the studio, where the noise seems to come from? It would mean leaving the security of the open door, to which I can flee if necessary. It would mean gambling everything on there being no one there.

I retreat inside the studio, lock the door and wait. After a while, hearing nothing more, I again take courage. This time I'm carrying a torch. I walk quickly round one side of the studio, my bare feet cautious on the dewy grass. No one there. I double back and go round the other side. The far end of the studio is joined to a low wall, too low to conceal anyone. Nobody could be hiding there. I return to the open door. I should be safe now – unless someone slipped in while my back was turned.

I scan the room quickly before locking the door again. I know I would be safer in the house. But I don't want to risk crossing the courtyard carrying my duvet. Perhaps I should ring the police. But, like last time, there's no real evidence. Reporting a strange noise and a bad feeling isn't enough. Again, if I ring Will he'll be scornful. He'll demand more information. As I think of him an unexpected thought comes to me, sparking fresh shots of adrenalin. Suppose it's Will out there? Suppose he's spying on me! It would be so unlike him that even the possibility is shocking. Unless he's got it into his head that I'm being unfaithful. Men can be stupid like that. With sex on hold, however complex the reasons, they can jump to the obvious conclusion. But are we really so far apart now, Will and I, that he could imagine I have a lover? The idea is so ridiculous I can barely handle it. Nevertheless, thinking it might be Will takes my mind from my earlier fear.

Hearing no more outside noises, I eventually drift off to sleep. But my night is patchy. Waking several times in the dark, I am relieved when at last dawn appears, painting my studio by stages in Davy's grey and cerulean blue. By the time daylight arrives I feel exhausted.

Josie

Early next morning, Esme appears on my doorstep, concerned about me.

'You slept in here? That was brave!'

'Oh God, I'd better tidy up. Yes, I did sleep here. For some reason it felt like a friendlier space. But, really, it's less secure than the house.'

'Looks like you had a bad night,' Esme says. 'As a matter of fact, I didn't sleep so well myself. I was worrying about your intruder. I should have insisted you stay with me.'

'When I said I can't let myself be frightened in my own home, I meant it.'

'I admire you for that. But were you all right? Did you hear anything?'

'Well,' I say, and stop. If it was Will sneaking around after all, I don't want to make an issue of it. 'I thought at one point I did hear something. But it was very faint, and when I looked around outside there was no one there. I think it was probably just my imagination after all.'

Esme looks relieved. 'I hope you're right. But it's still worrying. Have you rung Will?'

'No.'

'I think you should. You need him back. Apart from anything else, you need his protection.'

'It's a question of pride.'

'It often is.'

'I don't want to run after him.'

'And I dare say he's thinking the same about you.'

I say nothing.

'So, who's going to be the first to break the deadlock?'

I look away, unable to answer.

'Josie, this is serious. You've got to talk to him. If you want to stay together you've both got to climb down. Perhaps you could arrange to meet at a neutral place, talk about your differences and try to work something out. I know it sounds like a cliché, but it's the only thing to do.'

'OK.' I sound resigned. 'I'll ring him today.'

'Good. Let me know how it goes.'

After she's gone I go to the stack of paintings at the back of the studio. I take the outer one in my hands and turn it round. Something in me shakes with apprehension whenever I do this. There is the small girl, her yellow ochre hair across her shoulders, her eyes strong, her face indistinct. Each time the child from my imagination has to slide onto the canvas and meet the one in the portrait, I find myself wondering whether this is the child from my dream. I've tried so hard to catch her but I'm not sure I've managed it. I look into the eyes that stare at me, trying to quell the fluttering within me – is it fear or excitement? Then I lower the canvas and turn the child towards the wall again.

Will

Will opened his eyes and was surprised to find he was lying beside a claw foot belonging to an Edwardian chair. Rolling onto his back with a groan, he gazed up at a corniced ceiling with a paper lampshade dangling from its centre. Then he remembered where he was.

It had been good of Andy to give him a floor to sleep on at such short notice. Andy was his closest colleague at work, probably his closest friend, besides which he was divorced, so he might be expected to understand. But after an earlier attempt to confide in him had produced the dismissive observation that women were unfathomable, Will had been reluctant to turn to him again.

Nevertheless, it was Andy's doorstep that had beckoned when he'd left home and, after giving him shelter he'd asked no questions, which was the best thing a friend could do. But as he lay there staring at the ceiling, Will reckoned he couldn't spend another night at Andy's without attempting some kind of explanation. Before that, however, he had to get up and prepare himself for the day ahead. He got up stiffly, rolled up his mattress and headed for the bathroom.

As it happened, the day passed easily enough. It was a relief to resume his professional role. With a succession of clients in front of him and the necessity of dealing with their accounts, he could retreat into a world of calculations and forget his domestic difficulties. At the end of the day Andy dropped into his office and suggested picking up a takeaway on their way home.

It was when they were sitting in the kitchen eating curried chicken and saffron-coloured rice that Will finally made an attempt to outline the situation. It wasn't easy, because he found the whole thing so difficult to grasp. He couldn't explain Josie's behaviour. She was a complete mystery to him and a bloody unreasonable one at that. While he vented his feelings, Andy listened, occasionally nodding and grunting as if he understood. When Will had finished pouring out his tale, Andy got up and fetched two more bottles of lager from the fridge.

'The thing is,' he said after they'd opened their beers, 'women like to be understood.'

'But she's so difficult and so – so unreasonable …' Will began.

'Well, mate,' Andy said, 'if you want an opinion from me, first hear me out.'

Will admitted that an outside opinion would be helpful.

'The way I see it is this. She says she wants a child as much as you do. As far as that goes you're both in agreement.'

Will nodded.

'So, if we look at it rationally, the IVF solution is the obvious way to go. But if she won't agree to that there must be something about it that's bothering her.' He took another swig of beer then sat in thought for a while.

'Actually it's bloody simple!'

Will looked at him hopefully.

'Well, despite what she's told you – about not being afraid of the process and all that, it's pretty much what you suspected, isn't it? I mean, it's her body, after all – and all the clinical business – to a woman it must seem like a bit of an invasion. Bit scary, too, I should think. I mean, how'd you like to have all that done to you?'

'I know that and I've tried to be sympathetic. But it's mostly just taking drugs, isn't it?'

Andy waved his fork in the air and grains of rice fell onto the table. 'I don't think you're getting it, mate. According to you, she went as far as listing the side-effects. So, it's pretty obvious, isn't it? All *you* have to do is jerk off. She has to have some bloke going in with a bit of metal, scraping out her eggs.'

'But other women do it! Most women are prepared to go to all sorts of lengths for a baby!'

Andy took another swig of beer. Lines of foam framed his words as he spoke.

'You've always been pretty bloody protective of her up to now, haven't you?'

Will nodded.

'So why stop now?'

'But I've really tried. I've tried to listen to her, to understand.'

'Well, all I can say is it's a big thing for her. Maybe she needs a bit more time and a bit more support.'

Andy had struck a chord. Will felt chastened, but relieved, and suddenly less angry with Josie. He began to wonder if, after all, there was a way forward.

The feeling was fleeting. Andy seemed to be deliberately fiddling with one of the discarded bottle tops. 'Not wanting to pry,' he said, 'but whose fault is it she can't get pregnant?'

Will glanced towards the open door. 'Difficult to say,' he muttered. 'Don't really know. Tests were a bit inconclusive. Possibly a bit of both, really.'

Andy lifted his pint and squinted through the opaque liquid. 'Bit low on the old …'

'Yep. Something like that.'

'In that case, if you don't mind me saying so, you're bloody lucky.'

Will jerked his head up.

'I mean,' said Andy carefully, 'at least she's taking that on board, not screwing you – I mean, really screwing you, like some women would!'

'What do you mean?'

'Well, you know how some women would get around it?' Andy gave him a pitying look. 'Especially if it might be your fault after all.'

Will thought for a moment. 'Oh, Christ!' he said.

Josie

It's the third night since Will left home. I lie alone in our large bed trying to sleep, but my mind is too restless. Taking two nights to cool off is a bit pointed, I think, but three is beginning to cross a line. I know I should do something. I should try to ring him. Then again, it was Will who walked out – so, surely, it's up to him to return.

But as I turn it all over in my head, I realise it's not easy to paint myself white and Will black. Things are never that defined. They swirl together like globs of paint, one colour blending with another. Grey would be more appropriate. I think of Payne's grey: zinc white mixed with bone black, ultramarine and a smear of red lake like blood. The pun arrives unbidden. Pain's grey.

The light of a three-quarter moon is still lively on the curtains, the air still heavy. Feeling suddenly stifled, I throw aside the duvet, drop my legs over the side of the bed and slip to the floor. Drawing back the curtain, I push the window open and gaze out to where the garden disappears into black grottoes. There is no wind, not even the faintest breeze to lift the leaves. I wonder if there's a storm coming. I take a deep breath then release it as I hear the chock of a pebble hitting concrete. A spurt of faint cracking sounds follows. It *is* someone. But who? It has to be Will. No one else knows I'm alone. Is he spying on me?

Propelled by sudden rage, I snatch up my dressing gown. In seconds I'm through the front door and running across the courtyard. Then I'm down the steps, crossing the lawn.

'I know you're there!' I call. My voice is bold in the oppressive air. 'So you can stop playing games!'

Ahead I can see the dark bulk of the boundary hedge where it's been cut into an alcove. The moonlight shafts across it. In its light I can see the leaves shake. There is not enough breeze to make that happen.

'Will, for God's sake, stop lurking around!'

I dart towards the grotto. It houses a carved bench. I kneel on the seat and part the hedge behind. I'm just in time to see a tall shape detach itself. I climb down and run on. Only I know where the alleyways lead – which ones open onto the passageway and which are deceptive. Will is always forgetting which is which, and it appears he's forgotten now. I can hear him running on the other side of the hedge. I stop and stand still, knowing where he must come out. And there, from behind my fish statue, he suddenly appears in the lit arena of the lawn, like an actor bounding on stage.

'Wi–!' I begin. Standing in the monochrome landscape as if caught in one of his own paintings, a slight young man passes a hand across his hair and down the back of his head. It's a familiar gesture. But not Will's.

'Tom!' I cry in disbelief.

He groans and falls to his knees in the grass.

Tom is shivering as I lead him into the house. I take him into the kitchen and put the kettle on. He blurts out:

'Oh God, Josie. I – I'm so sorry. I never meant. I never – I didn't want …'

But of course he meant to. I know that. And, for all I know, he wanted me to find him and take pity.

I sit hugging myself in my night gown. He's sitting opposite me now with tea in his hand. I start to fire questions: 'Why were you out there? Were you stalking me? Didn't you realise I might be frightened? Did you know I was alone?'

He doesn't answer.

'Tom, this is so unlike you.'

He puts down his mug and puts his head in his hands. Then he takes his hands away in surprise. When he holds out his hands to me, I see blood.

'I think I've –' he begins.

'Oh,' I cry, 'your head!' I run and fetch a towel and wrap it tightly round his wounded forehead.

'I think I must have scraped myself on some branches,' he mutters.

I bend over him, concerned. 'How deep is it? Are you all right?'

'It's nothing. I'm OK.'

'I'll check it in a minute when it stops bleeding.'

I'm still standing beside him when we hear a noise, unnaturally loud in the middle of the night – a key inserted in a lock and turned.

'Oh, my God!' I drop onto my haunches. Tom clutches the towel to his head and we freeze there, waiting. The sound of footsteps is unnerving even though we know who it must be. As the familiar tread recedes up the stairs, I come to life.

'You must go!' I mouth at him.

I cross quickly to the French window and push it open. Holding the towel to his head, Tom takes off at a run, following the side of the house before disappearing round the corner in the direction of the drive.

After he's gone, I sit by the window shivering, half-supported on the chair seat, my body strained forward, listening. All that fills my ears is my own fast breathing. After several minutes, I hear the tattoo of Will's footsteps on the stairs, the creak of the penultimate step as he releases it and lands on the hall floor.

'Hello!' I call, moving quickly through the kitchen towards the hall. A second later I hear the crash of the front door and the rattle of glass in the photographs hanging on the wall.

Will

Will was sitting in his office thinking about numbers. Numbers had always been safe to think about. But now he was trying not to think about the number three. An uncomfortable number. Unbalanced, not properly divisible. Two and one, one and two. It was a number that could topple a kingdom.

He thought about going outside for a cigarette. Smoking was an old habit of his he'd long despised. But in a time like this it offered a little comfort. Of course, it didn't help that Katy also smoked. He winced as he thought of her. Trying to force his mind back to his figures, he looked down at his calculator: 433.34. Fours and threes.

A childhood storybook about King Arthur came to mind – the fellowship of the Round Table wrenched apart by a love triangle. Good old Arthur, the plodding and reliable king. How unexciting he must have seemed beside Lancelot, the exotic Frenchman.

He felt dull, small, how he'd always known he would feel once Josie saw who he really was. Returning to the house last night, at first he had been surprised to find her bed empty. Then he'd wondered whose bed she was lying in. But that was when he'd heard the sound of running feet. He'd looked out in time to see the figure of a young man disappearing up the drive. But who the hell was he? Where had Josie met him? She was certainly moving fast, he had to admit that. Unless it had been going on for some time. Was that why she refused the fertility treatment?

Then suddenly it all made sense. Of course, she was still hoping to become pregnant naturally. She was only waiting to surprise him with the news. But that didn't quite add up. Why hadn't she had sex with him recently to complete the deception? Nevertheless it was a neat explanation. He could address the details later.

He looked down and saw he'd been grinding his pencil onto his notepad in increasingly dense circles forming a raised lump of grey. He broke off and began drawing 3s all over the page, flipping them so they turned into waves and birds and breasts. When he'd filled the page, he crumpled it in his hand and dropped it on the floor. Gathering up his jacket, he went out into the street.

It was one of those long light evenings of early spring, the air musky with the smell of hawthorn blossom. It made him think of Katy. He remembered how she'd insisted on the number four being his talisman, his zone of comfort. Four, he thought, was a good number. Better than three.

Josie

It was stupid, I know, but a perverse part of me made me try. The board is laid across the garden table, its weathered face turned upwards. Across it is written 'Open Studio' in flake white, entwined with climbing roses to indicate the garden setting. I know that I should really be starting all over again with a complete sanding down. But that would mean erasing the careful lettering, the blooms and petals. Calligraphy is not my strongest suit. It's been a struggle marking out and keeping the letters perfectly scripted, so I'm trying to patch it up. But already I've smudged the opening serif, my hand unsteady as I attempt the sweep of the S. The air turns heavy and a drop of water falls onto the board, splashing the flake white lettering across the blue ground. I run towards the studio, carrying the board while the curved back of the O drips across the T below. I push the door open and lay it on the floor.

I stand looking down at the spoiled lettering, knowing there's no energy left in me to correct it. My attempt to repaint the sign was a pathetic pretence of bravado, driven by my need to believe that my life is continuing as usual. Abandoning the board, I go indoors in search of my phone.

It's already been two days after the incident with Tom. If only I'd taken Esme's advice. If only I'd rung Will before this happened. I realise now how foolish I've been, imagining that, while I put off ringing, everything would stay on hold; that time would somehow stop and wait for me to resume my life. While I prevaricated, events, of course, rushed onwards. I'm almost sure now that Will saw Tom escaping through the garden in the moonlight. So it's too late to try to convince him I'm innocent. My recent behaviour – my inability to communicate, my aloofness: it will all add up too neatly. He'll believe the worst. Even so, I pick up my phone and call him. His mobile's switched off so he must be with a client. Texting seems too impersonal. Instead I leave a voice message.

'Will, it's me. I'm sorry, I'm so sorry about what's happened. Please, we need to talk.'

Will

Will pushed open the pub door. The interior greeted him like an old friend. Andy waved from a far corner with exaggerated vigour. In front of him were a couple of beers.

'How's it going?' he asked.

'It's not!' Will's face was expressionless.

'Oh.' Andy was disappointed. He'd hoped Will and Josie would have made a move towards each other by now. Failing that, he'd hoped the atmosphere of the pub tonight might trigger a brighter response.

'Is this for me?'

'Sure, mate!'

Will took the pint in his hand.

'So what's the latest?' Andy said.

'You were right!' Will placed his drink down carefully. 'You know that guy I saw disappearing across the garden?'

Andy nodded.

'Well, I think I've worked out who he is. I think it was Tom, that nerdy student of hers who once took a shine to her. He used to linger in her studio after everyone else had gone. A dickhead.' He took a draught from his pint. 'And now I finally get a message from her. Left on my mobile. Not at a time I can talk, you understand. When she knows I'll have it switched off. While I'm working, for fuck's sake!'

'What did it say?'

'"I'm sorry!" That's what she said: "I'm so sorry!" *Sorry!*' Will slammed his fist on the table.

Andy put a hand on his shoulder.

'Will, it's OK! That might not mean –'

'Of course, it does!'

Andy held out the packet of nuts. In an automatic gesture, Will opened his hand and Andy shook the packet into it.

'Are you sure you've got it right, that you're not over-reacting?'

Will shook his head, nuts crunching in his mouth, then swallowed. 'That's just like her. She'd be sorry. She'd do it and then, yes, she'd feel guilty. Guilty as hell.' His voice cracked. A nut lodged in his throat threw him into a fit of coughing. Andy thumped him on the back.

When Will had recovered, Andy said: 'Would you like to go back to the house?'

'No. I'm OK here.'

'Are you sure?'

'Sure.'

'How about we order something to eat?'

'You go ahead. I'm not hungry.' Will drank the beer in one long draught, then slammed the glass down, watching the dregs run down the sides. He reached into his wallet and held out a ten-pound note.

'I could do with another one.'

He watched as Andy walked to the bar – probably wondering what the hell advice he could give now, Will thought. He didn't know Josie well enough to guess how she would behave, so he couldn't defend her. He'd been to their house a few times and seemed to find her a bit unsettling. That air of preoccupation she so often had. Plus her looks: skin like white sand, honey-coloured eyes – beautiful. Andy probably wondered what she saw in him.

Two hours later they were still sitting there. Andy was now beyond censoring the advice he felt compelled to offer.

'If I were you, I'd go back and pretend you didn't see anything. Tell her how much you've missed her. Make a pass at her. Try and get her back into bed.'

'She wouldn't have it!'

'She might. You never know.'

Then Andy confirmed Will's deepest fears.

'But if she did, you'd really know.'

'Know what?'

'Whether she was sleeping with him, and needed to set you up.'

Will's heart sank with the realisation. He was caught and they both knew it. If Josie welcomed him back, it would only prove her guilt.

Josie

As I enter the house, the landline is ringing. I put down my two bags of shopping and pick it up. I hear Esme's voice.

'Will's not back, is he?'

'Hi Esme. No, but thanks for asking.'

'I tried your mobile, but I couldn't get an answer.'

'Oh, sorry, I can't always hear it in the noise of the supermarket.'

'There are a few things I wanted to ask. First, how was last night? I'm still worried about that intruder.'

'You needn't be. I've discovered who it was.'

'Really?'

'Yes. It was Tom.'

'Tom?'

'Yes, Tom. You know, the guy who served us that time in Artco.'

'What was he doing at your place?'

'He said he was keeping an eye on me.'

Esme snorts. 'I've heard that one before.'

'Well, look, never mind. He's pretty harmless. At least I can stop listening out at night and wondering if there's someone there.'

'Are you sure he's harmless? I mean – lurking in the shrubbery!'

'Well, he was quite shame-faced. I don't think he'll do it again.' I ignore Esme's doubtful tone and hope she'll drop the subject. 'Anyway, what else did you want to ask?'

'OK. Well, I wanted to know if you'd rung Will.'

'Yes, I did. And I left a message saying I was sorry and that I wanted to talk.'

'And?'

'I haven't heard anything back yet.'

'I see. That's a shame. But you might have expected that. It's all part of the game – making you wait. So, actually, the third thing I wanted to ask might be timely.'

'What's that?'

'I wanted to invite you to stay over. Nathan's away on some conference or other and I'm on my own. The invite still stands, even if you're not being stalked anymore. I think it'd be good for you to get away for a bit.'

'No, I'm all right. Really. There's no need to worry about me.'

'Oh, go on. It would do you good to get away. And, besides that, I'd enjoy your company.'

I consider only for a moment before answering, 'OK. You've twisted my arm. I'll come.'

Actually, I'm curious to see where Esme lives. I haven't been to her flat yet. We've always met in my house or somewhere in town.

When I arrive, Esme is cooking. She takes me into the kitchen, which is as bone-white and clinical as she described, except its surfaces are strewn with vegetable peelings and scraps of onion skin. A smell of garlic seeps from the oven.

'Wow, I didn't expect this!'

'Why not? We've got to eat, haven't we? Anyway, lasagne's my speciality. It'll take about half an hour. Let's go and sit somewhere more comfortable.'

We go into the living room. Here the theme of the kitchen is reflected in white leather sofas on a stripped wooden floor. A large Mondrian-style rug lies in the centre. On it are two glass-topped coffee tables at right angles to each other. Cushions in black and chrome yellow, echoing the colours of the rug, are scattered on the sofas. A lemon-yellow wall is hung with modern paintings by artists unknown to me – perhaps friends of Esme's. On the far white wall is a layered rectangle in varying hues of red, a Rothco print.

Esme sits on a sofa and motions me to the other one. She's placed a tray with a sweating bottle of white wine, two narrow-stemmed glasses and a bowl of olives on the table between us. As she pours the wine she says:

'So, who exactly is this Tom who's been stalking you? When I met him at Artco you said he was an old student of yours.'

'He came to my summer school. He was the only man in the group.'

'Was he any good?'

'Well, yes, in a meticulous sort of way, he was.'

'Meticulous?'

'Nothing was allowed out of place. His work was so careful, so *anal.*' I take an olive. 'But now I'm straying into your territory!' Esme laughs. 'So I did my best to loosen him up. We all did. The women were the complete opposite of him – colourful clothes and messy grey-streaked hair.' I smile. 'Actually, I think they were rebelling. Not wanting to slip tidily into old age.'

'Rage against the dying of the light.'

'Something like that, yes. But they were living, vibrant; whereas Tom ...'

'Seemed to be excluding life?'

'Belittling it, containing it, holding it in check. He was so careful, so deliberate.'

'With people like that it tends to spill out in the end.'

As soon as she says that, I remember how, unexpectedly, every now and then I saw flashes of something more daring in his work.

'I know,' I say. 'And occasionally I saw something more in him. So I tried to catch it – I tried to free him up, encourage him to let out some feeling, some *colour*, for God's sake! Express himself. Be a bit radical. But everything is black and white for him. Everything. It's as if he lives in a monochrome world.'

'Perhaps he does. Did you ever check whether he was colour blind?'

'Nothing as simple as that, I'm afraid. He just can't go there. And he disapproves of my using so many colours – and my passion for them.'

'Colour is very important to you, isn't it?'

I nod.

'So, in a way he was attacking you.'

This surprises me. 'I hadn't thought of it like that.'

'Well, perhaps you should.'

'But I don't think he meant it. He's just very serious. He considers himself a real artist.'

Esme raises an eyebrow.

'In a garret,' I continue. 'You know the kind of thing. He's putting all his energy into his work. Hoping to make it.'

'What do you think of his work now?'

'I haven't seen it recently. But, from what he says, it seems to have taken a new turn since I first taught him. He says it's much darker. More daring.'

'Perhaps you should go and take a look at it. After all, he was once your protégé, so he'll expect you to take an interest. It might offer some clues as to his psychological state – can he really be trusted? But you'll need to be careful – take someone with you.'

'I suppose so. He was one of my more promising students, despite being so cautious.'

'Well, it seems now he's thrown caution to the winds.'

'Certainly sounds like it.'

Esme gets up. 'That lasagne must be ready by now. I've already made a salad. Let's go and eat.'

We go back into the kitchen and eat sitting on two high stools at either side of the breakfast bar. As she passes me the salad, Esme says:

'And now, tell me, have you spoken to Will?'

'No. He hasn't got back to me yet.'

'Give him time. At least it's a start.'

Wanting to deflect the conversation, I raise the question I've been putting off: 'You never tell me much about *your* relationship.'

Esme waves her hand dismissively. 'Oh, living with an academic is a whole other ball game.'

'You know, I haven't met him yet.'

'Haven't you? Oh, that's weird. No, I suppose not!'

'So, what's Nathan like?'

'Clever, witty, infuriating. All those things. But, actually, he's done well to get as far as he has. It's not easy to get a job like his these days. And he's still pretty young of course.'

'So he's quite a challenge.'

'He's a bit critical of my field, likes to argue with me about the value of psychology, that kind of thing. But it certainly keeps me on my toes.'

'I bet you give as good as you get, though.'

'You could say there's a deliberate rivalry thing going on between us.' She sips her wine. 'But then, if you're married to an aspiring don, you've got to, haven't you? Hold your own, I mean.'

We eat in silence for a while. Then Esme points towards the lasagne. 'Do you want some more?'

'Thanks.'

'Help yourself.'

I spoon some onto my plate. 'Well it sounds as though your secret of success is built-in positive conflict.'

She shrugs. 'Maybe.'

'I reckon half my trouble with Will is his mother.'

'Oh God, mothers and their sons!'

'You said that with feeling. I suppose you see it in your work a lot.'

'All the time.'

'So what's your own mother-in-law like?'

'Well, of course, Nathan and I aren't actually married so, strictly speaking, I don't have one. Nevertheless, I do have to deal with his delightful parents every now and then.'

'What are they like?'

She makes a face. 'Oh, I suppose they're all right really – especially compared with yours. Except that, looking at them, I keep on seeing why he's such a self-centred bastard!'

'But you still put up with him?'

'Oh, he's all right really. Anyway, it's high time you met him. I'll invite you to a dinner party or something. Then you can judge for yourself.'

After supper, we move into the sitting room where Esme opens another bottle of wine.

Next morning I wake to find myself under a faded Japanese silk eiderdown of duck-egg blue with blossom branch motifs. The room is furnished with simple bamboo pieces. Japanese prints hang on the walls, the sun illuminating them through thin curtains. I roll over luxuriously. I've slept well and feel refreshed, despite a slight pounding in my head due to the two bottles of wine we drank the previous night.

When I return home later that morning, I realise the mistake I've made. While I've been away, Will has been back. The door to the sitting room is ajar. Through it I can see beer cans on the coffee table. I go in. The room smells of cigarette ash. There are five stubs crushed together on a saucer. I carry it out and scrape them into the kitchen bin. But Will doesn't smoke. Is the stress getting to him or did he bring a friend round?

I pick up the phone and ring Will's office number. The brisk voice of Megan, the receptionist, answers.

'Hi!' I say, knowing my voice is only too easy to recognise.

'Oh! Hi Josie!'

'I just wanted a quick word with Will.'

'Will?' Megan sounds puzzled. 'Will rang in sick yesterday. And he hasn't come in today.'

'Oh! I didn't realise! I – I've been staying with a friend. I didn't know. I'd better get back home.'

'Yes.' Her voice betrays nothing. 'I hope he's OK by tomorrow.'

As I ring off I realise too late that my home number will have shown up on the office phone.

I go upstairs to the bedroom and push open the door. Will is lying across the bed, his arms flung out. Why didn't I check the bedroom before ringing? I know why. Because it's so unlike him. He's always so methodical, so correct. But then I remember I didn't see his car when I came in. It isn't parked outside. Why is that? Perhaps he went out drinking and was dropped off by a friend – the smoker. That has to be the explanation. Unless he deliberately hid it somewhere.

It's strange what a difference a few days can make. I feel as if I don't know him anymore. I look around the room. His jeans and sweater are discarded on the floor, a cigarette butt stubbed out in a glass on the bedside table. Oh, God, what kind of friend did he bring back?

I don't want to think about it. Don't want to jump to conclusions too soon. I go downstairs again. I decide that before confronting him I'll wait until he sleeps it off. Even then, he'll feel too grim at first. The best thing I can do is get out of the house and go to my studio. That will help pass the time. I finish tidying the kitchen then write a note on the back of an envelope and prop it against the fruit bowl:

Will, I'm in the studio. Come and find me when you're ready. J xx

When I come back at lunchtime, Will has still not come down. I go upstairs to rouse him. But as I enter the bedroom I already know what I'll find. There's no sign of him. The bedclothes are thrown back, the heap of clothes gone. He left while I was working. Does he need to avoid me that much? I sit on the edge of the bed then let myself fall sideways onto the mattress and pull the duvet over me. I move to where I last saw him lying, his arm flung across the pillow. I imagine there's still a vestige of warmth remaining from his body. But has there been a woman in our bed, lying where I am lying? It doesn't bear thinking about. I lie there, tightly curled, knees biting my chin, rocking myself beneath the weight of the bedclothes. Finally I make myself face the situation. Something has happened. Something fundamental. The fragile illusion of a little Eden shared by two people, an image fostered by childhood fairytales, is now in tatters.

After an hour of miserable contemplation, I go downstairs to the kitchen, tear off a crust of bread, spread it with houmous, and stuff it in my mouth. Then I return to the studio and yank out my painting of the artichoke. I dip the fattest brush I can find into a jar of white spirit and begin blotting everything out until all that remains are the bare lobes, faint bulbs of Hooker's green.

Will

Feeling too rough even to contemplate returning to his office, Will had gone back to Andy's. He knew he risked outstaying his welcome. He'd only intended to crash there for a couple of nights and, however friendly and supportive he'd been, it was clear Andy needed his space back. Then, of course, he *had* gone home. But first he'd deliberately concealed his car down a side lane. He'd intended to surprise Josie, catch her with Tom maybe, but she'd been out. In the empty house he'd helped himself to some beers at the back of the fridge, then opened the whisky. He didn't remember much after that.

Next morning, he'd woken, dressed and gone down to the kitchen, where he had found her note. Still in her studio – despite everything! He screwed the note into a ball and hurled it into a corner of the room. But the thought of facing her in her lair was too much. Instead he'd left the house in angry silence and walked the couple of hundred yards to his car.

As he made himself a sandwich in Andy's kitchen, bitterly sawing off two slices of the soft white bread and hacking at some cheese, a sudden memory from the early days of his marriage came to him. It took him back to a Saturday when he and Josie were walking hand in hand down the main street of a small village in the Forest of Dean. Beside the post office stores, they came upon a shop selling toys and baby clothes. Its window was laid out with so little sophistication that they wondered if the contents were second-hand. They laughed together seeing, amongst the array of bright plastic playthings, a few wooden toys that looked like old models gaudily repainted. Then they noticed that some of the clothes which had faded in the sunlight looked hand-made.

In a fit of enthusiasm, Josie had wanted to go in and buy something. She'd scanned the window, assessing the woollen hats and cardigans. A pair of tiny pink bootees lay pressed neatly together in a corner. Squeezing his arm, Josie had said: 'Let's buy them, as an encouragement!' He'd assumed it was meant as a joke. 'Plenty of time for all that,' he'd said laughingly, pulling her away.

He wished now that they'd bought the bootees, painted a room, got a crib. Then she might be on side with him today. But this had never happened. He remembered why. He pulled away because of the colour of the bootees: they were pink.

Josie

I'm still blotting out the artichoke leaves when I hear a light tap on the studio door. My heart sets up a quick pulse. Can it be Will? I dab my eyes with a corner of the oil rag, and open the door, paintbrush in hand. A man is standing outside in an overcoat with his back turned to me.

'Will?' I ask uncertainly, knowing at once that it isn't him, yet hoping I can somehow make it him. Yet it is Tom who turns round, looking down at the ground apologetically.

'What on earth are you doing here?' I ask.

'I'm sorry, but I couldn't just leave it like that.' He looks at me pleadingly. 'Please, can we talk?'

'Just a minute.'

I leave him waiting while I replace my brush. 'Let's go into the house.'

I lead the way and Tom follows meekly. We go through into the kitchen and I offer him a coffee. While the kettle boils he paces awkwardly about the kitchen floor.

'I think I might have dropped you in it!' he says at last. 'Did he see me?'

'I think so.'

I put our mugs on the table and take a seat. Tom sits opposite me.

'Josie!' he says. 'I'm so sorry. I've been a fool.'

'What on earth were you thinking?'

'I – I don't know.' He's been avoiding my eyes. Now he lifts his head and looks directly at me. 'I just wanted to make sure you were all right.'

'All right? You scared the hell out of me!'

'I know, I know! But I didn't mean it like that. I care about you Josie.' He reaches a hand across the table. I ignore it.

'What do you mean, you care about me? You've only ruined my marriage, that's all!' This is unfair, I know, but I can't help myself. After all, Tom's presence might have been the final blow that's keeping Will from coming back.'

'*I've* ruined it?' Tom leaves the question hanging.

'Yes!'

'I think that was already happening before I came along.'

'Came along!' I glare at him. 'Before you began stalking me, you mean!'

'You don't have to call it that.'

'That's what it was, Tom. I could go to the police.'

'No you couldn't! Because then you'd have to tell them that you cleaned up my wound and that you let me out quietly. And, considering Will had come back to the house, they'd want to know why you didn't call out and get his help.'

'The way things were, I didn't want Will to come to the wrong conclusion.'

'The way things were?' Tom echoes me softly. 'How were things, Josie? Or rather, how are they now?'

'Worse, of course, since I found you prowling in the garden.'

'But it's not all my fault, is it?' Tom persists.

'What do you mean?'

'I heard ... rumours,' he says quietly.

'What rumours?'

'I saw him with –' He clears his throat. 'I saw him in the pub.'

'So?'

'He was drinking too much, saying things, beginning to make a nuisance of himself. I think someone took him home after that.'

'When was that? Last night? You started stalking me long before that.'

There is a long pause during which Tom seems to be considering his position.

Against my better judgement, I ask: 'Was he with anyone in the pub last night?'

'A friend – male.'

I feel a temporary surge of relief, but not enough to be completely reassured. One more question needs to be asked.

'Was Will smoking at all? I mean, did he go outside for a cigarette?'

Tom appears to search his memory while I wait impatiently.

'Maybe. I'm not sure,' he says.

I let out a breath.

'I think you'd better go,' I say, getting up.

He follows me to the front door. As he leaves he turns back to me.

'Josie,' he says, 'Can I ...?'

'No, I don't want you calling again, if that's what you're going to say. Please keep away from me. You've done enough damage already.'

After he's gone, I begin absent-mindedly rinsing our mugs. I feel puzzled. So much is strange about the whole business. For a start, why was Tom stalking me at all? He's never seemed that kind of man. But what *is* that kind of man? Even assuming he is, why did he begin stalking me just then? His timing was extraordinary. How on earth could he have known my relationship with Will was foundering? After all, we'd barely admitted it, even to ourselves.

Leaving the mugs to drain I sit down. I must admit it's a relief to be puzzling over a new mystery rather than thinking about my relationship with Will. I sit on, unaware of time passing, until the light fades completely. I'm thinking of what Tom said or, rather, what he didn't say. There were moments when I thought he was on the point of telling me something important – something I ought to know. But what?

Will

Katy looked at him, the pack of cards in her hands.

'Are you sure you're OK?' she asked.

Will said nothing.

'You look as if you've been through a bit of a rough time. Is that why you want a clarification?'

Will thought this a strange term for an occupation he considered vague and murky at the best of times.

'I don't know about a clarification,' he said.

'Oh,' said Katy with one of her light laughs, 'that's just what we call it when you want more information following a reading.'

Will was aware of his duplicity. He was not coming for the cards.

'Which card stayed with you in particular after the reading?' Katy's face came towards him. He realised it was a genuine question and, with an effort, forced his mind back to the litter of strange images she had spread before him. But that was a while ago and they had mostly become an unpleasant blur. He could only remember one.

'Er, the Pope guy sitting on a throne.'

'You mean the last one, the Hierophant. I'll find him now.' Her fingers shimmied through the cards. She pulled one out and placed it between them. 'Here he is.' She looked up enquiringly. 'What do you want to know?'

This had not been a good idea. Will didn't want to know anything. Nevertheless he had to play it out. 'Well, all that number four thing. I mean, is that it? Is that all I am? Is there a possibility of moving on?'

'Do you mean in a particular area of your life?'

'Well ...'

'Career, maybe?' Katy raised a fine eyebrow. Without waiting for his reply she went on: 'No, I don't think so. It seems to me you're quite well set up there.' She glanced across at him. 'Relationship then.' She was busying herself with the cards again. Will said nothing.

'Let's see.' She lifted half the pack away as before, and put it into his hands. 'Shuffle!'

Again the cards that he'd watched dance in her hands became leaden in his own. He forced clumps of them together half-heartedly, then handed them back.

'Now cut the pack!'

Will took a few from the top and placed them on the table. It was becoming increasingly difficult to maintain this charade. He felt like throwing the cards across the floor.

Katy picked up the pack and creamed three cards from the top. She placed them face upwards on the table. The nearest one showed an effigy of a knight lying on a tomb with four swords displayed around him.

'Hmm. The Four of Swords.'

'Looks like I've got four again.'

It's a card of disappointment and exile. But don't worry, that situation's now passing, and the other two cards are pretty damn good.'

The card next to it was certainly more to Will's taste. It displayed a naked woman kneeling beside a pool, pouring water from a jug. Above her was a sky full of stars.

Katy's glossy nail with its half-moon cuticle tapped at the naked woman. 'The Star. This is a great card. It symbolises new hope.' She dropped her voice and added softly: 'A doorway of love is opening to you.'

Will was wondering if the card had any such meaning at all. He began to realise how much power lay in her chosen occupation. It was all so easy for her with her teasing eyes, her sly lips. She could have anyone this way.

'Does any of this speak to you, Will?'

Reluctantly, he nodded his head.

'All right. So let's see what the future holds. The Ace of Cups.' She tapped the third card with satisfaction then leaned back. 'Abundance, fertility, and an exciting new love affair.'

Will stood up, pushing his chair away. 'You're making this up!'

Katy flushed, but he saw it was with anger not embarrassment. 'If you think that, you can look it up yourself.' She went to a row of books between two sphinx-shaped bookends, pulled one out and tossed it onto the table in front of him. 'Go on, look it up, if you don't believe me! It's near the beginning.'

Will flicked through the opening pages until a picture of the Star card appeared. 'The Star brings new hope,' he read, 'being associated with new opportunities. In the realm of relationship, it brings new love.'

'The aces are on page 54,' she said icily.

Turning to the page, he read: 'The Ace of Cups represents the ultimate of love and happiness. It denotes great abundance, fulfilment, fertility.' He closed the book.

'I don't understand. How can they possibly ...'

Katy smiled. 'Because Will, the cards never lie.' She leaned over him and took the book from his hands, her lips still quivering from the smile. She parted them and he saw the wet gleam of her tongue. All he had to do was bend his head towards her.

Josie

I'm trying Will's number again. Over the past few days my messages have become increasingly desperate:

'Will. It's Josie. Please ring.'

'Will, we must talk.'

'I need to see you, Will.'

'Hi! It's Josie. Can we meet somewhere? Talk?'

'Will, we can't just leave it like this ...'

Which of these pathetic pleas am I going to leave this time? When I ring, Will never picks up. He must know by now that I miss him, and want to sort things out. Yet he still maintains a stubborn silence. I never would have imagined he'd behave like this.

As I pick up my mobile to make yet another attempt, the doorbell rings. I open the front door to find Frieda standing on the doorstep. She's clad in a capacious raincoat in bright bismuth yellow. Drops of rain are running down it. She bustles into the hall, shaking water onto the wooden floorboards.

'Just thought I'd pop round. See how you're both getting on!'

'I'm afraid Will's not here,' I tell her. I'm just about to add, 'He's at work,' when I remember it's Saturday morning.

'Oh!' Frieda sounds put out. 'Where is he?'

'He's gone out.'

'Where's he gone, dear?'

'I don't know,' I say lamely.

'Well, perhaps by the time I've had a coffee, he'll be back.'

Before I can say anything more, she hands me her raincoat, charges into the kitchen, and sits down with a sigh. 'Nice and warm in here with that Rayburn!'

I hang her coat up and follow her in.

'Wherever Will is, I hope he's not caught in this awful downpour.'

I fill the kettle. Its whistle, when it reaches the boil, comes as a welcome interruption.

I hand Frieda a delicate china cup with matching saucer.

'Thanks, dear,' she says. The saucer's come from beneath a small cactus. I managed to rinse it surreptitiously while Frieda was sizing up the unaccustomed mess in the room.

'You must have been busy lately,' Frieda remarks, waving her hand at the accumulated clutter. 'Been too busy, dear, trying for the baby – is that it?'

I am appalled by her remark. I want this woman out of my kitchen, out of my life if possible. 'Frieda,' I say, 'that's not –' I'm about to say 'your business' but she looks up sharply.

'Are you all right, dear?'

It's the first time she's ever asked such a question and, for a moment I wonder if she could be genuinely concerned about me. A mad impulse makes me want to enlist her support, as someone who cares about Will, someone who could perhaps put my case. It makes me want to pour out everything to this woman who, I know in reality, has no feelings for me at all – at least no positive ones.

'You – you're not ... are you?'

'No.'

I control myself. The impulse passes.

'I don't know whether you've seen Will recently but I'm afraid we're not getting on very well at the moment.'

'Oh? He hasn't said anything to me!'

Frieda is clearly taken aback. Not, I think, by the difficulties between us, but by the fact that she didn't know about them. Will evidently hasn't told her anything.

'Would you like a biscuit?'

'No, thank you, dear.'

Frieda takes a sip of coffee, then looks searchingly at me through her magnifying lenses. She replaces the cup thoughtfully on the saucer.

'I've been very careful not to say anything,' she begins. 'But now I really think I ought to, for your own good.'

This was unexpected. Perhaps she does know something after all? I brace myself.

'Of course, you realise how much we want Will to be happy?'

Josie nodded.

'So, you'll understand that we've been a bit concerned.'

'I didn't know.'

'Well, dear, in a nutshell, what we're concerned about – is all the art you've been doing.'

'My art?'

'Yes, dear. Of course, we understand it's quite a hobby of yours – I mean Will understands that, too. But it does rather seem to consume your life.'

She stares at me. I stare back.

'What are you trying to say, Frieda?'

'Well, just that we *have* wondered whether it was getting in the way.'

'In the way of what?'

'Of wanting a baby.' Without waiting for a response she goes on: 'What I mean is, we know some artists can get a bit obsessed. Their art ...'

'Their art what?' I ask her, my voice quiet. Does the woman imagine that painting has contraceptive properties?

'Well, you know, dear, for some artists their art becomes their baby. It becomes such an obsession that it leaves no room for a real one.' She gives a slight laugh. 'Baby, I mean. So you can see that we have been rather concerned.' She takes another sip of coffee, again replacing the cup carefully. 'And we wondered whether it's only Will who wants a family – and that maybe it's not quite your thing, dear.'

'And why wouldn't it be my thing?'

Frieda pulls the edges of her cardigan together. 'Because, you seem more devoted to your painting than to anything else – even poor Will himself.' She gives another small laugh. 'And, you know, he's quite a straightforward man really. All he wants is a loving wife and family.' She searches my face, then continues: 'Of course, he's devoted to you, but we get the impression he does rather suffer for it.' She lets her words hang unanswered, then turns a fat wrist to look at her watch.

'Well, I'd better be going. You never know, Will might have

turned up at ours, looking for me.' Pushing her cup and saucer away, she gets up.

'Don't bother to show me out,' she calls from the hall as she dons her raincoat.

As soon as she's gone, I pour the still warm coffee down the sink and rinse the cup. Instead of placing it to drain, I hold it over the tiled floor and let it fall.

Will

He couldn't believe he was doing this. Nor did he want Megan or Paula to come in and catch him at it. Before him on his computer screen were those same awful images, the ones he had first seen in Katy's flat. Instead of working, he was exploring the Tarot online, trying to grasp what it meant.

It was a strange experience. For a start, the terminology in itself was baffling. The four suits: Wands, Cups, Swords and Coins were straightforward enough, he supposed, but terms such as *Major* and *Minor Arcana*, *archetype*, *querent*, *lemniscate*, were completely alien to him. Still, he needed something to focus on, something that chimed with his bizarre situation. Being in Katy's flat – surrounded by her talismans, rifling through her books – even such slight acquaintance with her world was affecting him. And, already, his reading about the Tarot had set him thinking. It was difficult not to see the dark and light of everything – a bit like an artist, he supposed. He wondered if it made life easier, seeing things that way. The cards, he now realised, had dual meanings. That was the awful trick of them. For example, the image of a tower splitting, flames coming from its mouth, people falling, could mean either total destruction or the cracking open of a prison. It depended on how you looked at it.

Having grasped this premise, he began to feel angry with Katy. He felt she'd duped him and he wanted to have it out with her. He rang her number. When she answered, he launched straight in with his new information.

'I've looked up the Ace of Cups online and discovered that besides love and abundance and all that, it has a reverse meaning.'

'That's right.'

'In fact, for that particular card there are several meanings.'

Before she could comment, he began listing: 'change, insecurity, sterility, instability, unrequited love – that kind of thing.'

It pleased him to be meeting her on her own ground, for once. 'Which is, actually, much more relevant to my situation.'

'But that's only when the card is reversed.'

'And how do you know it wasn't?'

'Because it wasn't upside down.'

'Oh!' he said, caught out. 'But is it as simple as that?'

Katy's answering laugh was, he thought, a little patronising. 'It can be. But you have to really know the cards to be sure. You have to handle them a lot to understand their full meaning.'

After the call, Will switched off his phone. He had been irritated while she argued with him. He found it extraordinary that she made such claims for what she called her 'craft' when, to him, it was all random speculation. He refreshed a spreadsheet on his computer and applied himself to it. After a few minutes the figures began to soothe and steady him. As he let go of the Tarot cards and their meaning, he found his irritation with Katy subsiding. Instead he was thinking of the sound of her breath down the phone, her scarlet lips framing her words, and the black plumage of her hair.

Josie

Will has still not answered my message. He's been gone for several days, and now that the coldness is no longer palpable between us, I miss him. I miss especially his remembered warmth, his touch. All morning I've been trying to prepare my flower paintings for the open studio exhibition but my body, continuously aflame, is a constant distraction. I've decided there's nothing for it but to attempt to put my feelings onto canvas. It will mean another of my unsaleable pictures, but I don't care. I need to do something. For the next two hours I paint quickly and soon I've completed the whole image. It's rough, but as I stand back and look at it, it seems alive with energy. I hear a tap on the door.

'Tom!' I'm unable to quell the surprise in my voice.

'Josie, I'm sorry, I had to come. I needed to see you.'

Against my better judgement, I invite him in.

My canvas is on the easel, glistening with wet oils. It shows a nude figure of a woman, foreshortened, splayed in an attitude of desire – her haunches raised like fat wings to either side, her shadowed face half-drowned in a tumult of amber hair.

Tom's dark shirt is rolled up at the sleeves, open at the neck. He swallows when he sees the canvas.

'How are you, Josie?'

I fiddle with my paint tubes. 'I'm just getting ready for my summer exhibition.'

'Are you going to put that in it?'

'No, of course not.'

'Why not?'

'Well, you know what I do this time of year. I paint pictures to please the punters. I need all the money I can get – especially now.' I glance up at him quickly, realising I'm giving away too much information. 'I can't afford to put them off.'

'I thought you were more daring than that.' Tom is standing in the middle of the studio, no longer nervous.

'Why do you say that?'

'I know what you showed us in class and I can see what you've got here. I've also seen what you hang in your garden exhibitions. No one would think they were the work of the same artist.'

Stung, I look away. It's as if Tom has found me out, stripped away my covering. The throb between my legs intensifies.

'You won't stand up and acknowledge who you are. You want to be respectable little Josie – your work, your life, inoffensive.'

Is this really Tom talking? Careful, discreet Tom whose conservatism I once tried so hard to break down? And is he now trying to change me in return?

'You need to stretch your wings, stop being the bird in the gilded cage.'

'And what would you know about that?' Vulnerability is making me angry. 'What the hell do you know about that, Tom? Since when have you dared to break any boundaries yourself?'

Tom's face arranges itself into a slow smile. 'You haven't seen any of my work recently, have you?'

I regard him coolly. 'Is it still monochrome?' I ask, trying to resurrect the tutor in me.

'Some,' Tom says. 'But it's not so careful now.' He breaks off. 'Except here and there. Where it matters.' He gives a sly smile. 'Except', he adds quietly, 'the bits you need to see – or imagine you can see, within the darkness.'

I step back and the heel of my left foot brushes the leg of the easel. The canvas quivers.

'And has it changed your life? Has it made you more daring?'

'You know it has.'

He moves towards me. 'I began stalking you!'

I am standing in front of my canvas. Suddenly I know how I must look, my head positioned roughly between the painted thighs, my hair tumbled around my face. I draw a hand across my cheek. There's umber paint on my fingers and I realise I've left a smear. Tom comes over to me and, wetting his finger, rubs it away. Then he takes my head in his hands and puts his mouth to mine, his tongue feeling through my opened lips.

I stumble towards the half-broken sofa, falling backwards on its cushions, taking him with me. He drags my jeans down and pulls them roughly from my legs. I'm already climaxing as he enters me.

Katy

Katy knew how she appeared to Will. She knew how the lustre of her hair, the colour of her flesh, the perfume she wore – musky like the scent of undergrowth, lured him as it would a child to a forbidden place. So what she planned would be easy to accomplish.

Even so, she found herself wondering whether to go ahead. As the question raised itself again, she argued her case. She might not be in love with him, but she needed his energy, his calm sense of himself, his plantedness – as if he were a great tree rising from the earth. These were what she needed now. So she would do it. She would lure him into her trap. The first bit would be straightforward. But, after that, in order to keep him with her, she would have to create a sense of responsibility – one that would tie him to her. That was the bit that needed careful planning. The initial problem was, of course, the other woman. As regards her, Katy thought, perhaps it was time to stop scheming and consult the cards.

She went to a dark wooden chest standing in the hallway and opened a drawer. Reaching to the back, she brought out a small box swathed in a square of blue silk cloth. She lifted out a Tarot pack. It was one she used exclusively for readings relating to herself. The cards nestled and flew between her fingers and she felt their familiar dips and dents. They bore the marks of frequent handling. She could almost recognise each one by the creases on its back before turning it over.

As she shuffled, she focused on her quest. First she had to find the card that would represent her rival. It would be one of the queens. And here they were, springing to her, all four of them. She laid them side by side in the middle of the table and regarded them in all their finery. Which one was her opponent?

First up was the Queen of Swords. The painted woman was sitting bolt upright in an elaborately carved chair, her sword piercing the sky. Mistress of the air, she was too bold and imperious to represent Josie. Next was the Queen of Wands, staff raised, flower in hand, dressed in yellow with crimson regalia and flanked by lions. The black cat erect in front of her gave her away. This queen had Katy's wand, her cat, her fire. This queen, then, was her. Was Josie the Queen of Pentacles, then? Here was a real earth mother, head bowed towards the ground, pentacle cradled in her lap. Surely this was Josie? But then there was the last one, the Queen of Cups, sitting on a scalloped throne, head inclined towards a chalice, water lapping round her feet.

Suddenly Katy knew. This was Josie. This was the queen she was up against.

She laid the fire queen to her left and the water queen to her right, then began shuffling the remaining cards. Just a short three-card spread for each would do the job. She decided to alternate the spreads this time. It was something she had never done before and it gave her a small thrill of excitement. She placed the first card face down below the fire queen, the second below the water queen. These two cards would reveal their situations.

She turned hers over first and drew in her breath. It was the deadliest card in the whole pack. It showed a figure lying on the ground, ten swords sticking from its body. The meaning of it was clear – defeat and ruin. Quickly she turned Josie's card over. The King of Cups. Damn! Did she still have Will on her side or – a relieved smile spread across her face – could it be she had another lover?

She dealt two more cards. These would show personal influences. When she turned hers, she let out a gasp of delight. Now she had the best card in the pack. It showed a child sitting on a white horse, its head crowned with red roses, the sun blazing in the sky above. Relieved, she turned Josie's card. This was more like it: the bowed figure of a woman on a boat with seven swords sticking up from the prow like iron bars. Forces beyond her control were driving her out on a journey. The only way back would take a cool head and a deal of ingenuity – attributes Katy was pretty sure Josie didn't have.

The last two cards would reveal the outcome. She turned hers and shivered. On it was a dark-haired woman bound and blindfolded, surrounded by eight upright swords. There was no way out for this woman except, perhaps, through someone else's power.

She turned the last card. A pale crescent within a golden circle. The Moon. With a wolf and a dog howling up at it and a stream running below with a lobster-like creature crawling out. It held the energy of the female, the left-hand path of intuition. Josie had the card that should have been hers! Having it gave her power – assuming she knew how to use it. But the Moon was slippery and had another meaning: deception, double-dealing. So perhaps all it signified was her adultery.

She packed up the cards, swathed them in their silk again, and put them away. She suddenly felt tired. It was not late, but she decided to go to bed anyway.

Her night was restless, her sleep filled with visions of swords and sacrifice, a warring sun and moon. In the middle of it was the shining child, careering through the forest on the white horse, sun flashing on yellow hair, roses dropping from a woven crown.

When she woke, the tumble of cards in her dreams had fallen into a sort of pattern. She knew now what she must do. She must give Will what he craved, and quickly. The way to do it was, of course, delicious.

Will

Will approached the building in the half-light of early evening. A scent of hawthorn blossom was in the air. He looked up at the window on the fourth floor and saw pink light oozing between the curtains.

He stood at the Georgian front door, its shade of greyish blue indistinguishable in the gloom, and rang Katy's bell. For a long time there was no answer. He pressed it once more.

At last her voice came through the intercom: 'Who is it?'

'It's Will.'

A buzzer sounded. Seconds later the front door began almost imperceptibly opening before him.

The hallway looked different in the evening. The timed light switch set off an energy-saving bulb which at first barely illuminated it. The lift was waiting in its skeletal cage, but he ignored it. He began climbing the stairs. As he climbed, the light grew in brightness until the dim brown stair-runner turned purple and scuffs appeared on the treads. He was clutching a bottle of Chardonnay fresh from the chiller in the local off-licence. He could still decide against this. They could always just have a drink and talk. He could still turn back. But where would he go? Halfway up, he heard the click as the door softly closed downstairs. He was unaware that until then a pair of eyes had been following his progress up the stairway.

Josie

From high up on the edge of the valley I'm winding down the lanes, steadily descending towards the old Severn Bridge. As I drive I'm thinking about Tom. I can't believe I let him go so far. I realise I've dropped my guard and now suddenly I've plunged into new territory. I feel nervous, out of control. Sheltered by Will, I haven't felt like that for a long time. As I drop down towards Chepstow I change gear, relax my grip on the wheel, and let the mechanics of driving soothe and distract me. Ahead are the two uprights, white rectangles against the mottled sky. By the time I reach the bridge I've managed to put my worries about Tom aside. I decide I'll just have to restrain his ardour and keep him at arm's length again.

Crossing the bridge always lifts my spirits. Through its slung cables, I can see the mudflats of the estuary stretching away on either side. The expanse is exhilarating. Away to my right lies the little island of St Tecla, with its ruined chapel and lighthouse. The tide is out, so its causeway is exposed – black rocks patched with silver water.

Once I've crossed into England, my thoughts turn to my mother. Meeting her for lunch is a rare enough occurrence and, in the circumstances, perhaps humouring her will help take my mind off things. I picture her small pinched face. Her hair is dark brown and I wonder whether that's still natural or if she has to dye it now. Thinking of it reminds me of the time I tried to paint her. It was my first serious oil painting, done when I was about twelve. I remember I'd got her pale face and tight features near enough; it was only her hair that was wrong. I'd made it block brown. There was no thread of life or movement in it. But that was deliberate, because at the time I was trying to replicate mummy brown. I was obsessed with the colour. Ever since I'd heard its name I'd longed to block in my mother's hair with it.

Even though the pigment, I knew, was obsolete.

For mummy brown wasn't to do with my mother – or any mother, come to that. It was made from ground-up Egyptian mummies mixed with white pitch and myrrh to yield a rich dark brown. Some Dutch paintings, I'd read, were made from little else. I imagine Vermeer or Frans Hals spreading their flesh across the canvas, thin-scraping it with a pallet knife. What would it be like, I wonder, loading your brush with the remains of corpses, giving them resurrection, drawing fresh images from their powdered bodies?

As I drive towards my mother I feel the pull of them, the wizened mummies stretching back into the past. Then I think of the generations of women that have produced me. What if their experiences could be wrapped and bandaged, their memories preserved then ground up and used to paint a canvas? What picture would emerge?

As I get out of the car it occurs to me that, in a way, all art is a form of preserved experience, whether or not it's made with mummy brown. Pleased with that thought I walk towards the glass-fronted complex and go through the revolving doors.

I've made an effort to be punctual. Even so, as I rise to the top floor via the ribbon of elevators, I know my mother will be waiting. And I am right. Janet is sitting primly at a table in the far corner. I smile as I go towards her.

'Mum – Jan-et'.

We exchange kisses across the table.

'There's quite a queue,' she says. 'I thought we might wait until it dies down a bit.'

I sit down. 'You're early, as usual. Have you had time for a browse?'

'I did have a quick look at materials, but nothing really caught my eye.'

'What are you going to make?'

'Oh, something to wear for that golf do your father wants to take me to.' She laughs with slight embarrassment. 'You know how he is. If I didn't go to those, I'd hardly see him.'

'Don't you mind?'

'Well!' The question was too probing. She looks uncomfortable. 'The house can seem a bit empty sometimes.' She brightens suddenly. 'But that'll all change, of course, when you –' She stops and looks encouragingly at me, waiting for me to finish my sentence.

'When I have a child, you mean.'

She nods, her eyes bright.

'Well, it doesn't look like that's going to happen now.'

'Why not?' Her voice is sharp.

Her directness is not what I expected. I haven't come prepared for this conversation. I certainly wasn't intending to bring up the topic myself.

'Because Will's moved out.'

'He's what?' Her voice is so loud that heads turn at nearby tables. She adds in hushed tones, 'Why didn't you tell us this was going on?'

'I thought it would all blow over in a few days.'

'And now?'

'Now, I don't know.'

'But what's set all this off? What have you done?'

'What have *I* done?'

My mother looks away, her eyes scanning the crowded restaurant.

'Have you been neglecting him?'

'Mother, marriage is a two-way thing – or didn't you know?'

'You can get awfully wrapped up in things,' she murmurs.

'Will won't listen to me.'

'He's always seemed so reasonable to us.'

'But he won't let me have a say.'

'We used to worry about it, you know. When you were first married. You were so headstrong. We worried that one day you might lose him. But we thought you'd got past all that now.'

'Mother,' I cut in, 'whose side are you on!'

My mother begins fiddling with her napkin. 'Well, Josie, we've always tried to be fair, but you can be quite a handful sometimes.' She looks up and adds, more boldly: 'And then there's your art, of course. Maybe you don't want a child.'

'Mother, you haven't even heard what I'm saying!'

'Well, if there are difficulties between you, I'm sure it's about the child. In fact Frieda mentioned something.'

'Frieda! Have you been talking to her?'

My mother has the grace to look ashamed. 'Let's just calm down for a moment and get a coffee,' she says. 'The queue's died down now.'

'No! I want to know what Frieda told you!'

'All right, then. She rang us the other night. She said she thought things between you were a bit difficult … but we had no idea.'

'Oh, did she?'

'She didn't mean any harm. She's just concerned about the two of you, that's all.'

'Concerned? I'll say she's concerned! Concerned that her little boy hasn't gone running back to *her*, more like!'

'Josie, that's not fair! Your father says she only wants the right thing.'

'But who for? That's what I'd like to know!'

My mother reaches across the table and pats my hand.

'You know we all care about you – about you both,' she says. 'Look, please do let's get a coffee. I could really do with one now, and I'm sure it will make us feel better.'

Scowling, I follow her to the counter.

The girl serving coffees looks up. 'What would you like – cappuccino, latte, mocha?' She starts to reel off the list but I cut her short.

'I'll have a cappuccino, and my mother will have an Americano with milk.' We choose a couple of filled baguettes from a selection of sandwiches and make our way to the till. I open my bag looking for my purse.

'No. I – I'll do this,' Janet says.

I carry the tray, threading my way carefully around the tables, trying not to spill our drinks. As I put the tray down, liquid from both cups slops into the saucers. My mother fusses with the napkin, blotting it all up before handing out the baguettes.

'Thanks,' I mutter reluctantly.

We sip our coffees, grateful for something to do.

'Have you started it, yet?'

'What?'

'The IVF programme.'

'No, of course not. Mother, I told you, Will's moved out.'

My mother lifts her baguette to her mouth and takes a bite. Mayonnaise spurts from the side.

'This is what I hate about these things,' she says, indicating the baguette. She finishes the mouthful. 'So is that the problem – the IVF thing?'

'Yes – and no.'

'I know these treatments are expensive. Is it the money? Because if it is, you know you only have to ask.'

'It isn't the money.'

'So, what's stopping you? Is it that you don't want a baby, after all?'

'No. It's not that.' I know I'm sounding difficult. I take a deep breath. I'm a grown woman, now.

'It's an awfully risky process,' I begin.

My mother lifts her eyebrows in interested concern.

'There's a lot to consider.'

'But I thought you'd done all that.'

'We didn't get that far.'

'Why not?'

'I didn't. I didn't want to go ahead.'

'So what was all that about the other Sunday? When you both announced you were starting the treatment.'

'*I* didn't announce it: that was Will.' I want to add 'and he had no right,' but check myself, knowing this will only rile my mother, who has surrendered all rights to my father, and probably thinks I should do the same for Will.

'Well, I'm sure the doctors know what they're doing. After all, lots of women go through the process, don't they? They must think it's worth taking the risk to have their own child.'

'It's not exactly about the risk.'

'Oh? Then what is it about?'

'I don't feel it's right for me, Mum.'

My mother looks startled. 'What's not right for you? Having a baby, or having the treatment?'

'The treatment. I don't want to do it.'

By now we have almost finished eating.

'But Will said –'

'I know what he said, but I hadn't agreed to it.'

Janet considers a moment. 'Is that why he's left you?'

'I don't know, Mother,' I say miserably.

Two hours later I'm driving home again. The lunch was difficult from beginning to end, my mother probing me with insensitive questions while I became increasingly morose. What can I say to her that would make any sense? Replaying our conversation while I drive home makes me tense. But as I cross back over the Severn Bridge the tension eases and I begin to feel relief. The tide has come in over the estuary, and now the causeway to St Tecla's island is obscured by pewter-coloured water puckering in the wind.

As soon as I'm home, I retreat to my studio. The spring evening is balmy, the light still good. Working with my studio door open to the scents and sounds of my garden, I am not at first aware of Tom slipping in, until his arms enfold me and I feel his lips against my neck.

'Tom!'

I turn in his arms, trying to free myself. I hadn't expected this. I thought he'd be a bit more hesitant.

'Tom. Wait!' I push him away. He takes a step back, his face showing hurt and surprise. 'Tom,' I say in a softer voice, 'we have to think about this.'

'I thought …' he begins.

'I don't know what you thought, but you can't just assume.'

'But we –'

'Tom, I'm still a married woman.'

'But it wasn't just a one-off. I really care about you, Josie.'

'I know you do and I appreciate that. But it's more complicated. Look at all this!' I wave my arms. 'The house, the garden, the studio. I'm married, Tom. I can't just let it all go on a whim. And, more importantly, there's Will ...'

'Ah, Will!' Tom says hotly. 'As for him …'

'As for him what?'

'He's –'

'He's what?'

'He's gone off.'

'I know that!' I snap. 'What are you trying to say?'

Tom looks around the room as if taking stock. 'Can I sit down?'

I gesture to the sofa. Tom sits on one end hunched over, his feet neatly together on the floor. I drag over a chair and sit opposite him.

'What are you trying to say?'

He fiddles with his fingers.

'He's ... Well, I've ... I've seen him, Josie.'

'You've seen him? You mean you've talked to him – you've told him!' I leap up. 'How could you! How dare you – that was for me to do!'

He looks up at me, his eyes showing hurt innocence. 'I haven't spoken to him!'

'Then what do you mean, you've seen him?'

'I've seen him with someone else.'

I close my mouth. Feeling behind me for the chair, I sit down again. I'm shaking. 'Will? With someone else?'

Tom nods. 'A woman.'

'Who? Where?'

'I saw them in a café together.'

'When was this?'

'A while back.' Tom looks down at his hands. 'Actually,' he says quietly, 'it was what made me start watching you. I – I was concerned.'

'And you never thought to tell me!'

'I was just about to – after you caught me in the garden. I was wondering whether to, whether it was fair – and then Will came back.'

'So, after you thought better of it, when you saw me again, you decided not to mention it, not to say anything!' I am almost shouting. I feel betrayed, humiliated, by Will, and by Tom. At the same time I'm trying to absorb this new information. Questions are crowding in, providing a temporary barrier against the shock and pain.

Tom is looking again at his hands, unable to meet my eyes.

'But who is she? How did he meet her?'

'I think she's a client of his.'

'How do you know?'

'I happened to see her once, coming out of his building.'

'You happened to ... What does she look like?' I'm trying to imagine Will with someone else.

'She's quite … she's quite striking.'

'You mean she's beautiful. Is that it?'

'No. Not exactly. She's unusual.'

He looks up at me.

'And then a few days later I saw them both in the window of Raphael's Café.'

'Did you see them again by *accident*?'

He looks down again. 'Yes. Well, not exactly by accident.'

'You mean you were stalking them, like you did me?'

'Not them. It was Will. I was following Will,' he says sulkily.

'And have you been following her, too?' I ask, incredulous.

'No. Just Will. And then only at odd moments – at lunchtimes and sometimes after work.'

Seeing the look on my face, he adds quickly, 'I do go to work, you know!'

'Has he seen you? Does he know you're ...'

'No, of course not!'

'So where did you see him go?'

'He went to her flat – last night.'

'My God!' I'm beginning to tremble. 'My God, so you even know where she lives!'

Tom nods his head miserably.

'Where?'

'It's 24 Portland Street.'

A sudden realisation sends a fresh stab of adrenalin round my body.

'So he'd already – before he thought you and I – before he saw ...'

Tom nods again. 'He'd already met her.'

'You should have said something.' Despite the shock, my mind is already revisiting the past few weeks, seeing how that piece of information might have changed everything.

'You should have let me know.'

'But that's all I could have told you at the time. And then – there might have been nothing in it, at least until last night.' He breaks off. 'Oh, Josie, I'm sorry!'

'No, you're not! But I'll say one thing – you're bloody good at your job!'

'What job?'

'Spying!' I spit the word out. 'My God!' I say again and realise I'm shivering violently.

'Josie, are you all right? Can I get you anything?'

'Drink. In the kitchen. Cupboard by the Rayburn.'

As soon as he goes, I move to the sofa. I sit there breathing in and out with difficulty. When he comes back with a tumbler of Scotch, I almost snatch it from him. The liquid stings my throat and I feel the shivering gradually subside. Tom sits down beside me. Tentatively he puts his arm around me. I am too much in shock to remove it.

We sit there stiffly for a while, the whisky working its magic. 'But he won't think it's his fault,' I hear myself say.

'Why do you say that, Josie? The guy's a complete jerk. He ...'

'I know. I know!' The numbing sensation of the whisky is allowing me to slip around the arguments. 'But it's not as simple as that.'

'I know a guy cheating on his wife when I see one!'

It's heartening to have someone on my side, but it isn't enough.

'I know, I know,' I say again. 'But he didn't understand.' I hesitate, wondering whether to say more. In some way I feel I owe Tom an explanation.

'What didn't he understand, Josie?'

I take another mouthful of whisky. 'It was about having a child. We wanted one. It didn't happen. We couldn't agree how to go ahead.'

It sounds too simple. Tom is silent, considering.

'What did he want you to do?' he asks at length.

I shake my head.

'Did you go for tests?'

I nod.

'Did he want you to go for IVF?'

Tom is pressing too hard.

'And did you?' he says.

I refuse to answer.

'No,' Tom says, as if to himself. 'You did something else.'

We sit in silence, Tom with his arm still round me. I am still breathing in and out with difficulty, the air of my studio and the evening equally stultifying. After a while, Tom removes his arm and gets up. He walks towards the back of the studio.

'Do you mind if I look at some of your paintings?' he asks

The request is unexpected. 'All right,' I say, hesitantly.

He goes to a stack against the far wall. One by one he shifts the canvases, regarding them carefully as he does so. Then he goes back to the first one and slowly turns it round. There she is again, the little girl, yellow ochre hair curling round her face and shoulders. Tom props the painting on an empty easel, then stands back to look at it. From a distance the force and vulnerability of the child are inextricably fused together.

'As for you,' he says, 'you painted her.'

Josie

The midday sun lights a film of insects that have flown into my windscreen. I'm hoping they'll screen my face. I've been sitting here for over an hour, staring at the Georgian door. Farrow & Ball paints are unmistakable and Lulworth blue will always haunt me now. His hands have pushed that door, his eyes have glanced up at the window. But which one is it? Perhaps I should have come at night. There would have been lights on and I might have seen in. But what would I have seen – a red glow seeping between thin curtains? Just then the door moves. It's opening inwards. I stiffen. A young man comes out. The door slips shut again.

I notice the prick of adrenalin, the quickening beat of my heart, and feel irritated that my body can react so swiftly. I reach into the glove compartment feeling for the car sweets, keeping my eyes on the door. I put a black pastille in my mouth and suck it slowly, willing my breathing to calm, my body to recover. The door trembles. My heartbeat mounting again, I wait. No one comes out. A lorry lumbers past, obscuring my view. In its wake, I see the front door tremble once again. It wasn't shut properly. The young man must have been in a hurry and just let it go. I open the car door, my hand clammy on the steering wheel as I push myself out.

I cross the road. Beside the door is an intercom buzzer. I look at the list of names listed on the buzzers for each of the flats. T. and A. Wright live on the ground floor, M. Robson on the first. The second floor is simply marked Wilde – perhaps a man's terse entry. Beside the entry for the third floor is the name Katy MacLaren in bold black letters, a scrawl that is nevertheless perfectly readable. This must be hers. I push the door open and go inside.

The hallway is bigger than I'd expected, illuminated by the sun which enters through the blue and yellow stained glass window above the door. Shafts of light strike a wrought-iron lift which sits crouched, like a spider, in an alcove. Ahead of me the stairway ascends in a loose parabola, fringed by white banisters, bright against the mahogany steps and purple runner. I put my foot on the bottom step, the stairs creaking as I go up. On the first floor I pass a brown door with a brass number 2 on it. I go on up. The second floor has an olive-green door, the bottom of which is scuffed. I hover next to it for a moment, thinking I hear a noise from above. Then I climb to the third floor. Here the door has been painted to match the stair-runner. On it is a small black pentacle, hardly distinguishable from the purple ground.

I pause. Perhaps I'm wrong and it's the top flat after all. Just then I hear a sound of scuffling behind the door. I start up the last set of stairs. I've reached the turn in the banister when I hear a click from below. I go swiftly up three more steps, then crouch down and watch through the banisters as the door opens. A young woman with dark hair steps out. The first thing that announces her is the clink of her bracelets tumbling against one another as she fumbles in her shoulder bag for the keys. There's a purple cloak over her arm and her bag is patch-worked with yellow crescent moons.

Josie

'It can't be her!'

I'm slumped on the end of my sunken sofa, while Tom sits on a chair opposite me. I invited him over. It's against my better judgement, but I need to know more and he's the only one who can tell me.

'He'd never go for anyone like that!'

I'm still struggling to imagine Will with a woman in a long black skirt, kohl-circled eyes, a moon-studded bag, and silver stars dangling from her ears.

'She doesn't always dress like that,' Tom says. 'Sometimes she looks almost normal – at least she was when I saw her with Will, but she did have the earrings and the bag.'

He stops, seeing the pain on my face.

'If she was all dressed up when you saw her, I expect she was going to see a client.'

'A client!'

'Yes, to give someone a reading or something.'

'You mean she's a …?'

'Some kind of clairvoyant? From the way she looks, I'm guessing she's something like that.'

'But Will hates that kind of thing. In fact not long ago he was complaining –' I break off and raise my hand to my mouth in disbelief as the realisation comes to me. 'Oh God, Tom! It *is* her! He told me about her just after she'd come to see him.'

'What?' He is puzzled.

I take my hand away and look at him in shock. 'One night he was going on about about a fortune-telling woman whose accounts he'd agreed to handle. He was really scornful, and I – Oh, God, Tom, I stood up for her! I actually stood up for her!' I shake my head, still incredulous. 'It must have been her! How else could he have met her?'

Tom shifts in his chair. I think for a moment he's going to come over and put his arms round me. To my relief, he remains sitting.

'Why would he be attracted to her with all that?' I ask, not expecting an answer.

'Perhaps because she's so unlike you?' he offers.

'But the things she believes in!'

'I know.'

'It's all the stuff he hates. You don't know what he's like, Tom. He hates anything like that. I mean *anything* that's remotely illogical. I daren't even mention female intuition, for God's sake! And if we're watching a crime drama on TV, he can't bear it if a detective says he's got a gut feeling about something.'

I look at him in desperation and then burst out: 'Given that he hates everything the woman stands for – what the hell does he see in her?'

'I don't know,' Tom says. But his tone lacks conviction. I imagine him conjuring an image of Katy's painted eyes and long black hair. We sit miserably in silence while I suppress my tears. I want him to stay so I can find out more. I want him to leave so I can howl undisturbed.

Suddenly Tom claps his hand to his knee and stands up. 'Come on. This isn't doing you any good. Let me take you out.'

'I don't think –'

'Please, Josie, let me take you out for dinner.'

'I'm not very hungry.'

'I don't care how little you eat. I think you need to get out of the house.'

I give him a tired smile. I'm feeling numb and confused and haven't the energy to resist.

'OK,' I say, 'as long as it's not The Yellow Freesia.'

Tom drives us to a country pub a few miles away. I didn't want to go into town and risk people seeing us, and tongues wagging. Settled at a corner table in a dimly lit alcove, I'm thinking that perhaps he was right. I do feel less tearful out of the house, in a public place. Tom raises his pint.

'Here's to you, Josie,' he says.

I raise my red wine in answer and our two glasses clink together. A few drops of beer spill onto the table. Then I hear a familiar voice. 'Where would you like to sit?' It's Megan. I lean urgently towards Tom.

'Will's receptionist just came in!' I whisper, 'I don't want her to see us!'

'But we've ordered the food now.'

'I know, but I'm not ready to ...'

'Not ready to what?' Tom raises his voice, refusing to join in my conspiratorial whisper. It's as if he wants people to see us.

'Tom, please!' I clutch his arm.

We hear Megan's voice again: 'Actually it might be cosier round there. Shall I have a quick look?'

There's nothing I can do. I sit there, trapped and helpless, as Megan puts her head round the end of the alcove.

'Josie!' she exclaims.

'Hi!'

'How nice to see you!'

'Nice to see you, too!'

A man's head appears beside Megan's.

'And Dai,' I say. 'It's not often I see you.'

'Once a year at the Christmas party, isn't it?'

Tom stretches his hand across the table.

'I'm Tom,' he says.

'Yes,' I add quickly. 'Tom's a former student of mine. We meet up from time to time.'

Dai and Megan shake hands with him.

'Just to catch up,' I add weakly.

Megan turns round as a waitress comes into sight.

'Oh!' she says. 'Your food's just arrived. We'd better leave you to it.'

'Well, bye for now,' says Dai. 'Nice to meet you, Tom.'

'And you.'

When we're alone again, Tom pushes his plate away, puts his elbows on the table and confronts me: 'So were you thinking of not introducing me, then?'

'Of course not!'

'I suppose you're ashamed of me. Even though your husband couldn't care less about being seen with his fancy woman, you still don't want anyone to see you with me. Is that it?'

'Stop it, Tom! I don't want to have a row in the middle of a pub.'

'Especially when your friends are only a few yards away.'

'They're not my friends. I told you, Megan works with Will. I barely know her husband.'

'So?'

I touch his arm in appeal. 'Please, I don't need this. I can't cope with you being difficult on top of everything else.'

In response, he pushes his plate further away and puts his head in his hands.

'Tom, don't!' I take a mouthful of food from my fork, then pull his plate back into place.

'I thought you were the one who *could* eat,' I say.

'I've lost my appetite.'

'Oh, Tom, for goodness sake, just eat up!'

Tom gives me a look of unconcealed resentment before reluctantly picking up his fork.

Will

In his working day at the office, where he would have welcomed a sense of continuity in his life, Will was beginning to feel that things were far from normal. He was unsure whether he was being treated differently or whether it was his own guilt unsettling him. Whatever it was, he was unable to resist the suspicion that everyone there knew what was going on. He hadn't said anything, but most of the staff were women, and he supposed they had a nose for these things. He scanned the spreadsheet on his screen and deleted another duplicated item.

A light tap on his door announced Paula holding a cup of tea with a ginger biscuit balanced on the saucer. 'I thought you could do with this!' she said. Will accepted it in silence, merely nodding to her as she left the room.

Did she normally say something like that or did she somehow know the turmoil he was in? He drained his cup, then saved the file and closed his computer. It was near enough time to go home and he needed to get out. His sports bag was already in the car.

As he drove to the leisure centre he was trying to remember how it had once been at the office – at least on Monday mornings, with Megan asking him brightly what he'd done over the weekend. When had she last done that? And Paula? Was there anything different about her? Didn't she use to flirt with him a bit when she brought him letters to sign?

Stripping off in the changing room, he wondered if Paula had felt safe to flirt with him before, secure in the knowledge that he was a dependable married man. He pulled on his swimming trunks. So what was he now? A man playing away from home? A man on the prowl? He piled his clothes in the locker and went to the pool.

Diving in, he set off in a furious front crawl. He reached the end of the length and slewed round, the water shivering ahead of him. Deciding to swim back underwater, he duck-dived, his arms reaching down, the tiled pattern of the pool's mosaic centrepiece coming towards him. Then he floated to the top, took a draught of air and dived again.

As he swam, his thoughts went to Katy. They were forever going to her. He was a man obsessed. He was remembering the thrill of excitement he felt when she led him into her bedroom. That first time. The flicker of the candle flames had made the whole room seem alive. She'd put on some hypnotic Indian flute and tabla music which twisted round the walls, winding between dissonance and harmony.

He crossed the central mosaic again, its circles shimmering through the water like rings of flame.

She had given him a cup of red wine, which she had first held up to a picture of a snake goddess. It was the richest thing he had ever tasted. He drank it slowly while she wreathed her body in time to the music, twining and untwining herself in front of him, draped in a diaphanous black garment. The sight of her veiled body undulating like that was intoxicating. This was the vision that bewitched him every time he thought of her. It was like nothing he had ever known.

His feet touched the bottom and he shot upwards, shaking water from his hair and eyes as he broke the surface. He launched into a fast crawl, his thoughts scattering as a family burst through the door. Eager to be in the water, the children raced ahead. One jumped in; the other ran to the end and picked up a ball, throwing it onto the water and tumbling in behind it.

Will swam five more lengths dodging in and out of the children as they threw the ball between them. One of them dropped it and the ball skittered across the water, narrowly missing his head. After that, he slowed to a lazy breast-stroke. He couldn't remember when he had last felt so liberated. He wove one last time between the other swimmers before climbing out. As the pool door swung behind him, he caught an image of the father supporting a small boy who was kicking his legs and flailing his arms.

Standing in the shower with blades of water hitting his body, he felt a momentary longing for Josie, for his old life of security. He stepped out and began rubbing himself down. But it was he who had provided that, not Josie. Now he had crossed the line, it was gone, too. He slung his towel over his shoulder and headed for the changing rooms.

Josie

When I come in from the studio there's a red light blinking on the house phone. A message from Esme.

'Hi, Josie. Giving a dinner party on Saturday week for some of Nathan's colleagues. Would love it if you could join us. If you want to come on your own, that's fine. But you're also welcome to bring someone with you – Will, if you like.'

I decide I don't want to bring Will, or anyone. I want to go on my own. But I could do with some new clothes. After being closeted with my paintings, it's just the excuse I need to leave the house and go into town.

Mid-morning, without bothering to change out of my painting clothes, I tie my hair back, slam the front door and get into my car. The roadside is rimed with mud from yesterday's heavy rain, the hedgerows splattered. I feel truant. The duties of the garden, the studio, my work, still hold me. I've become so used to pushing through pain and tiredness in an effort to achieve anything, it's difficult to let go. Halfway there I decide I should go back. I pull into a lay-by. But as I turn the car round, the pale cone of the Sugar Loaf trembles in my rear mirror and suddenly my weight of misery shifts. I turn the car back again, defiantly. As I drive, I see bluebells already patching the roadsides. I feel strangely carefree.

I park and make my way towards the town centre. Walking along the high street I think of Will. Might I bump into him? Do I want to bump into him? No, not looking like this. I wish now I'd bothered to change. The clock on the market hall tower shows 11.30 – too early for Will's lunch hour. So there's no danger of seeing him yet. I go quickly on up the street, stopping to peer into several women's clothes shops. A few steps inside is sufficient to scan the rows of hanging clothes. It's colour I'm looking for as much as style. Most of the rails present the usual monochrome choices with the occasional bright green item as a concession to spring. Green must be this year's fashion accent. I come to a shop that seems more rebellious, so I go inside. Sifting through a rail of dresses in a riot of hues, I select one and disappear into a booth where I discard my painty jeans and saggy sweater and remake myself in a dress that billows slightly from the waist. It's cleverly patterned, with a mix of bright colours on a magenta ground. I regard myself approvingly in the mirror. The effect is daring yet restrained.

Now I need shoes to go with it. There's a selection poised on glass shelves at the back of the shop. I lift one down and fiddle my foot into its pointed toe. I step towards the mirror, rolling up my jeans. The shoe is bright red and strappy, with a high heel. I limp across the floor, then remove it. I try another shoe, and another, before returning to my first choice. Wearing both shoes I find it easy enough to walk across the room. After a couple of turns in front of the mirror I decide to buy them.

I stride back down the street, large carrier bags banging against my legs. In my mind I'm swathed in a cocktail of colours masking my scruffy clothes, lifting my step as I walk.

'Hi, Josie! Haven't seen you in ages!' It's Paula, on her way out of the office. So it must be lunchtime now.

'Hi!' I say brightly. 'No, I've been busy.'

'Oh?' Paula adds encouragingly. What more does she want to know?

'With my paintings.' Can't she see the paint marks on my jeans?

'Oh! Yes, of course!'

'And you?' I say, switching the focus.

'Me? Oh, I'm fine, thanks!'

'Good.'

I smile at her and carry on down the street. There's no snub in such a withdrawal. The meeting, after all, has been only a passing encounter. Then a sudden draft of air lifts the hairs at my neck. My God! There's Katy MacLaren striding towards me in full sail, dark cloak in billowing profusion, stars nodding at her ears.

As she approaches I shrink towards a shop window. She has no idea what I look like, so I should be safe. I slink past her, camouflaged in Will's dull sweater. But as she goes by, her cloak brushes my shoulder. I continue on without looking back. Was it my imagination or did the black circled eyes narrow in the elfin face? Did she catch and then exhale, a sudden breath? She's psychic, isn't she? Shouldn't she know?

Katy

How had Will's wife recognised her? This was the question in the back of Katy MacLaren's mind as she fingered the cards, her mother looking at her anxiously from across the consulting room table. But she kept it to herself.

'We're almost there,' she said, speaking into her mother's face, half-whispering, as if fearing they could be overheard.

'Has he?' her mother asked.

Katy nodded.

'And is he?'

'Yes, he's almost ...'

'So when do you think you'd ...?'

'Soon. I'll need you to hold the fort for me a little longer, though, just until ...'

'Until?'

'Until the time is right.'

'I suppose you would know, dear.' Her mother sighed. 'But it will be a relief when you feel he's ready. This hole and corner business – it isn't exactly fair on ...'

'I know, Mother, but it will happen soon, I promise.'

Her mother took her hands and squeezed them. 'You're such a clever girl!'

Josie

'Wow!' says Esme as she opens the door. 'You look great.'

She kisses me on the cheek, then leads me through the hallway. I can hear voices from the front room, a half octave of laughter. Esme is wearing olive trousers and an oyster-coloured blouse tied at the front. I enter the room behind her, aware of myself as the other guests must see me: a swirl of raw sienna, crimson and magenta, floating on red heels. Heads turn.

'Let me introduce you.'

A middle-aged man rises to his feet. There's a pleasing gravitas about him. His thick hair is white, matching the sofa he's been sitting on, and his eyebrows are tinged with silver. He's wearing a dark brown jacket with leather elbow patches.

'This is Dominic, head of Nathan's department.'

Dominic squeezes my hand. His palm is warm. Sitting beside him is a woman with a powdered face and strong features. Her hair is iron-coloured, tightly bound. She's dressed in a charcoal-grey suit brought to life by a silk scarf in Bohemian orange. Her figure is trim, her posture erect.

'And this is his wife Isobel.'

I shake her hand. Grey eyes examine me briefly, then drop. Esme indicates a young man standing at the fireplace, leaning on the mantelpiece. 'And this is Nathan.'

'So, we meet at last!' Nathan smiles, his eyes appraising me. 'Well, well! Esme's *femme fatale!*' He detaches himself from the mantelpiece. He's tall with spindly limbs and sandy hair. His shirt is open at the collar. Instead of shaking my hand he kisses me lightly on the lips.

'Now you're all here,' Esme says quickly, 'I'll just go and attend to things in the kitchen.'

'Do you want any help?' I ask.

'No, don't worry. I'm fine.' Esme disappears leaving me at the mercy of her guests. Nathan hands me a glass of white wine.

'I'm not going to say I've heard so much about you,' he says, 'because really I've heard very little. Esme's been keeping quiet about you. Purely, I think, to spark my curiosity.'

'Oh? Is that the kind of thing she does?' Isobel says.

'I think every man needs a wife who can keep them on their toes,' Dominic offers.

'It goes with the territory, I suppose.' I sense the inadequacy of my comment. I've only been there a short time and already I'm feeling challenged. Then Isobel comes to my rescue.

'So nice to have an artist among us,' she says.

'Thank you.'

'Have a crisp or something.' Nathan offers me a dish with a selection of crisps and nuts in glass pockets.

'Thanks.' I put a handful of roasted peanuts in my mouth, grateful for the conversational respite. I take my time chewing them while Nathan and Dominic lapse into university chit-chat and Isobel sits quietly, sipping her wine and keeping her own counsel.

By the time we are ushered into the dining room, I've gleaned something of the dynamics between them. Dominic is a kindly man, warm and paternal. His wife appears less kindly. It seems as if she nurses some secret pain that takes priority. Nathan exudes an air of amused authority. He is, as I expected, good-looking and arrogant. I can imagine how he would play a room of students, eyeing the women, vying with the men, delighting in his own casual wit. I'm also wondering how difficult he is to live with.

When we move through, I'm pleased to find myself placed beside Esme. I haven't been in the dining room before. I suspect it's not a room they use much. It's almost entirely taken up with a rectangular metal table. Candles in glass holders throw golden yellow shapes across its mirrored surface, their restive flames bringing it to life.

Esme carries in the first course on a stainless steel tray. She sets it on the table and hands out plain white china bowls filled with fennel and asparagus soup. The noise of conversation dips as spoons sink into it.

'Delicious, Esme!' Dominic says with a fulsome smile. 'You always were a superb cook. At least, I'm assuming it's you and not Nathan here,' he adds jovially, slanting his spoon at Nathan.

Nathan raises an eyebrow non-committally.

'Of course, we're lucky to get someone with youth on their side. Most of us are getting on a bit!'

Nathan inclines his head in acknowledgement.

'He's a metaphysical man,' Dominic muses. 'Unusual to have that, really.' He bends again to his soup.

'Seventeenth-century going on twenty-first,' says Esme, glancing towards me, 'with a giant leap in between.'

Already I feel out of my depth. I'm trying to think who the metaphysical poets were. I vaguely remember reading John Donne at school. Was he one of them?

'You make it sound incongruous, Esme,' Isobel says. She turns to Nathan. 'Is it?'

'Not at all,' Nathan replies. 'I like the metaphysical wit. I find it quite contemporary.'

I'm almost sure Donne was one of them. I remember something about his play on geometry.

'Weren't the metaphysical poets nearly lost to obscurity?' It's Isobel again, fortified by a glass of wine. 'I mean until they were rediscovered.'

'By old T. S. Eliot. That's right. Imagine if that hadn't happened. I, for one, wouldn't have a job!' Nathan laughs. 'But with due respect to Mr Eliot, it doesn't necessarily mean he understood them.'

'Really?'

'I don't think he appreciated their wit. I think he was just rather taken with their mysticism.'

Esme unexpectedly enters the conversation again. 'From what I've read, I think he understood them perfectly well. I think he realised they were deliberately moving away from wit to something more significant.'

'More's the pity,' Nathan jokes, attempting to regain his authority.

'I mean, I think they were trying to express a different kind of reality,' Esme persists, 'but using reason to argue their point.'

There is a momentary pause while everyone tries to take this in. Then we hear Isobel's fluting voice. 'Where reason is concerned, I think Donne was the most down to earth. Some of the others ventured so far into the unknown, didn't they?' She gives a slight laugh. 'I always think they should be called the meta*mysticals*.'

Dominic clears his throat. 'Ah! The *via mystica*.' He catches his wife's eye.

'But so many great writers and artists try to explore the unknown – the numinous side of things, don't they? Isobel continues smoothly. 'Really, one has to admire them.'

Nathan lays down his spoon and wipes his mouth with his napkin. 'Why,' he says lightly, 'this seems to be turning into quite a seminar!'

Esme turns to me. 'As an artist, what do you think they were trying to express?'

I tip my bowl and load the last spoonful, aware that all are waiting for my reply. I have no idea what to say. Then it occurs to me that between them, Isobel and Esme are offering me a chance to jump into my own territory. I pause.

'I don't know much about the metaphysical poets,' I say cautiously. 'But if you mean the place a poet or artist enters, the place where they go to find inspiration, I think it's very difficult to define.'

'Exactly!' Esme says. 'And it's the job of the artist to *express* what they find there, isn't it? Not analyse what it is.'

I nod, relieved. 'As an artist, I'm only too happy to leave the interpretation to others.'

Isobel enters the conversation again: 'Yes, where the artist is concerned, I always feel over-analysing has the dreadful potential to kill things, don't you?' I bless her silently while we concentrate on the soup.

Then Esme joins in. 'Where artistic inspiration is concerned I agree with Isobel: it can be dangerous for the artist to be too introspective. But, actually, there *is* a name for it – the place or state of mind the artist enters.' She looks round the table challengingly.

'I always thought such things were nameless,' Dominic says.

'Maybe to you. But it's our job to try and pin them down.'

'So, what would you call it then?'

'Liminality.'

'Ha! Walking on the edge, you mean. Not following the herd. Pretty risky thing to do.' Dominic moves his empty bowl to one side, leaving the remark hanging. There is a general murmur of agreement.

'It's a place with nothing to hold on to, no reference points at all. Most people find it very frightening.' Esme stands up and starts gathering the soup bowls. 'I should know. I see it all the time in my clinic.'

As there is no immediate comment anyone can add, there's a temporary hush as Esme reloads the tray and carries the bowls out. Nathan gets up and follows her. His voice is audible from the kitchen: 'Why did you have to bring up that liminality thing?' and Esme's reply: 'Well, why ever not?' After that there is some clattering of crockery interspersed by low muttering, then Esme's voice again: 'Nath, can you get the plates while I take in the tagine?'

Nathan returns with a pile of dinner plates, Esme with a large dish covered with a Moroccan-style ceramic dome. She lifts the lid, releasing a waft of spice, then starts cutting into a dense cone of meat and vegetables while Dominic obligingly passes plates along the table.

'Please help yourselves,' she says, gesturing towards a dish of rice and an oil-drizzled green salad.

I sense a general relief at the interruption of food. Dominic clears his throat. 'Wonderful meal, Esme,' he says in his fullest voice. 'First class cook.'

There is appreciative agreement, before Isobel puts down her fork and looks around at us.

'To my mind, creativity and academia don't always go together, do they?' She gives an almost apologetic laugh. 'In fact, they often seem to be curiously at odds.' I wonder how much wine she's had and whether that's what's prompted her to revisit the subject.

After she's spoken, Dominic gives a low chuckle, as if enjoying a private joke. As if encouraged, she pipes up again: 'As for trying to analyse the poets and artists, I always think it's what none of them say that's so difficult to get at.'

'Exactly!' Esme sounds triumphant. 'It's what they don't say. But isn't that just it?'

'Isn't it rather what they *can't* say?' I put in. Though my voice is quiet I hope it carries conviction.

'A big subject,' Dominic says, nodding sagely. 'A very big subject.'

'Does anyone want any more?' Esme lifts the lid of the tagine again.

'I think I'm full,' Dominic says. 'But it was certainly a triumph, wasn't it?'

There are nods and noises of agreement as Esme gathers up the plates and carries them out. Nathan reaches across for the rice and salad dishes and follows her out. We hear muffled exchanges from the kitchen and then Esme's voice: 'Oh, for God's sake, Nathan, just get the desserts, will you!'

By the time they return, the conversation has picked up again but is now on safer ground. I am talking about the difficulties of nude drawing, a subject it is easy to make amusing. If Will had been with me, of course, it would have been different. As the thought crosses my mind, I try not to think about him.

When we move back to the living room for coffee, we break up into groups. Dominic and Nathan sit together on the sofa. I can hear snatches of laughter – university in-jokes, I assume. Isobel has gone to the bathroom. Esme is obviously a bit the worse for wine, which I find amusing.

'So nice to have a free spirit among us,' Esme says, pulling her fine eyebrows together as if searching for the right words. 'And I love that bohemian thing. Your studio –' she waves her wineglass in the air, 'it's like something straight out of St Ives.'

When Isobel reappears she joins Nathan and her husband. From snatches of conversation I overhear, it seems she's holding her own with the two academics. I'm glad I am no longer involved. Having said my piece, I feel relaxed now, enjoying easy banter with Esme, who is slowly becoming less coherent.

At 11.30, Dominic rises. 'I think it's time we made a move,' he says. Isobel gets up gracefully and they say their goodbyes, Dominic hugging the women, Isobel shaking hands.

After they've gone, Nathan comes over and sits beside me.

'I hope it wasn't all too much for you.'

'Oh, God, Nathan, don't be so patronising,' Esme says.

'Actually I found it all very interesting.'

'Give the poor girl some more wine.'

'No, I'm OK thanks,' I say quickly. 'Besides, I've got to drive.'

Esme waves her glass again, splashing wine on the floor.

'Well, give her a bottle to take home then. She could do with it.' Turning to Nathan she adds, as if confidentially: 'When she lets herself go, she's a bloody good painter, Nath.'

Nathan smiles. 'So I've heard.'

'I thought she hadn't told you much about me,' I say.

'That doesn't mean I haven't heard about your work. Very intriguing.'

'She needs to stop painting bloody flowers.'

Nathan flashes me a look.

'I've heard some of your work's quite pornographic.'

'Oh, come on, Nath. You're deliberately winding her up.'

'OK, OK!' Nathan raises his hands in mock surrender. 'Esme's right. They're symbolic rather than pornographic.'

'She needs to go further, be more abstract, more surreal.'

'Maybe,' I say, 'but I'm waiting for inspiration.'

'What kind of inspiration?' says Esme.

'Oh, I don't know,' I say vaguely. 'Something totally different.'

Nathan looks amused. 'Well, if that's what you want, I've got some books with really weird pictures.'

'Really?'

'Yes, by the metaphysicals. They're a bit crude, though. Like yours, they appear pornographic, but really they're just symbolic. So they won't exactly turn you on.' He laughs.

'You've intrigued me.'

'I have?'

'Yes. I'd love to see them, judge for myself.'

'Oh!' He shrugs. 'Well, if you're interested, I'll lend you one.'

'Thanks.'

Soon afterwards I get up to go. 'I've had a great time,' I say. 'Really interesting. Thanks so much for inviting me.'

In the hallway, after I've kissed Esme, Nathan slips his arm round me.

'What about that book?' I say, extricating myself.

Reluctantly he goes to fetch it.

Josie

I wake with my body flung across the bed. It's already late morning. My red-heeled shoes are dancing across my brain, yet I feel more alive than I have for a long while.

I phone Esme.

'That was a brilliant evening. The food was fantastic and I really enjoyed the company.'

'Thanks.' Esme sounds a bit flat, which surprises me. 'Sorry if I got a bit squiffy at the end.'

'That's OK. How are you feeling now?'

'Fine. But I'd pre-loaded a bit to begin with.'

'Is that why you threw a few cats among the pigeons?'

'I like doing that kind of thing.'

'And you brought me in to help. Was it a set-up?'

'Not exactly. I just wanted to throw an artist in amongst that lot and see what happened.'

'I don't think Nathan was quite comfortable with you doing that, though.'

'Oh, he's all right. He thrives on it. In any case,' she says, turning the subject, 'you certainly held your own.'

'Really?'

'Yes. They were all rather impressed by you, I thought. Especially Isobel.'

This pleases me more than I expect. 'But wasn't she a bit too far gone to tell?'

'Oh, never mind that. She's got a good head on her and from what I've heard she's a pretty shrewd judge of people.'

'She certainly enjoyed your wine.'

'It was rather good wine, though I say it myself. Did you take a bottle home?'

'No.' I don't want to talk about the wine. I want to know more about Isobel. 'What does Isobel do?' I ask.

'She's retired now. When she was young, she used to be a ballet dancer, I think.'

I have a momentary image of her pirouetting on points. 'That would explain a lot'.

'The slight severity, you mean?'

Isobel has suddenly become a wonder to me. She's no longer wearing grey: she's dressed in white – the fragile plumage of a swan. She's turning, bending. I see the arc of her arm, the arch of her foot, her utmost grace and balance. She's serious about her art.

'Yes, and now you've told me that, it makes sense of all that championing of the artist. I wondered why she defended it with such feeling. It's because she is one herself.'

'Oh yes, of course. I suppose you're right. I should have realised that,' she admits.

'Actually I rather admired her. She certainly knew how to give Dominic a run for his money.'

'Actually, I think something happened to her that put paid to her career. A broken leg or something. I've heard rumours but never quite liked to ask.'

'Or maybe it was just getting married and having children.'

'Oh, just think of it,' Esme says. 'How awful to have to make a choice. Thank God we didn't live then.'

Putting down the phone, I wonder if she's right. I wonder if things really have changed so much – whether we do have a choice now or whether much the same sacrifices are still required.

I wander around the house feeling restless. I enjoyed myself last night – meeting new people, being challenged. It's given me new things to think about. I need more of that.

Nathan's book is lying beside me on the kitchen table. I begin looking through the illustrations. Nathan was right. Some of them are surprisingly explicit, but they're strangely soulless. They're also crude to the point of naivety. As I flick through I notice the same images appearing again and again in different styles. Couples entwined, lying beneath trees, or half-submerged in water. I find them disturbing. I'm certain they represent a language of symbols and colours, but I can make no sense of them. I close the book.

My head feels muzzy and I need to go out. As it's Sunday afternoon I decide to do what everyone else does – visit a garden centre and buy some plants.

Two hours later I return with a boot-load of bedding plants – pansies, begonias, geraniums and a selection of trailers. I unload them on the patio then let myself into the house. As soon as I go into the kitchen, I realise Will has been home. He's left an unwashed coffee mug on the kitchen table. I run upstairs to the bedroom and open the wardrobe. Most of his clothes are missing. This is what I've been dreading. I sit down heavily on the bed. The feel of him so recently in the house is disturbing, his presence lingering, as if he's somehow there and not there. His insubstantiality creates in me a kind of panic. I get up again and move mechanically around the room, hanging up my clothes, tidying the place. I wonder what would have happened if I'd been here. Would we have spoken to each other? If so, what would we have said? We've moved beyond words, beyond explanations. It's as if we have to play something out to the end before we can engage with each other. And yet, I think, we will have to speak at some point, if only to sort out what to do next.

I return to the kitchen, trying to force myself to address the situation. Since he's taken his clothes, he must be moving in somewhere. Is it with Katy? I conjure an image of her flat, with hanging pentacles, an altar to a female deity. I try to picture Will living there, and the whole thing seems like madness. Surely this can only be a temporary passion. He'll come round in time. For a brief moment I imagine that somehow things can return to normal and I can resume my old life. But it's a fleeting illusion. I know I'm cut adrift now, whether I like it or not.

I cross to the sink and rinse Will's mug. As I put it to drain I hear the crackle of approaching tyres on the gravel. Has Will come back for more of his things? Did he want to see me after all? Hope flashes through me again. Then I hear a tread on the path. It's not Will's. The steps come round the side of the house and a figure peers through the window in the back door. I go to the door and open it. Frieda is standing there, dressed inconspicuously in brown trousers and a padded anorak.

'Oh, my dear, I – I didn't mean to disturb you. I just wondered if ...' For once she seems unsure of herself. I finish the sentence for her.

'If Will's here?'

'Yes, dear.'

'Well, the answer is no, and I don't expect him back in the foreseeable future.'

'Is he all right?' Frieda's voice is meek. 'I mean to say, I haven't seen him for quite a while. I know things haven't been ... good between you, but, all the same, I did think he'd … I mean, he wouldn't normally let me worry like this.'

'Quite,' I say, 'but one doesn't really know what to expect from him these days, does one?'

Frieda opens her mouth as if to defend her son, then shuts it, for once seeming lost for words.

'I rather think he's moved out.'

'Oh!' Frieda seems astonished by this information. 'But … but where's he …?'

'Where's he gone? I think I can probably tell you that.' I keep my voice flat, concealing a feeling that is almost triumphant. After all, if Katy is going to steal Will, then she can bloody well have what goes with him: his mother.

'I'm not completely sure,' I say, 'but I think he might be living in a flat on the outskirts of town. Would you like some tea?'

Frieda licks her lips, but it's not tea she wants.

'No, dear, thank you. I haven't time to stop. But if I could just ask you where?'

'I don't know,' I say, 'after all if he hasn't told you himself, I'm not sure it's for me to ...'

'Please!' Frieda's lips pucker.

I shrug. 'Chester Crescent.'

Frieda looks up sharply, a smile beginning on her face.

'And the number, dear?' Her voice is authoritative now.

'Are you sure you won't have a –'

'The number, dear.'

'It's 24.'

'Which floor?'

She stands, head bent to one side, looking up at me expectantly.

'Third.'

'Thank you, dear.'

Without further ado, she bustles out of the door.

After she's gone, I sit a while, processing what's just happened. Despite everything, the small victory over my mother-in-law is enough to raise my spirits a little.

Then my mobile phone buzzes. It's a text from Tom. 'Need to see you. Can I come round this evening?'

I text back: 'Have to get out of here. I'll come to yours.'

Will

Coming to the house had not been easy for Will. He knew he might encounter Josie, and was at first relieved that she was out. But her not being there he'd found, if anything, more difficult. If she had been there, he thought, they might have had an awkward or antagonistic encounter. As it was, her absence was unexpectedly potent. When he went up to the bedroom, there was a tangle of her clothes across the bed and, on the floor beside it, her leather boots, one pointed at a slight right-angle to the other, as if her legs were still inside. He opened the wardrobe and there were her jeans, her long cardigans, and the two cotton shirts of his she sometimes wore over leggings, the sleeves loosely rolled.

He knelt down, reaching to feel for his suitcase under the bed, pushing aside her shoes. He drew the case out and laid it on the bed beside her clothes. Quickly, indiscriminately, he began filling it, squashing together trousers and shirts, bundling them inside. He snapped the suitcase shut and hurried down the steps. When he reached the front door he stopped. This is my house, he thought. Why am I behaving like a burglar? I'm still paying half the bills.

Leaving his case beside the front door, he went into the kitchen and boiled the kettle. So, where was she? He scrutinised the Monet calendar he had picked up last Christmas thinking it would please her. There was nothing on it. So, she didn't want him to know where she was. Was that it? Doubtless she was out with Tom. He could feel the anger returning, the well-rehearsed arguments insisting his innocence: why should he have to put up with a wife who refused to have his children, was unable to explain anything to him, then took a lover? Everything he'd done was justified – his leaving, his finding someone else. None of it could be helped. He'd only done what any man would do in similar circumstances.

He poured the boiling water over a tea-bag and stirred it with one of the many silver teaspoons Josie had picked up. She'd collected them here and there at antique shops. Despite his self-justifications, he felt an unexpected tenderness for her. She loved oddities like that, she loved the mismatch of them, the character. She'd once said it was like bringing other people's stories into the house. Other people. He thought of Tom coming into the house. A bad story. A bad find. His anger returning, he drank the tea, left the mug on the table as a sign that he'd been back, and went out, slamming the front door behind him.

Josie

I approach Tom's house, a terraced property down a narrow backstreet within half a mile's walking distance of the town centre. I've never been here before. Despite Esme's advice, I felt I needed to come alone. The street is shadowed, the houses shabby. His front door is black, badly painted. As soon as I knock I hear footsteps running down the stairs. Tom opens the door into a dark hall, and stands a moment, blocking me from coming in. He seems surprisingly nervous.

'Wouldn't you rather go out for a meal?' he says, adding quickly, 'I'll pay.'

'No, thanks.' I shake my head then smile at him encouragingly. 'In any case, it's time I saw your work. You said you'd made a breakthrough.'

I push past him into the hallway. It's not so much a hall as a passageway made gloomy by maroon paint below a dado rail. Above the dado the walls are a dull mix of what looks like sap green and Payne's grey. I wonder if Tom painted it himself.

'Where's your studio?'

'In the spare bedroom. Don't you want a coffee before we go up?'

'No, thanks.'

I lead the way upstairs. Some small canvases are propped on either side of the stairs, leaning against the wall and the banisters. I take in a vague murk of dun-coloured landscape as I pass. It's difficult to see as the only light is shed by a feeble bulb hanging above the stairway. I reach the landing at the top.

'To your left,' says Tom's voice behind me.

A cold northern light enters the studio room through a sash window. It's the right light for an artist, of course. Canvases are hung all around the walls, some enormous, some ridiculously small. All are in monochrome except for some stabs of violent colour. Two easels stand either side of the window, their backs towards me. I cross to the window and turn round to see.

The canvas on my left shows a group of people on a city street. Tall buildings rear up behind them, dim roofs against a twilit sky. The group appears to be either on their way or coming from a party. The monochrome figures are indistinct, defined by the angle of the head, the curve of the cheek, the suggestion of touch or gesture rather than individual features. The central character, a middle-aged man, is bending forwards, eagerly following a woman in a long skirt striding ahead of him. The man has part of him opened up, as if the viewer possesses X-ray vision. The opened section is intended to be a shocking revelation, which only the viewer can appreciate. White light illuminates a visceral heart with a safety pin grotesquely puncturing both the right and left ventricles. It is unclear whether the heart is being held together or cruelly pierced. Another woman is pursued by a man whose lit window into his intestines displays a coiled snake winding towards his genitals. A fat man bringing up the rear, has a cut–open wedge of distended stomach, as if a Santa Claus figure had swallowed a sack of toys, while a young woman hurrying ahead of him is slashed open in the head, revealing a slice of cerebrum which emits an almost star-like radiance. I look away and the brightly lit apertures linger behind my eyelids.

Having had my fill of this painting, I turn towards the one on the other easel: a portrait of a woman's face. Even with such barely defined features it's perfectly recognisable. Except for one eye – an eye that is disturbingly penetrative, its glossy pupil lit with dazzling convex patches. As I look, I can feel Tom waiting for my reaction. I keep my face blank.

I move away from the window and scan the walls of hanging canvases. They all follow the same theme: apertures cutting into the body. Except in some of them the flashes of illumination show instead in a crook of an arm, in the interstices between two figures or in the void between two hills. Again and again, these small, insignificant areas take on unexpected importance as concealing flaps are peeled back to reveal a sudden brilliance of nature – incongruous fish or mammals or birds. I can follow the progression. The more benign canvases are technically less impressive. The ones where he breaks into the body are his most recent works.

Tom is standing in the middle of the room watching me intently as I examine his work. His face shows both apprehension and pride. He should be proud, I think; the execution of the illuminated segments is immaculate, the organs viscerally accurate to the point of repulsion. He should also be apprehensive.

'What was your inspiration?' I ask him, noncommittally.

'In my monochrome phase,' he replies carefully, 'you told me to be less meticulous, to allow some shadowy areas.'

'I didn't say you had to. I would never say that. I just suggested that there were alternatives.'

'Yes, that's right.'

I think back to his earlier canvases, remembering how his monochrome precision denied any spontaneous flights of fancy.

'I said that because I thought you might be limiting your imagination.'

'And you urged the use of colour. You were always urging that.'

I fall silent, considering. Had I done that? Did I urge him towards what I love?

'I hope I didn't force you into that,' I answer carefully. 'I mean, I hope that was ultimately your own choice.'

'You were a good teacher. You didn't force us to do anything. It was just that some of us couldn't help adopting your own enthusiasms – especially if we admired you.'

I look again at the paintings that surround us. The colour has arrived all right, but with such intensity it's breaking out with manic force.

'Apart from me, where has your inspiration come from? Or can't you say?' I wait for his answer, aware I still haven't actually commented on his work.

'First I tried making my figures less detailed.'

'I can see that. That's good.'

'Then I made the buildings more abstract.'

'I like that too.'

'Then I went to the Body Worlds exhibition and saw the bodies.'

'Gunther Von Hagens?'

'Have you seen them?'

'Yes.'

'And what did you think?'

I pause, considering my reply. I remember the slight apprehension I felt arriving at the gallery in Brick Lane, climbing the stairs, turning the corner and seeing the first of the bodies. It was a man, standing at the entrance to the gallery, his entire skin removed, showing the crimson bandings of his muscles. Strangely, I felt no horror. The peeled bodies cut open to reveal the beauty of their inner organs had inspired, not revolted me.

'They were beautiful,' I say finally.

'Why?'

I know the answer.

'Probably because their organs were clean and treated. Plastination I think he called it.'

'Yes. Too clean.'

I walk back to the window and look again at his large canvas. The right and left ventricles are squelched and dripping, and there is slime on the intestines.

'But it made them acceptable.'

I see the look on Tom's face. Has he led me into this deliberately? I feel ashamed. Unable to meet his eyes, I look down at the floor and study the uneven floorboards.

'I know what I said,' I mutter.

'Yes. And that's not what you taught us. You told us to break boundaries, to express ourselves no matter what. You said art was the great opener. You told us to challenge everything.'

I'm still studying the floor. I glance up. Tom is in full flood, his face flushed.

'You told us to dare, to make uncomfortable, to take risks.'

'I know.'

'To risk offending – *to risk offending*!' He is shouting now, punching one hand into the other.

'*I thought you believed in that. I thought you believed in me!*'

He strides towards me. I see his anger at my betrayal. 'And now you don't believe those things! What's happened to you? You don't believe those things any more!'

But did I ever, I think. Did I – or was it just my training? I raise my head and meet his eyes. Then suddenly I know. My training was right. I was right. The real question is something else. Is Tom right?

'So what are you trying to say in your work?' I ask.

'Isn't it obvious?'

'Maybe. But I'd like to hear it from you.'

'People are not what they seem.'

'You mean they hide things.'

'They try. They walk about trying to look normal most of the time.'

I wait for him to say more.

'But it's all just a mask. However much they try, they can't outwit the animal inside.'

'But are all people like that?'

'Most of them.'

'What about the others?'

'Well, maybe some manage to be better than that. But I should say they're pretty rare.'

'Like the woman with the illuminated brain?'

'Yes. Like her.'

I consider a moment. The woman is the only enlightened figure in the room.

'OK, I think I get it,' I say slowly. 'But if it's what I think, that's actually an old idea.'

Tom looks up.

'The Fall. Everything in Man, fallen, degenerate. Everything except the intellect.'

'So?'

'It's Thomas Aquinas.'

'So?'

'So do you believe that?'

'I hadn't really thought about it.' He sounds bored, disappointed. 'Do you?'

'Not entirely,' I say. 'But it's an idea.'

'I suppose there could be something in it,' Tom says grudgingly. 'The intellect, reason, maybe ... maybe it can save you ... sometimes, from acting on animal instinct.'

'Is that what you're saying?'

'For God's sake! I don't know.' He kicks suddenly at the wall leaving a shoe-print above the skirting board. He has been interrogated and found out. He has not been approved.

I am thinking about instinct. I'm remembering Tom stalking me. Neither of us has yet mentioned the portrait on the easel, the woman with the gimlet eye. Neither of us has acknowledged who she is.

'Tom, I need the loo. Where is it?'

'Oh,' he says. 'It's downstairs, turn right at the bottom.'

'Thanks.'

I descend the stairs, turn left and let myself out of the front door.

'No wonder they won't hang them on the wall!' Esme says. Her lips are poised above the thick rim of a large coffee cup. We've met at Costa this time. 'And, in answer to your earlier question, of course, we do sometimes get patients to bring us their artwork. And, yes, it can tell us quite a lot about them.'

'I thought so.' My cheek is resting on my palm. I dunk one end of a dry almond biscuit into my coffee then turn it over, trying to moisten it without making it soggy.

'In a way, though,' I say. 'Tom's paintings are brilliant. I should have told him that.'

'That's because you're such a good teacher.'

'His earlier works – the ones with flashes of light and creatures in hidden places – aren't quite so skilled, but in terms of content I think they really have something.'

'Then that's what you should tell him.'

'Yes. Except ...' I stop.

Esme puts her cup down carefully.

'Except', she says, 'you don't want to see him again.'

I shake my head.

'Then I don't think you should – and certainly not on your own!'

'But he thinks I've betrayed him – rejected his art. He said as much. He was shouting at me.'

Esme raises her cup again thoughtfully.

'He thinks he was following me – in his work, I mean.'

Esme places the cup in its oval saucer. 'Yes,' she says. 'Following you.'

I feel a slight shiver run through me. 'I could have overlooked *that*,' I say. 'I did overlook it.'

'But not this,' Esme says quietly. 'Not the eye. And you're right. I don't think you should see him again. At least, not on your own.'

We finish our coffees and get up. At the doorway, Esme kisses me lightly on the cheek. 'And remember, you can ring me any time if you're at all worried.'

Will

As Will drove the familiar route to the leisure centre, he replayed the arguments for his innocence – the ones he couldn't get Andy to buy, but which he found irrefutable.

His temper cooled. In some ways he had the upper hand now. He wondered what Josie would conclude after his visit. It would be obvious he intended to stay away, but she wouldn't know what his plans were. He thought perhaps he ought to tell her. But how could he when he didn't even know them himself? He hadn't decided whether he and Josie should divorce or what would happen to his own home. Nor, he realised, did he want to think about it. The disjunction he felt every time he visited the house was bad enough. But, in any case, he was still being more than fair to her. She had the house to live in, whereas he was in limbo at the moment. Andy had had enough of him and he wasn't contemplating sleeping on anyone else's floor. He'd booked a B&B. It would do for the time being.

Nevertheless, as he approached the leisure centre, he began considering his next move. He couldn't remain in limbo for ever. But what were his choices? He had no intention of living with Katy. Even the thought of it was absurd. The kind of things she had in her flat made Josie's quirky selections of *objets d'art* ridiculously tame.

He parked the car and sprinted up the stairs to the gym. He stripped off, donned his shorts, did a few stretches and was soon warming up on the stair climber. He was still thinking of Katy. Even if he could put up with all her weird stuff, living with her would be impossible; she was so controlling about her flat. For a start there was the mysterious locked room. He had no idea what that was about. He supposed it housed magical equipment. He could insist on her showing him, of course. But perhaps he didn't really want to know.

He got off the stair climber and stepped onto the running machine. As he gradually built up speed, he thought about the odd regime Katy insisted on. He could only visit her at lunchtimes and after eight o'clock in the evening. She said it was because she did her Tarot readings earlier in the evening. To date, he had not been allowed to stay overnight either. Apparently it was because she liked to meditate first thing in the morning. He'd accepted that. It even gave him a grudging respect for her. However silly her occupation, it showed she was at least attempting to put some mental discipline around it.

He slowed down to a steady pace. Irritating though Katy's strictures were on one level, he had to admit he found them strangely exciting. Stealing off from work for sex in his lunch hour seemed deliciously errant. He felt a frisson of desire at the thought of it.

Adjusting the machine, he upped his pace again with the increasing speed. After five minutes he was running flat out. It was exhilarating. As he ran, he felt relief in the freedom of his body. He couldn't remember feeling like this before. As long as he could remember, he'd felt restricted. He slowed and jumped off, and went over to the weights. Panting slightly, he raised his arms, pushing against the pressure. He pumped his muscles in rhythm, feeling almost invincible as he held off the load. Yes, he'd been restricted for too long. He'd been the dutiful husband and son.

His mother. Good God! He hadn't seen her in quite a while. He'd been ignoring her messages along with Josie's. How extraordinary that he'd managed to avoid her for so long! He upped the weight on the bar, the speed of his repetitions dropping as he adjusted to the new resistance. In the last few weeks, she'd only once presented herself at reception, to be told firmly by Megan that she should meet her son away from work. Fearless in all other situations, his mother retained an old-fashioned respect for what she perceived as the male domain of work. At the same time she couldn't come round and see him because she didn't know where he was.

He climbed onto the rowing machine and pulled his knees towards him, stretching and releasing in mechanical motion, forwards and backwards, forwards and backwards. By now he barely noticed what he was doing. He was still thinking of his mother. Then it occurred to him that she must have gone to see Josie. Oh, God! Had he inflicted that on Josie – the task of telling his mother they had separated? If so, how on earth had Josie coped! He'd had a welcome reprieve, caught up in a scenario so extraordinary he'd been unable to think beyond it. But all this time his mother would have been building up a debt of anger and outrage that would descend on him in one great landslide of reproach. He got off the rowing machine and headed for the pool. He needed to put all this out of his head. He didn't want to think about his mother, or Josie, or the future, or anything other than sleeping with Katy. He wanted to enjoy his newfound freedom for a little longer.

Frieda

Frieda was standing outside a tall Georgian front door under a grey sky, twisting her neck in an attempt to look up at the windows of the flats above. The door, she noticed, had been recently painted a newfangled but nondescript colour. It was almost the same shade as the sky. What was wrong with good old-fashioned reds or greens? Her annoyance helped combat the apprehension she felt. Which floor was it on? Three. Not wishing to linger on the doorstep, she pressed the bell. After a few seconds a voice crackled over the intercom:

'Is that Natasha?'

She grunted.

'OK, come in!'

The buzzer sounded and she pushed the door open. As soon as she was inside, she marched straight up the stairs to the third floor. She stopped outside a purple painted door and lifted the metal knocker. Before dropping it, she faltered. The door was marked with a black pentacle. She frowned. This couldn't be the one, surely? Josie must have sent her on a wild goose chase. That would be just like her – that little madam with her oh-so-innocent eyes! Frieda's hand was still poised holding up the knocker. She let it fall. She heard a scuffling from inside, then the door opened. A young woman stood there dressed like a priestess, dark hair hanging down her shoulders, eyes ringed with black, and a floor-length skirt. She looked at Frieda in astonishment.

'Oh,' she said, recovering. 'I thought you were Natasha. She usually comes at this time.'

'I'm sorry, I think there must be some confus –' Frieda began. She was about to turn away when in the corner of her eye, she noticed something familiar in the hallway. 'I'm sorry,' she reiterated, 'I thought ...'

'If you want a reading,' Katy said, 'you have to make a booking.

But if you'd like to come in for a moment, I'll look in my diary and find a date.'

She swung the front door wide and Frieda went in. Katy led her down the passage. The door to her bedroom was ajar. As they passed, Frieda glimpsed the edge of the bed, a mahogany four-poster draped with black. Beyond the bed was a candle burning on a chest of drawers. It illuminated a tatty picture of a snake-tailed woman with three faces.

Frieda followed Katy like a zombie. She had half-expected someone shady, but nothing had prepared her for this. Katy led her into the consulting room. It was mercifully light and airy compared with the bedroom, but there were several strange objects on display – a winged statuette on the window-sill, and a collection of mystical paraphernalia on a side table – a marble egg, a pewter goblet and a crystal wand. On a far shelf were two phallic-shaped crystals and a pregnant woman crudely fashioned out of orange clay. As she gazed speechless at it all, Katy advanced towards her with an open diary.

'I could fit you in next week,' she began, then glanced at her watch.

'Actually, it looks like Natasha's not coming. So, as you're here, I could squeeze you in for a short reading now if you like.' She ushered Frieda towards a central table.

'Take a seat.' She pulled out a wooden chair.

Still in a hypnotic state, Frieda sat down. An arc of cards was lying spilled in front of her. Among them she saw a goatish devil figure, an armoured skeleton on horseback and two shrieking figures falling from a burning tower.

'Sorry about that. Rather a challenging reading. I was just pondering it.'

Hands shaking slightly, Katy hurriedly gathered up the cards, covered them in a blue cloth and reached for a new stack. As she shuffled them, she said: 'I'm sorry, I was a bit distracted. I haven't asked your name.'

Frieda opened her mouth, but before she could reply, Katy added, 'Also, before I give you the cards, do you have a particular question you'd like to ask?'

As Katy looked up enquiringly, Frieda shot her a look across the table – the most severe she could muster. This woman had no right to take what was not hers.

'Yes,' she said. 'Why is my son's jacket hanging in your hall?'

Josie

As usual I wake to the dawn chorus. A constant state of nervousness overlays my exhaustion. It's an insistent nagging at the back of my eyes. The energy may help me to finish some more flower paintings. But that's still a struggle because I've lost interest. Instead I'm haunted by the illustrations in Nathan's book – pictures full of secrets.

I get up. One thing is certain. However tired I am, I need to earn some money. I can't rely on being supported by Will any more.

The drizzle prevents me doing much gardening today beyond tidying some soggy branches. Not wanting to keep crossing the grass and creating more mud tracks, I retreat indoors. Sitting by the warm stove, I fall into a short, disorientating nap. This is how I manage my lack of sleep at night.

I am woken by a thud on the back door window. The rain has stopped and there, in a haze of fresh sunlight, stands Frieda, mouthing at me through the glass with fish-like exaggeration.

I get up. My limbs are moving, but my mind is bleary with daytime sleep. I gaze in incomprehension as if at a stranger, then go to the door and open it. Frieda pushes past me.

'I had to see you!'

'Oh?'

'It's something dreadful! You need to know.'

If I can just drink some tea, I'll be able to think. I fill the kettle and put it on the hotplate, Frieda fidgeting all the while.

'Don't worry on my account.'

'Well. I – I need some.'

I fumble for the biscuit tin, prise off the lid and hold it out to Frieda.

'No, dear, thank you.'

I take one myself and bite into it.

'That woman. She's …' Frieda hesitates as a new thought comes to her. 'You know Will's …?'

I nod.

'Have you seen her?'

My mouth full of biscuit, my hand shakes slightly as I force the ochre fluid out of the teabag. Once I have some tea inside me, I can cope with anything – even Frieda. I add milk to the cup and a dash of cold water. I drink half of it quickly. The effect is miraculous.

'Yes, I have.'

'Oh!' Frieda sounds incredulous. 'How? When?'

I pause, wondering how to respond. I can hardly tell her about Tom.

'When?' Frieda insists.

'I saw her coming out of her house.'

'Did you speak to her?'

I shake my head.

'You've seen what she looks like?' Frieda looms towards me. I nod.

'So, you'll know.'

'Know what?'

'Well, I can tell you what!' She breaks off.

I move away from the stove and sit down at the table. Seating herself opposite, Frieda brings her face close to mine over the table top. She lowers her voice to a whisper and pronounces conspiratorially:

'She's a *witch*!'

She sits back triumphantly.

I stare at her.

'I tell you, that woman's a witch and she's laid a spell on my son!'

I lift the teacup to my mouth, still staring at her.

'You poor dear! No wonder you couldn't hold him against such wicked powers!' She reaches across the table and takes my spare hand. 'But we must help him.'

I blink at her. I want to withdraw my hand but Frieda's grasp is firm. 'The poor lamb is in a trap. You and I must work together to get him back!' She lets go of me. 'I know I can count on you. Whatever difficulties you two have had in the past, I know deep down you love him.'

'I don't think', I say slowly, choosing my words, 'Will wants to come back to me.'

'Nonsense, dear. Of course he does. He just can't see it at the moment because of her.'

'I really don't think he does,' I repeat.

'Oh, but he can't want a woman like that!' Frieda explodes. 'She's ... she's ... Have you seen her flat?'

I shake my head.

'It's absolutely frightful! Full of shrines and wands and things. And to think that's where ...' She shakes her own head in an attempt to clear the unpleasant vision she's called up. 'Will's not that type of man, at all. He'd never go for a woman like that. Never!'

Still searching for words, I nod my head again. That much I can agree on.

'There's no doubt about it. I've read about these things,' Frieda says. 'There *are* witches nowadays. And they do all kinds of spells and whatnot.'

'I agree it's strange,' I begin, 'but ...'

Frieda, lost in her own thoughts, shakes her head sadly. 'The poor lamb! The poor, poor lamb!'

I am reluctant to respond, but saying nothing only makes me seem complicit. Before I can think of a response, Frieda takes hold of my hand again. 'So I need you to help me, dear. We need to bring him to his senses, get him to see reason.'

'Assuming I want him back, of course.' My voice is unexpectedly assertive.

Frieda lets go of my hand. 'But, surely –' she begins.

'And even if I did, I don't know what you think I can do.'

'Do?' Frieda glares at me. 'My dear, for a start you can agree to that treatment. That HMV or whatever. If you'd only agreed to it in the first place, none of this would have happened.'

This is more familiar territory. I study the wooden knots on the tabletop.

'Well, it's the only thing that'll get him back! Surely you know that?'

I lift my head and regard her quietly.

'I think it would take more than that now,' I say.

Josie

'Darling, it's me.' My mother's voice at the other end of the phone is unusually brisk and businesslike.

'Hi Mum.'

'We've just seen Frieda.'

'Oh?'

'Yes. She came here yesterday to talk to us. And now your father and I are very concerned. About Will.'

I wait.

'You see, Frieda thinks he's gone off with –'

'I know, Mum. She's just been round to see me.'

'Oh, yes, of course. She said she was going to. So now you know.'

'Know what exactly?' I ask.

'About the witch business.'

'So you believe it too, do you?'

'Well, no one would have expected it of him, but it does explain –'

'What?'

'His strange behaviour. We never imagined Will would be the sort to just go off like that. That's why we thought you must have driven him to it. But now – now it seems he was lured.'

'Well, if ...'

'Against his will.'

'I'm not sure ...'

'Of course, now we know that, the whole thing's obvious.'

I hold the phone away, reluctant to hear what might be coming next. Have my parents really swallowed that crazy theory? I can hear my mother's voice, as if from far away.

'Frieda explained the whole thing to us. It seems there are quite a lot of women these days who go in for that sort of thing.'

'What sort of thing?' I bring the phone back to my ear.

'Well, you know – spells and so on.' I can detect my mother's discomfort from her breathing.

'Spells?'

'Yes.' She sounds impatient.

'What kind of spells?'

'Oh, you know the kind of thing.'

'You mean like sacrificing babies and black cats?'

'Don't be silly, Josie!' There is a momentary silence, before she adds, 'Well, if you're not going to take it seriously –'

'Well really, Mum, how can I?'

'I don't see why not. After all, you know what Frieda saw – some sort of devil-inspired cards, incense burning, crystal balls. Oh, and in her bedroom there was a horrible shrine to a three-headed snake woman, and a lot of black drapes everywhere. I know it might all sound rather mumbo jumbo, but Frieda says –'

'And what does Frieda actually know about it?'

'Oh, Frieda knows a lot,' my mother says triumphantly.

'How?'

'Things she's read. That some women nowadays call themselves witches, some even meet in covens, do spells, dance naked – all kinds of things – and for an innocent young man like Will –'

'Mum, for goodness sake!'

'Don't you "for goodness sake" me! You should be grateful we're so concerned. We only want the best for you. You know that.' My mother sounds suddenly tearful.

'All right. I'm sorry.'

'So we're thinking, if he's been led astray like that. I mean, if he's in her power, it all makes sense.'

'Does it?'

'Listen, your father and I are sure he loves you really. Deep down. We're sure he does. It's just that he's been overcome by this woman's ...'

'Spells. I know. You said.'

'Well, it makes sense, doesn't it?'

'I don't know what kind of sense you're looking for, Mum.'

'Now you're just being deliberately difficult,' Janet says crossly.

'Here we are, trying to help, and all you do is question our judgement.'

'Mum, there's no need to get so upset.'

'Oh, I think there is! You obviously don't want our help. You're going to sit there locked away in your studio fiddling with your paintings, and let him go. You won't lift a finger, will you, to try to get him back?'

'I didn't say that.'

'No, you didn't and you don't need to. In all this time, what have you done to make peace with him? And, more to the point, what have you done to try to give him a child?'

'Not that again, Mother.'

'Well, it's at the bottom of everything, isn't it?'

'It's not something that –'

'That what?

'That I can talk about.'

She gives a snort. 'Not talk about? It's no wonder he's gone off.' Her voice breaks. She sounds tearful again. 'Is it any wonder your father and I despair of you! You won't help yourself and you won't let us help you. It's not as if we don't try.' I hear her blow her nose in an effort to compose herself. 'Well, if you simply won't listen, I don't know what any of us can do. I really don't!'

Josie

'Actually, in some ways, they're quite right!'

Esme's eyes are shining with suppressed amusement. We are sitting in my studio, two chipped mugs of coffee on the table in front of us.

'They're right?'

'Yes. She *has* cast a spell over him.'

I lift an eyebrow.

'Known in medieval times as a *glamourie*.'

She pauses to see the effect on me, before adding: 'Of course, today that kind of spell's called sex. And, naturally, every one of us can cast it!'

'So we're all witches?'

'Absolutely!'

She laughs and I join her. It feels good. I like seeing myself like that: a witch with powers equal to Katy's.

'Mind you, we have a host of other spells which are much more sophisticated.'

'Do we?'

'These, for example,' Esme says, her eyes embracing the stacks of canvases propped against the walls, 'are *your* spells.'

'I suppose you could say that.'

'I would definitely say that. What do you think art is, after all?' Esme picks up a stray piece of charcoal and begins idling with it on the table. 'Anyway, she probably relies on other powers besides sex.'

'Like what?'

'Well, you know! Stop reacting to your mum for a moment and think about it.'

'You mean she does have some –'

'Occult power, yes. And it could still be sexual in origin, but she might also know how to use it.'

'She knows how to use it?'

'Come on, Josie, you know perfectly well what I mean.'

I'm still puzzled.

'I mean in the sense of harnessing it.' Esme faces me. 'You, with all your intuitive awareness, your artist's path or whatever – surely you know about these things?'

I shrug.

'Well, what about everything you've been telling me? The dreams, the girl appearing. Are you going to tell me it's all bollocks?'

'N ... no.'

'Because if you really think it is, then you've sure gambled a hell of a lot on it. Your whole relationship for starters. Not to mention this house, the garden, your livelihood –'

'Stop!' I put my hands over my ears. Esme waits. She begins fiddling with the piece of charcoal again, rolling it under her finger.

'You're saying I'm crazier than she is?'

'Not at all.'

'What then?'

'I'm saying we all believe in something. We all follow an inner mentor, even if it's just our so-called conscience.'

'And it's no more than that?'

'I'm not saying that either. The truth is I don't know. But then nobody really does. They just have to keep following inner promptings and hope somehow they're doing the right thing. Unless, of course, they have rules to follow.'

'You mean like in religion?'

'Yes. And, in a way, that's what Katy's doing.'

'But how?'

'Well, really! I know you're an artist and all that, but where's your analytical faculty?'

I laugh. 'Some of us prefer to leave that to you lot!'

'Well, think about it. It's a question of belief.'

'And?'

'Katy believes in it.'

'So?'

'So she believes in what she thinks the Tarot cards are telling her. She also believes in the power of spells when she casts them – at least, I assume she casts them.'

'I wouldn't know about that.'

'When she kneels at her shrine, or lights a candle in front of it or whatever, she must believe in the power of the snake goddess.'

'What possible difference can it make whether she believes or not?'

'It makes all the difference in the world.'

'Does it?'

'Because it affects how she behaves. And that, in turn, affects how people respond to her.' She stabs the tip of the charcoal stick into the wood. 'And therein lies her power!'

I reach across and lift the charcoal from her hand.

'Stop marking my table!' I tell her.

'I thought you artists were free and easy!'

'We are. But only within a certain discipline.'

'That', says Esme, 'is exactly my point.'

Katy

Katy walked into her consulting room, unwrapped the blue silk cloth, and took the pack of cards in her hands. Usually she found the weight of them reassuring. They held their own power, of course, but it had always been a power she could contain. Now she felt she was losing control and the cards were beginning to take over, pushing her towards her fate. She shivered. If she hadn't seen it so clearly in the spread last time – the time when Frieda came, if the cards hadn't spoken …

One card would confirm it, she thought. A single card at this point would be more powerful than a whole spread. Just one card and she would know. But first she must ask the question. Slowly she began to shuffle the pack, the rippling sounding louder than usual. Her hands were shaking. Before she was ready a card fell from the pack and landed face-down on the table. She put her finger on it. Then she sat for a long time, steeling herself to turn it over.

Will

Megan looked up from the PC on the reception desk as a young woman entered the office, hair neat, neck draped in a peacock blue scarf.

'Would it be possible to see Will Jones?' the woman asked.

'Do you have an appointment?'

'No.'

'Well, I'm terribly sorry, but he has clients all afternoon.' She made a show of looking regretfully at a list on the desk.

'It's not about my accounts.'

'Oh – can I ask what it's about then?'

'It's a personal matter. If I could just have a quick word with him.'

'He doesn't usually take personal visits at work.'

'Just five minutes. It's very important.'

'Well, I ...' Megan hesitated. The woman had a quiet authority which made it difficult to refuse.

At that moment Will walked through the door. He was late back from lunch. The young woman went towards him.

'Hello!' she said 'I'm Esme. And you're Will Jones, aren't you?' She extended her hand.

Will ignored the hand and gave a brief nod, accompanied by a polite frown. 'I'm sorry – should I know you?'

'I'm not sure we've met exactly but I think you know who I am. I wonder if you could spare me five minutes before your next client. It's very important.'

Will glanced at Megan. 'Who's my next appointment?' he asked

'Miss Greenway, but she hasn't turned up yet.'

'All right.' He turned to the young woman. 'I can give you five minutes. But that's all.' He motioned her through the door into his office.

'It's good of you to see me,' Esme said, stretching her hand towards him again.

This time Will shook it stiffly. 'Have a seat.'

She drew back an armless grey chair and sat down. From the other side of the desk his jacketed shoulders were black against the daylight.

'How can I help you?'

'As you probably know, I'm a friend of Josie's. We've seen a lot of each other recently.'

'Oh? I don't think ...' Will began.

'I'm sorry if you think I'm being intrusive, but I'm a bit concerned about her.'

'Josie?'

'Yes.'

'Well, I ...' Will cleared his throat.

'I know you're not together at the moment, so you won't know.'

'Won't know what?'

'That someone's been stalking her.'

'What?' Will leaned forward slightly.

'His name's Tom.'

Will's expression relaxed. He leaned back in his chair again.

'Is that what she told you?'

'It's what I know.'

'Then', Will began, shuffling a pile of papers, 'you need to be aware, if you're not already, that he's her lover.'

'Not anymore – if he ever was,' said Esme.

'Well, I'm sorry,' said Will, picking up the pile of papers with both hands and tapping it on the desk, 'but that's no business of mine.'

'I think it is. He took advantage of the fact that you'd left her, and came on to her.'

'I seem to remember he was an old student of hers.'

'That doesn't stop him being a stalker.'

'I've no doubt Josie can handle this perfectly well herself.'

'I don't think she understands the danger.'

'And you do?'

'I'm a psychologist.'

Will placed the neatened pile of papers carefully down on the desk. 'What kind of danger?' he asked.

'He's obsessive.'

Will folded his hands together and leaned his weight forward.

'Josie thinks she's thrown him over, but she hasn't.'

'And how do you know this?'

'She's heard noises outside her studio, in the evening and at night. That's how it all started. And she's been to see his paintings. There's one –'

The door opened and Megan's head appeared.

'Thought you'd like to know Miss Greenway's here,' she said brightly.

'Thank you,' said Will.

Megan hovered, awaiting further instructions.

'I'll just be a few more minutes, Megan.'

Megan retreated and closed the door.

Will turned back to Esme. 'I believe you were saying something about a painting?'

Esme leaned forward. 'Yes. There's one that's particularly disturbing,' she said.

That evening Will went round to Katy's. As he walked from his car towards her house he was trying to dismiss what Esme had said, but not entirely succeeding. He hoped she was making a bit of a drama out of it all, perhaps thinking she could help Josie get him back. Of course, Esme couldn't know it was already too late. Whatever feelings he still had for Josie, he could no longer protect her. She would have to cope on her own. He sighed as he reached Katy's front door. He'd been given a key now, so he let himself in. He looked around. Was he being followed, as Esme claimed?

He had barely reached the first floor when someone darted forward from the floor above and shrieked at him through the banisters:

'What are you doing coming up here, visiting this hussy?'

'Mother!'

He began sprinting up the stairs towards her. She'd been lying in wait for him. How she'd got in he had no idea.

'She's not only a hussy, she's a witch! She's bewitched you, taken you away from your home, your wife, from *me*!'

'Mother, stop!' He took hold of her arm and began hurrying her down the stairs.

'She's a witch, I tell you. A witch! What is my son doing with a witch?'

She carried on protesting as he marched her across the hall and out into the street. He propelled her round the corner and into the first pub he could find. Placing her in a corner seat, he went to the bar. By now she had stopped shouting and begun snivelling instead. In an attempt to calm her down he bought her a large Cinzano. After several sips she began crying in earnest, claiming that she'd lost her son to a she-devil.

'Don't be ridiculous, Mother,' he said. 'She's not a witch or a she-devil. She merely has an unusual occupation.'

'I'll say it's unusual!' His mother was recovering from her sobs and rediscovering her indignation. He assumed it was the effect of the Cinzano. He made another attempt to make Katy sound normal.

'Mother, it's just her job. She's a Tarot card reader.' But he couldn't help wincing even as he said it.

'You mean like a sort of gypsy fortune-teller, is that it?' She dabbed at her face with a handkerchief. 'I thought you had more sense!'

In truth she was right and he had no defence. He had no idea why this woman held such an allure for him.

'It was bad enough when you chose that – artist,' Frieda continued. 'We had trouble enough accepting her. But this –'

'I knew you'd be like this,' Will said, cutting across her and affecting indignation himself. 'Completely unreasonable. That's why I couldn't come and see you. I didn't want this kind of scene.'

'Unreasonable!' Frieda's voice ascended to a shriek. 'Where's *your* reason gone, that's what I'd like to know? You'll be the death of your father if you carry on like this! You've no thought for others, not your parents, your wife –'

'Mother,' Will cut in sternly, 'my choices are for me to make.

Nothing to do with you. In any case, things haven't been that easy with Josie as you know only too well.'

'As for that one, I always said she was no good for you. So at first I didn't mind you falling out with her. I even thought it might be for the best.' She took a long swallow of her drink, 'But she's a bloody saint compared with this one!' She glared at him. 'How you can ...'

He knew there was no stopping her. She'd go on haranguing him until there was no endurance left in him, until he'd either have to start shouting back or walk out. That's when he decided to tell her. He raised his voice. 'You want to know why I'm with her?'

His mother barely heard him. She was still in full stream. 'You want to know why?' he said again, more forcefully. Then, cutting across her outpouring, he told her something that made her stop mid-rant, shocked beyond words.

Josie

It's the middle of the night and I'm in my studio. The purple-black Prussian blue I've spread across the base of the canvas, oozing it straight out of the tube, is furtive and beautiful. Nathan's book is lying open on the table beside me displaying one of its strange pictures. A crazy flock of blue eagles – and I'm unable to resist them. They're rising from the bones of abandoned skeletons – not feeding on them but headed away, soaring into the night sky. I'm painting them, and I'm doing it in the light of a full moon shining in through my window. My eyes feel as though they're shining, too, but not like in Tom's painting – not with that horrible gleaming intensity. I think of Tom's painting and what was unspoken. It was my face on his canvas, my face with an alien eye, searching, spying.

I push my brush into the corner of the canvas. Is Esme right to be worried, I wonder? I twist it so its fibres scratch out white-blue patterns as on Chinese porcelain. I don't feel worried myself. But nor do I feel in control. I feel possessed, almost exhilarated. Is this a phase of the separation? For days I've been gripped by an unstoppable energy that is stealing my sleep, lifting me off the ground. How high will I have to rise before it lets go of me and I come crashing back to earth?

I squeeze another slick of Prussian blue onto my palette, stick my brush in and lift it out, watching the dark substance hang from its tip.

The eagles I am painting are large and crude. I begin stroking out their blue-black wings. I decide I'll never cover the canvas like this. I need to be bolder. I squeeze more Prussian blue onto my palette and begin spreading it across the canvas using my palette knife. I'm careful to leave gaps in it, ones of varying sizes. I want to put some bones in the painting.

I scratch out a ragged wing, thinking about 'Dippel's oil'. He made it from ground-up animal bones and considered it an elixir. But by all accounts it was viscous stuff. How his laboratory must have stunk from its distillation! I put down the palette knife and pick up a rag. I imagine his laboratory filled with egg-shaped vessels, bubbling chemicals. I wipe the blue off my knife and apply it again to the wings. When the painter Diesbach went there to mix some red pigment, Dippel was out. I can see Diesbach helping himself to some leftover potash and beginning to mix it with iron sulphate. I can see him looking puzzled as he mixes. For, instead of the rich red he expects, a rose colour has appeared. He adds more potash and the mixture turns purple. He adds yet more, and now a dark blue emerges. When Dippel returns they stare at it together. Then Dippel works it out. The potash was contaminated with his animal oil and it was this macabre ingredient that produced the new colour. Prussian blue.

I wipe the blue off my palette knife with a rag. That must have been a *eureka* moment. Until then almost the only blue pigment had come from lapis lazuli – far too expensive for most artists. So Dippel's oil became famous. He went on claiming it was the elixir of life, and even drank it, thinking it would prolong his life. I squeeze another slick of the blue pigment directly onto my brush, where it hangs in a small, stiff, elongated globule. It was said that, when he was found dead, his body had turned blue.

It was just a rumour, of course. Like all the others. At the time there were so many superstitions, whispers of his powers. It was even claimed he experimented with human cadavers, attempting to transfer the soul of one into another. I shiver, suddenly feeling alone in the dark night. Surely none of it is true – it's all so far-fetched? I deposit the globule on my pallet, twisting it off with my brush. Except that Dippel lived in Castle Frankenstein. I put down my brush and pick up the oil rag. I wonder why that isn't more widely known, the connection being so obvious. Eighty years after his death, Shelley and his wife Mary visited Lake Geneva. Castle Frankenstein stood nearby in all its crumbling glory, the old tales of Dippel's bones and cadavers still clinging round it.

I dip my rag in the blue and draw it lightly across the wings. Then I stand back to have a look. In one corner of the canvas three blue eagles are caught in the skirl of smoke from a furnace. Two fly up, one falls.

It is then I think I hear a noise. Slight, almost natural. Possibly just the flurry of wind in last year's leaves.

Will

When Will turned over and stretched out his arm, his fingertips grazed bare skin. He drew his hand back quickly. It was a while since he'd spent the night with a woman. He opened his eyes. The darkness obscured everything in the room. If he stretched his arm out again, he would touch her. And if he leaned right out and stretched his left arm as far as it would go, he could probably touch *it* – her shrine. The candle that burned before it all day was out. He tucked both arms down by his sides and closed his eyes. It was only a ridiculous picture of a snake woman, after all. He began sinking back into the hollow of sleep. A mute thud brought him to consciousness. He listened, his eyes once more open in the darkness. He could hear Katy breathing, softly, rhythmically. Another noise, muffled and faint, came to him. He imagined it came from down the corridor. His thoughts went immediately to the forbidden room, the one she kept locked, the one he'd never been inside. That little room was her holy of holies. It housed her 'greatest magic'. In time, when he was ready, she'd let him see. Whatever it was, she said it would concern him utterly.

He lay awake listening for some time. Hearing nothing further, he drifted back into sleep. At once he found himself inside the unknown room. There was a presence there, something hidden in a smoky mist that climbed the walls and spread itself across the ceiling. He heard a cry. Two eyes were coming at him out of the mist. One was Josie's eye, captured in paint, the other an eye so horrible, so intense, he could only turn and run. And so he ran. But the eye pursued him. Detached, floating free. He felt he would never escape it. He ran until he had no breath left in him. Caught, wriggling like a skewered insect, he came to consciousness, disorientated by the strangeness of the room, the bed, the darkness. Astonishingly, Katy was still sleeping peacefully. He lay panting, reluctant to wake her. As his breathing slowed, he eased himself from the bed and felt for the wicker chair where he'd piled his clothes. He dressed, stole down the stairs and let himself out of the building.

The night air was warm. He opened his car door and sat inside. His hands were shaking, making him clumsy with the keys. He started up the engine. Soon he was speeding along the empty, tree-lined lanes. He drove fast, as if the eye were still pursuing him. Was he really driving home in the middle of the night, or was this a lucid dream? He drove on, Esme's words circling his mind: it's not really *her* eye, it's *his*. The eye was penetrating, fearful. It was the same eye that had followed him, peering through keyholes, blinking in the shadows, waiting. Waiting for what? Surely he was being a fool! Following an eye that had followed him. It was ridiculous! Nevertheless he drove.

Josie

I put my brush down carefully. That sound I just heard – what is it? The wind in the trees, a gusting of last year's leaves, a breath? At least the door is locked. I keep still and listen. Yes, there it is again. A breathing in the night. Behind the door, beyond the window pane. A sigh stifled by the darkness. Long exhalations as if the breeze were forming words: *Josie, Josie* ... Then a rubbing at the windowpane. I hold my breath. A shadow crosses the glass, a footfall outside the door, and now the door handle jerking down and up, the door frame shaking. The frame is flimsy, the lock thin. I back away to the far end of the room, dropping down onto my hands and knees. Quietly, carefully, I shift a pile of canvases and hide behind them.

The door bursts open, splintering the frame.

'Where are you?'

It is Tom's voice, broken and savage.

'You've been avoiding me.'

I stay quiet, crouching, breathing swiftly.

'You've thrown me over, haven't you? Just when I needed you.' His voice is wheedling now. 'Josie, I followed you. I followed you in my work. I foll –. Where are you?' He is lunging through the room, pushing aside paintings with one hand. He stumbles into the shadows at the far end, snatches at the furthest stack. The paintings tumble forward exposing me. He drops down, knocking me back across the floor. My head hits the skirting board. His coat is open, his trousers loose. I half-raise myself, clawing at his face, trying to thrust him off. I grab a painting, cramming it between us like a shield. The canvas buckles beneath his weight. My head bangs on the floorboards as his bulk falls across me, pinning me down. My arms flail. He is scrabbling at my night clothes, shoving them up, and I am raising myself up, screaming, pummelling his back. My head bangs down again ...

Katy

Katy woke. It was too dark to see, but the lack of warmth coming from the far side of the bed told her Will was no longer there. Where had he gone? Had he heard something? She got up quickly and went into the corridor. First she listened at the bathroom door. She heard nothing. Then she went to the adjoining door, opened it quietly and looked in.

Everything seemed undisturbed. Through the window came a faint light from the street outside. Outlined on the shelves were her magic toys, as she liked to call them: a star-tipped wand, a pointed hat covered with silver moons, a stream of coloured ribbons, a selection of quartz crystals and goddess figurines. All neatly placed. Only, some of the coloured ribbons were pulled out and lay abandoned on the floor and the little white crystals were formed into a star. In the middle of the room, three-parts hidden beneath a crimson coverlet, magically suspended in a world of dream, was her most precious object of all. The one she had so far concealed from Will, the one that would scare him more than anything – more than the snake goddess, the Tarot cards, the talismans. And from it, thrumming all around the walls and ceiling, came a rhythmic sound. The whole room vibrated with the insistent pulse. It seemed to her as if the room itself was alive and breathing. Katy closed the door quietly again and went back to bed.

Lying there alone, suddenly she craved human warmth. Where was Will? Why had he gone? Had he discovered her secret just when she was on the verge of revealing it? This was their first night together. He'd arrived late and she'd intended to show him in the morning. If he hadn't found out her secret, why had he abandoned her so soon? She needed his strength. She needed it now more than ever. The image of the card floated in the air above her. It would never leave her now. Silently, she began to cry.

Josie

'Josie, Josie!'

It's my mother's voice, funnelling through a labyrinth of mist and confusion.

I feel my eyes flicker.

'Are you OK?'

I try to lift the weight off my eyelids so that I can see. But, instead, my vision dissolves into fog again.

'Oh, thank God. She's opening them!'

I am only aware of the fog pressing closer. I move my hand.

'There may be some temporary damage.'

It's a young woman's voice. Who is she? I can detect the faint mixture of dry dust and chemicals. I can also smell my mother's slight perfume as she bends over me again. It's the same perfume she wore when I was a child.

I try again to raise my eyelids. This time I manage to push back the fog a little – enough to register a dull stab of light. I close them again.

'Josie.' My mother's voice is soft. 'You're in hospital.'

'Wha ...?'

'You've had a bang on the head.' My mother takes my hand and squeezes it. 'But you're going to be all right.'

I can feel throbbing in the back of my head. I lift my eyelids again, peering hard through a filmy layer of white mist. Snatches of my childhood litany come back to me. *Lead white, flake white, bone white* ... I can see my mother's pewter scarf and short hair. Beyond that, I can make out metal uprights over several beds, a criss-cross of ivory painted rods propelling swivel lights and minute television screens. Hospital. The word is semi-transparent, hollowed out with chrome yellow and flake white edges. There is a general swish and hubbub, the sound half-audible, half-swallowed.

I try to raise myself on my elbow, but miss the edge of the bed and sink down.

'Don't ... don't try to move, darling.'

The mist is thinning now to small threads, the throbbing to a focused point of pain. I realise I have a bandage wrapped round my head.

'There was quite a gash,' my mother says, 'and quite a lot of blood. But they say it's not as bad as it looked.'

I point towards the jug of water. My mother supports me as I take a few small mouthfuls. Then I motion for an extra pillow. My mother helps me wriggle to a half-reclined position. After a while, I find my voice enough to ask her again what has happened.

'It was Tom,' Janet says. 'He was ...'

I suddenly see myself in my studio, crouched behind the paintings, hearing his approach.

'But who –?'

'You mean who rescued you?' My mother looks at me earnestly. 'Will.'

I gaze at her with incomprehension. She nods.

'It was Will who rescued you. He came in the nick of time, and sat with you in the ambulance. Then he called me.'

'But how did he ...?'

A sudden nausea rises in me. I retch into the tin kidney-bowl while my mother holds it. Afterwards I sink down gratefully. A young nurse, hair in a tight bun, bustles over.

'I'm sorry to disturb you, but we need to have a look at your daughter. If you could give us a moment?'

'Oh yes, of course!' My mother disappears as the curtains are swiftly drawn round my bed.

'Now, Josie.' The nurse's voice is firm but patronising. 'Doctor Gillingham is here. We need to check a couple of things.'

A tiny woman in a white coat comes through the curtains.

'Is this the Concussion?' she asks. 'Right.' She peruses my patient notes then turns to me.

'We'll start with your vision.'

At her command, my eyes follow a number of fingers she holds up, moving them from one side of my face to the other.

Then she asks me a few simple questions. Once she is satisfied, the doctor draws back the curtains and hails Janet, who is waiting at the far side of the ward.

'I think she'll live!' she says briskly. 'Not much to worry about. But she does need rest.' Then, seeing the anxiety on Janet's face, she adds in a subdued voice, 'It was a nasty bang, but we see worse.'

Janet nods, and the doctor continues: 'She may need some counselling for the trauma. I believe we can arrange a referral for her here, if necessary.' My mother nods again. 'Have a word with one of the staff.'

'Thank you,' Janet says as the diminutive medic strides out of the ward.

Back home, my mother takes charge. The doctor has told her I'm suffering not just from the blow on my head but also from nervous exhaustion, so she makes me stay in bed.

Once I surrender to her command I find I am, at first, too comatose to be conscious of my mother's attentions. Instead I inhabit a dream-state devoid of colour, a monochrome landscape in which the figure of a man is pursuing me. Sometimes I escape, other times I lose my footing, fall, and am engulfed in his shadow.

While I travel through my gloomy dreamscape, searching for the scattered pieces of my life, blown and broken by my trauma, Janet lets me sleep undisturbed. Sometimes I half-wake to find myself propped against pillows, my mother lifting spoonfuls of warm soup to my lips. She makes me drink some before letting me sink again into my fevered world. I remember her doing that when I was a child recovering from minor illnesses. In the days when I called her *Mummy. Mummy*, I think I called her. Or was it *Mummy Brown*. I know I called her that in my head. But did she know that? And, if so, did she know why? I think I'm on morphine. I must be.

The pages of my notebook open before me, flicking themselves over before my eyes. A page is suddenly illuminated. The description of the mummy unwrapping. Someone invites me in and suddenly I'm in a Victorian parlour, waiting for the

Unveiling of the Priestess of Amun. No, I think, not unveiling – nothing so sacred. Unrolling. There are gasps as the outer covering is cut open. Then the unwrapping begins, the mummy propped upright to facilitate. There's so much unwinding, swathes of ecru-coloured bandage, acres of it filling the room, yellowed with palm oil. As the layers are ribboned away they release sweet pungencies – incense, balsam, infusing the room, drugging the senses as the priestess is unclothed. Precious blue scarabs made of azurite fall from the shrouding. Minutes pass. More still. And now the final swathe floats down, the last veil shadowing the dark-brown kernel of the body. Enamelled eyes appear. White with black pupils staring from brown lids. Proud Priestess of Amun. Exposed, defiant. Mock eyes fixed on the watching crowd. Her naked corpse is tiny, shrivelled into itself.

As she floats into darkness she reaches out with brown arms like the child.

Days pass. My mind filled with questions, broken arguments; forebodings. My dreamscape lifts, shifts and the child appears again, weaving through oceans – waif-like form, lips parting, arms stretching. I stir in my sleep, wanting to reach out, touch ... The child comes near, so near. Flashes of wet black hair, a woman's pale face turned to me and staring, arms enfolding, holding, pulling the child down, its saffron hair weed-floating ... sinking, drowning, gone.

I wake in tears.

The ochre traces of the child, like funeral flowers tossed on water, herald my emerging. They are my first flash of colour, striking through the dark. Then, gradually the monochrome vistas yield a reluctant sepia. Days, words, hours slowly take back their hues, drawing me into life. At first I lie with the curtains drawn, dimly conscious of the familiar outlines of the room, its furniture, the pictures on the walls. I ask for the curtains to be opened and, with the light of day restored, all the ochres, cadmiums, chromes and lakes swirl into view again and I begin to reinhabit my familiar universe.

In my more lucid state, I reflect on the strangeness of lying in bed at home and having my mother look after me. The last time this happened was when I was ten years old. It is strange, too, having another human presence in the house. Living each day as intensely as I have, I've begun to forget how long I've been alone now, how long we've been apart, Will and I.

Meanwhile Janet busies herself about the house and adds some final touches to the garden. She has managed to cancel the summer painting class, but the garden and studio are due to open in three weeks time. There's no question of delaying this as I've put up posters and advertised it in the local papers. But as I'm making such progress, she thinks I may be recovered by then.

'I want to see him, Mother,' I say one morning. 'I want to thank him.'

To my surprise, my mother says: 'I don't know if that's a good idea.'

'But he rescued me!'

'I know, but ...'

'But what?'

'It's just ... I don't want you to get your hopes up.'

I'm puzzled. What does my mother think? That, because he rescued me, we'll rush back into each other's arms? But surely that's just what she wants?

'Mother, it's not ...' I begin.

Her face is closed.

'He's a caring man,' she says hesitantly. 'I'm sure he still cares about you.'

'Then, why shouldn't I see him?'

'It's not –'

'So easy. Is that what you want to say?'

'I don't want you to get hurt.'

'Mother!'

Janet looks uncomfortable. 'There was a time when maybe you could have let bygones be bygones,' she says. 'When perhaps you could have worked something out. But now ...'

I wait for her to finish.

'It's that woman,' she says at last.

'Katy?'

Janet seems to shiver at the name. 'Yes.' She sighs. 'She's got him so he can't escape.'

'Mother, Katy's not a witch.' Yet, as I speak her name, I imagine a faint spider's web across the rose madder.

My mother turns and gazes out of the window. 'That's as may be, but –'

'But what?'

'Whatever she is, she's put a spell on him all right!'

I turn over. If my mother is determined to believe Frieda's nonsense, I haven't enough energy to argue with her. Instead I find myself thinking of Esme and wondering why she hasn't come to visit me yet.

Now that I'm recovered enough to move from my bedroom to the living room, Esme has finally been allowed to visit me. I hear her greet my mother, then stride into the living room, where she finds me lying on the couch.

'My God!' she says. 'I thought by now you'd look better than this!'

She puts a carrier bag on the table, then bends to kiss me.

'I've brought something I thought might inspire you. A couple of Nathan's old metaphysical books. I told your mother they're just picture books, something easy for you to flick through. She looked awfully suspicious, though. God, she really is being protective of you, isn't she!'

'Yes, I don't know what's come over her. She's quite ferocious all of a sudden.' I stretch my arm towards the table. 'Thanks for the books.'

'I sneaked them out of Nathan's study.'

I smile. 'Won't he miss them?'

'I doubt it.' Esme sits down next to me. 'You know I had my worries about Tom all along. But you didn't listen to me, did you? And now all this has happened.'

I hang my head like a shamed child. 'You were right,' I say. 'But it could have been a lot worse.'

'I don't see how.'

'It might have been if Will hadn't turned up.'

'Well, yes, I know. Your mum told me.'

'He rescued me. His timing was extraordinary! How he knew I was even in danger –'

Esme cuts in before I can say more: 'Are you going to give evidence?'

'Against Tom, you mean?'

'Of course, against Tom. Who else?'

'I don't know.'

'But surely, you have to.'

'That's what my mother thinks. But I'm not sure if it's the right thing.'

'Does she know you already slept with him?'

'No, of course not.'

'So, to her it's pretty straightforward.'

'Yes. And I think she feels a bit betrayed. She's put in all this work to nurse me back to health and I won't help bring Tom to justice.'

'Look, Josie, I think I'm with your mum on this. Give a statement and there's a better chance of a conviction. On Will's evidence alone, it's not guaranteed. There's no need to feel guilty. Just because you slept with him once doesn't mean he's innocent!'

'I know. And I hear what you're saying. But I haven't completely decided yet. I need more time to think.'

'Sure, it's your decision, but you know you can always talk to me if you want to.'

'Thanks.'

We can hear Janet clattering crockery in the kitchen.

'By the way,' Esme says, changing the subject. 'Did you know that when Will rescued you he took away a painting?'

'Did he? What painting?'

'Didn't your mother tell you? He took a painting you'd shielded yourself with. It was a mess, bloodstained. He didn't want you to see it in case it upset you.'

Just then Janet appears with a tray of coffee and biscuits.

'Mother, did Will take a painting of mine?'

'As a matter of fact he did,' Janet says reluctantly.' I was going to tell you when you were better. It was in a bit of a state. He said he'd try to get it cleaned up.'

'Which painting was it?'

'All I know is he said it was unrecognisable.' She sets the tray on the table and goes out again.

Esme turns towards me and speaks confidentially. 'I don't think your mother wants to be reminded of it all. She didn't like it when we were in the studio together cleaning up.'

'You cleaned up the studio together?'

'Yes. That's when I came over before and she wouldn't let me see you. She said you weren't well enough. Look, I'm sure she's getting on your nerves by now. But I have to tell you, she's been doing a great job getting you better. Whatever else, you can be grateful she cared enough to drop everything and look after you.'

'I know. In fact everyone's been pretty amazing – my mother, you, even Will. I suppose I should say, especially Will; though how he came on the scene just then, I really don't know.'

Esme pours out the coffee and hands me a cup. As she sits back again she says, 'Actually, I may be partly responsible.'

I look at her in surprise.

'I'm afraid I have a confession to make. I did rather stick my neck out. But I'm very glad I did.'

'What did you do?'

'I went to see Will and told him I was worried about you. I mean, about Tom stalking you.'

I slap my cup down on the table. 'You did *what*?'

'I knew you'd have stopped me if I'd asked you. So I –'

'You barged into Will's office?'

'Yes.'

'What did he say?'

'He didn't believe me at first. In fact he seemed a bit uncomfortable. And then he shuffled a bit and ...'

I'm staring at her. I can see she's worried I might be furious with her. Suddenly I let out a snort of laughter.

'I don't believe it,' I say when I can get my breath.

'Well, it's absolutely true. You should have seen him!'

I'm laughing almost uncontrollably. I put my hands over my face as my laughter turns to tears. Once I start crying, I can't stop. The release is extraordinary.

When I can listen again, Esme tells me how Will responded, how concerned he was once she convinced him of the danger. 'So I think he still loves you,' she says. 'He seemed so sad, somehow. And something else. So lost. I think the situation's got out of hand for him.'

'But he's got *her*,' I say at last, reaching for the box of tissues.

'Maybe for now. But what good is she to him, except for a fling?'

I dry my eyes. 'My mother says he's caught somehow and can't get out of it.'

'If your mother really believes he's caught by a spell ...?'

'Actually, I think there may be more to it. But she wouldn't explain. She went all tight-faced and refused to say anything.'

'Well, what do you think?'

'All I know is that she's managed to get her claws into him one way or another. But it does seem strange – Will going for someone like that.'

After my mother's silences, it's a relief to be able to speculate about Will with Esme.

'Sorry to state the obvious,' Esme says, 'but they do say opposites attract.'

'I know. But even if it's true for Will, I can't see what Katy gets out of it. In fact, I can't see why she wanted him in the first place.'

'Perhaps she's after his money?' suggests Esme.

'What there is of it! No, she's after something else – she must be. But I can't work out what it is.'

'How would you work anything out with a woman like that?'

'The whole thing's nightmarish. I don't like thinking about it too much. I keep trying to piece Will together as he once was. But now he's someone else, someone I don't recognise.'

Esme reaches across and takes my hand. We sit in silence for a moment. Then I say: 'Well, whatever else, I'm grateful that you did go and see Will.'

Janet's voice calls from the kitchen: 'If you're going to help with the garden, you'd better get out there before the rain starts.'

Esme gives me a conspiratorial smile: 'That's the deal I made with your mother, for allowing me to come round. I don't think she quite approves of me.'

'Really?'

'Yes. She seems wary of me. Probably thinks I encouraged the break-up.'

'But you told me to ring him!'

'I know. Anyway, when I asked to see you earlier, I offered to help with the garden. We did a bit together while you were still comatose. And now I've said I'll do a bit more. I don't think I'm much good at the intricate stuff but I could do something straightforward like mowing the lawn.'

'Well, if you're up for it, that would be great. It's not as big as it looks, but you'll need the strimmer for the edges and for going round the fish.'

'You mean that yellow thing on a plinth I can see from the window in your studio?'

'Yes.'

'I can't wait to see it close-up,' Esme mutters as she leaves the room.

Josie

Even though I'm sufficiently recovered for my mother to go home, she still insists on coming over almost every day. She's in her element, guiding visitors round the garden, drawing attention to various plants, explaining the special effects of the grottoes. This means I'm free to paint. I've rigged a cloth across the middle of my studio so that while people look at the paintings I can keep at my work relatively undisturbed.

Although my floral pictures are selling well this year, I have no desire to paint more of them. I searched for the portrait of the child. When I couldn't find it, I felt relieved. This must be the one Will took. I have a vague memory of snatching it up, and I'm glad it's no longer there to plague me.

Although I'm starting to feel like getting back to work, there is one painting I can't look at. The one with Prussian blue eagles that I was working on that fateful night. Yet it's the one that changed everything. I've been painting in a different way ever since. How many new works do I have now? I look around my studio. Propped against the wall are several canvases, all of them semi-abstract images. I have no means yet of understanding them, but I feel they represent something bigger than anything I've done before.

Esme still comes every Saturday, but not to help with the garden. Instead she concentrates on showing people my flower paintings. She's a good saleswoman and sells well, puffing up the emerging importance of 'the artist' and saying these are early pieces, still affordable and therefore something of an investment; though I know that really she despises them.

One Saturday the weather is particularly hot, which means that several families come, their children running into the sprinklers, shrieking and spraying each other. It has taken all three of us, my mother, Esme and myself, to keep a close watch on the plants and make sure they don't get trampled.

As soon as the last visitor departs, my mother makes her excuses and goes home, worn out by the heat and the effort of the day. Esme and I sit in the courtyard. On the table in front of us are two glasses of chilled white wine, a bottle of Chardonnay standing in a padded cooler, and a bowl of olives. I spear an olive and put it in my mouth.

'I wish you were my agent,' I say.

'Do you really?'

'You do a great job of bigging me up!'

Esme smudges her finger on the cold glass. 'Well, I suppose I could give it a go.'

'Are you serious?'

'Of course. But I'd only handle your real work.'

'OK,' I say slowly. 'But you'll want commission. What is it usually? Ten per cent?'

'Should be fifteen but, as it's you ...'

'Done!' I say with a quick laugh, then add more seriously, 'I suppose it's worth a try.'

'I'll say!' Esme nods her head encouragingly. 'I could begin by taking a couple of your canvases to Artco?'

'Artco?'

'Yes. They'd look good there. It's somewhere to start, anyway. And then I can try to interest a dealer.'

'Fine.'

We sat looking out across the garden. I lift the bottle from the cooler and pour more wine into our glasses. The evening sun lies on our shoulders like a liquid shawl.

I sigh. 'This is bliss.'

'Isn't it!'

'Do you want more olives? I can go and fetch some.'

'No. Just sit there.'

'You know,' I say after a while, 'recently I've been feeling almost happy. I'm beginning to stop worrying about what's going to happen. It doesn't seem to matter anymore. Maybe I'm learning something new, like how to live in the moment.'

'That would be quite a feat,' Esme says wistfully. 'If only we could all do that! She leans her head back against the top of the chair, the sun on her hair. 'Actually if we could, I'd probably be out of a job.'

'Really?'

'Yes. Most people live in the past and the future, which is why they're so fearful. Very few actually live in the present. It's hard to do that.'

'Until you find yourself somehow just doing it naturally.'

Esme says nothing. We sit in silence, our wine glasses sparked by the sun's withdrawing rays.

'So you're not worried about what will happen with this place, with Will?'

'Strangely, not at the moment.'

'You don't think the two of you might get back together?'

'What, after Katy?'

'Yes.'

'Really! You think that's possible?'

Esme wriggles upright in her chair. 'Oh, don't be such a prude! Of course it's possible! If people kept splitting up every time there was a little dalliance.'

'But this isn't a little dalliance, is it?'

'With a minx like that, I don't know what you'd call it! She's about as suitable for Will as one of Nathan's students!'

I glance at her, startled. 'You don't mean –?'

'Of course. It goes with the job. Well, it goes with Nathan anyway. He depends on sexual response to maintain his ego. Surely you noticed?'

'And you don't mind?'

'Yes, of course I mind. But I wasn't blind when I met him. I knew what I was taking on.'

'And you're sure he still loves you?'

'Oh, he loves me all right. Couldn't do without me. And, of course, it gives *me* a certain licence, too.'

I look quickly across the table. 'Have you used it?'

'Occasionally!'

'With men?'

'Mostly!'

'I see.'

The sun has lowered its rays but the air is still warm.

I say quietly: 'And me?'

Esme is looking at me, the light retreating behind her head.

'Yes, of course, with you, if you were into it.'

I look down.

'But I'm not sure you are,' she says.

'I'm not sure, either,' I say carefully.

After Esme's gone, I remain sitting in the courtyard, thinking about what has passed between us. In some ways I feel flattered. The thing has been spoken, it is out there now and it explains the intimacy between us. I hope we'll always have that, at least enough to keep the closeness of our friendship.

As I slowly finish my glass of wine, I start exploring this new feeling I tried to explain to Esme. Even the sexual freedom Esme has opened up seems part of it. I feel as if I'm floating unfettered on a sea of possibilities. And, though the idea of it may be clichéd, the feeling itself is not. Maybe life is like that after all, busily presenting one face then another as if in a constant state of renewal. It doesn't mean people aren't important, but it's a way of coping when things come to an end.

I pour myself more wine. I can feel something loosening and shifting in me and I suddenly wonder if I can let it all go. Is it significant that I've allowed Will some slack so that he can push beyond the bounds of convention, discover other possibilities? Maybe that's all I could offer in the circumstances, and maybe it's enough.

I lean my head back and watch the last fronds of a crimson sun straddling the hillside. I am in an extraordinary space. All choices seem suddenly open to me. Life has closed one door and seems to be opening another – several, in fact. I can find another lover, even experiment with Esme if I want. I stare across at the mountains. There's just a faint stain of rose on the skyline now, and soon even that will disappear. But tomorrow the sun will climb back, burst out again in lemon yellow. Everything is in a state of play.

Then it comes to me that the child, too, is a form of play. Teasing, mercurial. I don't know in what dimension the child exists. Is it Esme's liminal place – the one on the edge of things, or is the child merely a figment of my imagination? Whether the two are the same or different I don't know. But, for now, such questions don't seem to matter. How would it be, I wonder, if I could always suspend judgement like this? If I could stay in this place, accept the shifting paradigms – might I reach a new equilibrium?

Josie

As the summer progresses, the weather settles into a steady heat. Every day I am greeted by the sun. I feel as if my own head is somehow carrying it. Each morning its strong first rays warm the western facade of the house. Taking my coffee outside, I can sit on the bench, lean my back against the wall and feel the heat already stored there. I'm finding it easy now to get up early on these light mornings. I've fallen into the rhythm of it. It means I have enough time to tend and tidy the garden before it opens.

Although I can manage it myself, my mother still drops in every now and again to give me a hand, and Esme still comes every Saturday.

While the garden absorbs me, I remain in my liminal place, with grief somehow suspended. I'm living in the moment, going with whatever the garden decides to bring. Day by day the groups of people who visit are like new ideas appearing on a canvas. Some are contemplative, strolling round slowly then sitting quietly in a bower. Others – especially the children – are excited by its oddities, its sculptures, its dead ends and surprises. As they wander round, I retreat to my studio and continue my paintings.

On the last Saturday morning in August, I am tidying up, waiting for visitors to arrive. Dew lies heavy on the grass and I'm kneeling among its crystal flashes, trimming the curved edge of the bed. I hear Esme's car coming down the drive, then the sound of the car door closing.

'I knew I'd find you in the garden,' Esme says. 'Hard at it, as ever. Can I do something?'

I hand her a pointed trowel and a cushion. 'You could dig out these dandelions if you like.'

She kneels down and starts to prod at the edge of the lawn.

'Not really me, all this earth and mess, but I'm getting used to it. In any case, I suppose it's good for me to have a go.'

We work quietly together for a bit.

'You know, we never did have much of a chat about it in the end,' Esme says.

'About what?'

'Your reaction.'

I put down my trowel. 'Do you mean to your fancying me?'

'No.'

'Because that's flattering but ...'

'I know. And that's OK. But I wasn't thinking of that.'

'What then?'

Esme hesitates. She seems apprehensive. 'I was thinking about Tom.' She looks at me. 'You haven't talked to me again about him. And I haven't liked to ask.'

'I didn't feel I needed to.'

'Most people would be traumatised.'

I straighten up. 'Did I tell you I was offered counselling at the hospital. They said they'd refer me.'

'And did you take them up on it?'

I laugh. 'I think I'd only have been put on a very long waiting list and ended up seeing you!'

'Completely unprofessional!'

'I suppose so. But it would have been quite funny having them pay for me to see you. But no, strangely I really haven't felt the need. Partly because he didn't actually ...' I leave the sentence hanging, and pick up the trowel again. 'Also because I saw what he was battling with, and how he hated himself for it.'

I glance at Esme and see her nod her head. I'm surprised to find I want not only to explain myself but to defend Tom. I want Esme to understand. 'Maybe I also felt a bit responsible, using him when I was at my lowest.'

'Yes. But, as I said before, that doesn't mean it was your fault.'

'I know.' I brace myself. It's time to tell Esme my decision. 'Actually, I've thought a lot about it and I've decided not to give evidence. I don't want him convicted. I don't think he's bad enough for that.'

'Are you sure?'

Expecting an interrogation, I've rehearsed my reasons. 'He didn't mean to injure me. He was drunk. I think it was as much an accident as anything.'

'That's as may be. But even so ...'

'And I want him to get help, not go to prison.' I stick the trowel into the soil. 'Actually, I have spoken to him since. Not face to face. On the phone. He rang me – though I know he's not supposed to. He was crying. He said he was appalled at what he'd done. And he agreed to go for counselling. That's the deal I made with him.'

'And you're sure you're doing the right thing – that you won't regret it if he goes free? Whatever you've said, you know it's still not too late.'

I shake my head. 'You might think it's strange, given all the people you counsel who've had this kind of thing happen to them. What he did was wrong. But, like I said, I bear some responsibility. I used him. And I wanted to open him up, I'd made quite a campaign of it. But I see now it was all too much for him. He tried. He tried for himself and also to please me. In his own twisted way, he thought he was doing what I wanted.'

'But that's just the problem, isn't it?' Esme persists.

'No. It's not as simple as that. Maybe it is to you and maybe it is in law. But it's not simple to him and not really to me. He thinks I betrayed him. Prison would be the worst thing. He'd see it as the ultimate betrayal. And I couldn't live with myself, knowing that I helped to put him there.'

'But what if he –'

'I know what you're going to say, but I don't think he'd do it again. It was a crisis point for him. Something he'd been driven to – an explosion of years of repressed feeling. And who knows what that might mean for him now. If I have to give evidence, that's what I'll say. Then the law can decide.'

I gather my tools and stand up. As we climb the steps towards the house, I'm wondering whether Esme will continue to challenge me. But, as we reach the courtyard, all she says is: 'That was a strong choice, Josie.'

Katy

Katy and her mother sat in Katy's consulting room, both looking at the image on the card.

'You know what it means, don't you?' Katy's voice was quiet, her face unnaturally pale. Her mother nodded.

'But it doesn't always mean that. It's not always so straightforward.'

Katy looked at her. 'That's what I thought, at first. What I hoped.'

'But you've done another spread?'

'I've done one every day.'

'And is it always the same?'

'Always.'

'But you don't have to accept it. You can get help, before it's too late.'

Katy shook her head.

'So even if you ...?'

'Even if I ...'

Her mother swallowed hard, unable to speak. Her voice, when she found it again, was hoarse.

'And you think you'd risk, you'd lose ...?'

Katy nodded.

'Have you told Will?'

'No.'

'So he only knows ...?

'Yes, that's all he knows. And, Mother!' Katy gave her a fierce look. 'That's all he's going to know. At least for a while.'

'Oh, so you see it as *your* choice, do you?' Her mother was suddenly angry. 'And it doesn't matter what I think, what he thinks, what'll happen to ...? *We* don't have a say. *Nobody* has a say, only you. Is that right?'

Katy looked down at the card, the one that had turned up in

each spread – the figure in black armour on a white horse. 'It's only too plain, isn't it?' she said slowly. 'You know it as well as I do. And there's no point in denying it.'

She regarded her mother steadily, willing her eyes to remain dry, resolved to stay strong. She held her mother's gaze a long time. In her mind she was returning them both to the time when she was still a child, conjuring the youthful image of her mother spreading the cards in front of her, her mother's voice, powerful, compelling: 'You can't deny your own fate. It's waiting for you. You just have to make the best of it.' In her mind Katy went back even further and conjured an image of her grandmother, seeing her old creased face, her practised hands dealing the cards, her pale green eyes searching the images for their wisdom. Then, swooping forward to the present, she saw herself as if from a great distance, a guardian of magical knowledge – one in a long female line. For in every generation, without fail, a female child had come.

She knew her mother had been there beside her in the vision, and had seen it all. Nevertheless, when her mother spoke, her voice was pleading. 'But you've already fulfilled your role. Surely you don't need to make this sacrifice?'

Katy looked away and silence fell between them again. After a long time, she said slowly: 'There's no point fighting it, Mother, it's going to happen anyway. So there's no point getting rid –' She broke off. 'Besides, if I did, there'd no longer be a way of holding Will.'

She felt a sharp spasm of pain curdling her lungs, and knew that even though her mind was made up, she would need all her mother's strength to hold her to her purpose – at least until the time came when there could be no turning back. She looked at her mother. When she spoke once more, there was strength as well as fear in her voice.

'It's my fate,' she said.

Her mother put her head in her hands.

Josie

The last day the garden is open is the first morning that the weather begins to break. I always knew it wouldn't last. The hot summer has held through the last six weeks while visitors have shared its glories. I guessed that Will would leave me this – the final enjoyment of my handiwork before telling me we have to sell up. I know that, whatever has happened, he will feel some responsibility towards me.

After his dramatic rescue, I've been disappointed that he hasn't been in touch. I want to know what's happening with him. I haven't seen anything of Frieda, which is a relief, but also a puzzle. One way or another, I sense everything will be unravelled when the garden closes.

As it's the last morning, I'm only working fitfully in my studio. The sky is overcast with the approaching rain, the mountains obscured by its glazed screen. Although my mother has come over again to give me a hand, I expect very few people will visit. So, after all the heat, I suppose the gardens will close with a whimper rather than a bang. It doesn't matter: I've done well enough. Only a few flower paintings remain and, as if it's a harbinger of the future, Esme has already sold one of my new works at Artco.

Esme placed astronomical prices – or so they seem to me – against my new paintings, and wrote an article in the local paper stating that they were the daring and experimental work of a powerful new talent. She conducted a formal interview with me for the article and then rewrote my responses, making them more defiant. When she showed me the piece, I laughed and let it pass, recognising in it some tamed parts of me made free again.

I look out idly over the garden. My mother let in two women earlier. A mother and daughter, she thinks. Rather strange-looking people, she said when she popped her head round the door. I am slightly curious. If they follow the usual pathways, they will emerge from the hedge beside the fish sculpture at any moment, and I will see them for myself.

The older woman appears first. Her hair is black with streaks of white that are visible even at this distance. She wears a magenta shawl pulled tightly round her. She looks back and seems to be calling out to someone who has lagged behind, her earrings nodding vigorously as she moves her head. Then she turns and hurries back behind the hedge, re-emerging with her arm around a younger woman who is bundled in a dark cloak. The two of them walk slowly, the younger one keeping her head down. As they come up the garden, I see the bag dangling from the young woman's shoulder. Purple with chrome yellow crescent moons. I stare at the bundled figure. As they approach, a sudden flurry of wind lifts the cloak and tosses it aside. Then I see the thing I've been dreading. I've refused to contemplate it, but perhaps I've suspected it all along. Now it is unmistakable, pushing out under the dull gold robe, announcing itself in a soft, smooth swell.

I run out of the studio and into the house. My mother is in the kitchen. I am trembling. I can feel the colour draining from my face. As soon as she sees the state I'm in, she hurries over.

'*She's* here!'

My mother needs no further explanation.

'Does she know you've seen her?'

I shake my head. Still trembling, I let my mother lead me to a chair.

'She doesn't know I know who she is.' The words come out jerkily. My mouth is frozen.

'You stay there. I'll deal with this.' Janet walks briskly from the room.

By the time she returns, I've stopped shaking.

'She's in your studio looking at the paintings with her mother. I left them there.'

I cannot speak. I nod dumbly.

'I'll get them to go.' Without waiting for an answer Janet leaves the room.

When she returns, she says simply: 'They've gone.'

She draws a chair over and sits next to me. She tries to take my hand but I snatch it away. 'You knew,' I say. 'You, Dad, Frieda, you all knew, but none of you told me. None of you!'

'Darling, we were trying to protect you.'

'You said Will was caught. You said he couldn't escape. You implied it was an awful spell she'd laid on him – which to me seemed fanciful. I thought it was sex. But it was far more than that. She was much more cunning.'

I can feel the last remains of hope dissolving. Until that moment I hadn't realised how much I'd clung on, believing in the triviality of the thing, waiting for sense to prevail, for Will to come back. But that can never happen now. Katy has won. And now I know why she went after him. She didn't really want Will, not for himself. She wanted a baby and she wanted his support. But how could she trick him like that? More to the point, how could he let it happen?

I want to sweep everything off the table, lay down my head and howl. Instead I sit in the chair, my fists curled so tightly they are hurting me. My mother sits beside me in silence, her arm round my shoulders. Then she says: 'There's a haunted look about that girl.'

'I'll say there is. It's her black arts – her witchery.'

'No, not that. It's something else.'

'I stood up for her,' I'm almost shouting now. 'I told everyone she wasn't a witch, that there was no such thing, that I didn't believe –'

'Maybe she isn't.'

'Oh, but all of you were right, weren't you? All along. And now she's come here, to look over the place with her mother, to see what it's like. So that when I'm gone, when I'm shoved out, if she wants to, she can live here with Will and –'

'Hush!' Janet tightens her arms round me. 'You can't be sure that's why she's come. You didn't see the way she looked. There could be something else. You don't know what she's thinking.'

'Yes, I do! It's what she's been scheming for: Will's salary, his security, to raise her child.' My mind is streaming with a mass of questions and possibilities. It's the only thing keeping me from falling into despair. Then an idea comes, presenting itself as a spark of hope. 'But supposing, after all, it isn't his. What if she's just using him for another man's child?'

The moment of hope hovers. My mother brings it gently down.

'I don't think she's far enough on for that.'

'But it could still be someone else's.'

'Do you think Will would leave you for a – a slut?'

I can't understand why my mother is defending her. Can't she see how conniving the woman is? As if in answer to my unspoken question, she says:

'I don't want to make her seem any better than she is. But when I saw her walking back up the garden, I thought there was something ...'

'Oh, God, the garden's still open! There might be more visitors.'

'It's all right, I've put the *Closed* sign up. In any case the weather's too bad now. We weren't likely to get anyone else.'

I look up at the window. The sky has darkened to a lemon grey, and pellets of rain are pattering against the glass.

'I think you need to see Will.'

I blink at her.

'It's time the two of you talked properly.'

The rain sets in for the afternoon, weeping against the windows. As the sky darkens towards evening, my mother rings Esme, who offers to come round and spend the evening with me. When she arrives, my mother reluctantly leaves for home. I'm still in shock and subject to waves of violent shivering, so Esme lights a fire and wraps me in a blanket. Together we sit in the heat of the flames while I pour out my despair.

'I wish I'd agreed to the IVF.' I've been saying this so many times it's become a mantra. 'I wish I hadn't tried to follow a child, for God's sake, a witchy dream child.' I start crying again. 'And the child's left me, too. She's left me and that bitch has got her instead!'

'Don't say that. It doesn't make sense.'

'Oh, yes it does,' I sob. 'I saw her in my dreams. And – and I saw Katy take her away and drown her. She'll be a rotten mother. I know she will. Why can't it be me? Why can't I have the child?'

'But Josie,' Esme sooths, 'you were following your heart. You can't be sure you made the wrong choice about the child. You can't know that.'

But the child seems a mockery now, a testimony to my credulity. I tell Esme I'm glad Will has the painting. I don't want it restored, I don't want to see it again. Let it stay ripped and stained. It saves me doing the deed myself.

Esme tries to convince me I've done nothing wrong, but she can see this isn't the time to argue the point. She gives up remonstrating with me, goes into the kitchen and heats some soup, then does her best to persuade me to eat it. I only want to drink more alcohol, but Esme makes me cups of tea and cocoa. When she's calmed me down, she starts to give me some concrete advice.

'As soon as you're over the initial shock of this, I want you to take control, look at the situation squarely. Do you think you can do that?'

I feel a tiny glimmer of hope.

Esme continues. 'It's all right, I won't ask too many details about your financial affairs. I just think, now the garden's closed, you need to start looking ahead.'

Her voice is brisk, practical.

'First of all, in terms of the house, do you think Will can afford to buy you out?'

'No, I don't think so. We've always had to struggle a bit as it is.'

'And since your separation, has he continued paying his share of the mortgage?'

'Yes.'

'I'm sorry if I seem intrusive, but I'm trying to help you keep your head in all this.'

'I know,' I mumble.

'I think you need to see a solicitor. If you haven't already got one, I can give you the name of mine. She's very good.'

'Thank you.'

'And meanwhile, you can always come and stay with me.'

I look at her with something of my old determination. 'I know I'm a wreck at the moment, but you've already been a great help. Now I need to process this on my own.'

By the end of the evening, Esme has managed to raise me from my emotional quagmire onto some sort of solid ground.

After she's gone, I sit looking into the fire. Most of the coals have fallen and settled but, every now and again a flame reaches to a blackened log, licking the air around it. As I watch I think of all the pigments made by burning wood and bone. Bistre from beech wood; bone black from charred bone; ivory black from burnt ivory; vine black from charred grape vines; bone white from the ash of burnt bones. Lamp black from the soot of oil lamps.

I grow too hot and throw off my blanket, but it does no good. My heart is a hot ball in my chest. I can flail angrily at fate but nothing can change what has happened. Grief will crush me for weeks and months to come, sapping my life, my energy. I need something to hold on to. I remember Esme telling me to look at the situation clearly. I know all hope of reconciliation with Will is lost. All hope, too, of somehow, miraculously, manifesting the child. But there *is* one thing, I think. It's not much – but at least I know where I am now. I sit with my black litany: *bone black, vine black, lamp black, carbon black*, burning with pain, trying vainly to surrender to this truth. Knowing I no longer have any choice about it. That soon I must begin the agonising process of moving on with my life.

Will

Why was it, thought Will, as soon as you moved in with someone, the magic fell away? He was seeing Katy in the mornings now, her face devoid of make-up, her head bent over a plastic bowl while she endured the daily bout of nausea. He hadn't realised quite what a toll pregnancy took on a woman. He knew the first three months were the worst but, even though she was not quite past that, she seemed to be ill all the time. The flat was becoming unkempt, Katy dragging herself around it, pale and weary. She'd had to cancel clients and call in her mother to help on an almost daily basis.

He could see what a fool he'd been. Katy had assured him she was on the pill. He rather doubted that now. If things weren't so appallingly difficult, it would almost be hilarious. In his rash bid for freedom, he'd become entangled in a family of clairvoyants with only his own future child for anchorage. He didn't belong, he had no bearings here. More than that, between them, Katy and her mother had tricked and deceived him. He'd thought Katy was deluded, with her Tarot nonsense, but now he was discovering just how powerful she really was, and with the realisation came a kind of grudging respect. He could see how her paraphernalia, her magic toys, as she called them, cloaked a subtle determination. From the very beginning she had known how to manage him, to make sure he gave her what she needed – and all under the guise of fulfilling his desires.

Yet, he had to admit, Katy was a strange mixture. Now that she had what she wanted, she didn't drop the magic act at all. She kept the candle burning before the snake-tailed goddess, and every day she knelt at it and performed a ritual. Witnessing this, it seemed to him as if, after all, she were hanging on to something less calculated, something intangible, and credulous. So what did she really believe? He felt, as always, that he didn't know her, had no idea what made her tick, which worried him.

Away from her now, sitting at his desk waiting for his next client, Will found himself yet again speculating about the young boy of his dreams. All this was his fault. He'd wanted a child so much. And now he would have one. It was his only consolation. But what would it be like with Katy as its mother? And as for the grandmother – in her way she was just as bad. What's more, if she and Katy were so skilled at deception, who knew what else they had in store for him? He felt hopelessly caught, unable to figure it all out. The responsibilities newly thrust upon him were more than he had ever imagined. He put his head in his hands. Now that he had so much more to cope with, his far-off days with Josie were beginning to seem like a remote paradise. It was Josie who seemed artless to him now, Josie who wandered in an unearthly, imaginative haze, not Katy. He sighed. He would have to tell her about the child: there was no more putting it off. And what then? He'd have to turn her out, make her leave her home, her beloved garden. He buried his head in his hands, dreading the thought of it.

Josie

As I paint my pictures, allowing the shape of a bush, a tree-branch or another subtle twist or configuration from the garden to suggest itself within my work, I feel as though I'm unravelling, as if my physical and emotional grounding are slowly slipping away. I am painting on a different level now. I've lost control of my art – I've become subject to its whims and fantasies. It is a frightening place to be. Emotions come on me suddenly and with no warning, pain so agonising that I have to leave my painting and bury myself in the sofa, shaking and crying until the worst of it has passed.

My dreams are empty, my nights dark as my days. The child no longer comes to me. She seems now like an omen of bad fortune. A child that wishes me no good. A child that has summoned me like those three terrible witches in *Macbeth*, offering to grant my desire, then cruelly tricking me.

As the days pass I look out each morning towards the mountains, seeking anchorage. There is only one piece of wreckage in the turmoil – the surreal experience that flashed on me that sun-drenched day in the garden, when I saw how everything – the world, all existence – was in a state of flux. It was like a glimpse of paradise where everything seemed possible. I can't imagine reaching that state now. The immediacy of painting is the only thing that absorbs me. And so I have no choice but to paint on, feverishly, manically, hoping my art can somehow release me.

Will

Will was sitting at his desk. He had said goodbye to his last client of the morning. Opening his briefcase, he took out a sandwich. Lunchtimes were the least enjoyable part of the day now. He no longer went out to a café. He couldn't afford that luxury. And he no longer went to the flat for a lunchtime tryst. There was no sex on offer. Hadn't been for weeks. Katy wasn't up to it. He supposed that was just another sacrifice the child expected of him. He unwrapped his sandwich. He'd made it himself, so the filling was unimaginative – just two slabs of cheese, spread with brown pickle.

He was about to take a bite when his mobile rang. He picked it up and was surprised to see Josie's name appear. This time, the first in months, he took her call.

'Josie!' His voice was surprised, apprehensive.

'Will.'

He didn't know what to say, so he waited.

'Will, I've been wanting to thank you.'

'You did. You left a text. Several in fact. I'm sorry, I didn't …'

'I mean in person.'

'Oh.'

'Will, we need to meet, to talk.'

'I know. I've been waiting.'

'For the garden to close?'

'Yes.'

'That was thoughtful of you.'

This was not what he'd imagined. Josie getting straight to the point, without emotion or reproach.

'Josie, there's something I have to tell you.'

'I know.'

'You know?'

'I saw her. She came to the garden.'

'She what?'

'She came to the garden with her mother.'

'How do you know? Did she say anything?'

'Will, I could see.'

'Of course. I – I didn't mean ... I meant how did you know it was her?'

'Oh, I've known for a long time.'

Will was silent, and Josie felt reluctant to explain. She said quietly: 'It was Tom. He'd been following you. He told me where she lived.'

She thought she heard Will swallow. 'And you went to her flat? She never said.'

'I saw her come out one day.'

'I see.'

'She's hard to miss.'

Will cleared his throat. The conversation was moving too fast, too soon. He didn't want to talk about Katy. Didn't want to try to explain. Instead he said:

'Josie, there's something else.'

'Oh?'

'I don't know whether your mother told you, but I took a painting.'

Josie waited.

'It was the one you grabbed hold of to protect yourself. It was mangled. There was blood all over it, and I thought ... Well, at any rate, I took it with me. It's a portrait I think, but it was difficult to make out. I've taken it to a restorer. I don't know what he can do with it but …'

'You've taken her to a restorer?' Josie gave a bitter laugh. 'I've been dreading that painting. Dreading seeing her again. She's been the cause of everything. You don't know …'

Will was astonished. 'But I thought you'd be pleased. I thought –'

'I'm sorry, Will. I appreciate your efforts but really, I don't want it back. Especially now.'

Will was silent. He was thinking that whatever efforts he tried to make were, as ever, either misjudged or too late to be of value.

But he pulled himself up, not wanting to miss this opportunity.

'Well, anyway,' he said, 'what you were saying before. We need to meet.'

'Yes.'

'Good. When?'

'When are you free? Do you want to come to the house?'

'If you'd be OK with that.'

'When do you want to come?'

'I'll come tonight.'

Will pressed the red icon to end the call. He felt relief. Relief that he didn't have to break the news. Relief that Josie was so calm about it all. At the same time, he wondered what he'd feel seeing her, being inside the house with her again, after so long.

As he drove to see Josie, Will was surprised to feel so nervous. The day's rain had finally stopped but spurts of water sprayed from his wheels as he turned into the driveway. He was not coming home. There was no place for him here anymore, and no warmth. There had been once and he had valued that. But he knew now it wasn't possible to stay still. Life pushed you forward, pulling out tricks unexpectedly. And if you tried to seize what you wanted, there was always a catch. As the longed-for prize came within reach, there was never any warning of the cost.

He opened the car door and got out. A light was on in the hall. He tapped on the front door, trying to sound informal, not wanting to be like a stranger coming to the house. He could hear her footsteps pricking across the hallway. She pulled open the door and, for a moment, they stood awkwardly, looking at each other.

'Hi,' she said brightly.

He followed her into the kitchen where the Rayburn sat cold and unused. The house being old and the walls made of stone, it was chilly at the best of times, so they normally left it on all through the summer.

'The Rayburn's off,' he said. It was a stupid opening remark.

'I was trying to save on fuel.'

So, he had walked right into it. Without preamble, the conversation would go straight to money. That was usually all that was left of an abandoned relationship.

'Drink?'

'Yes, please.'

Josie had her back to him. She was reaching to the top shelf of the cupboard for the wine glasses. 'Red or white?'

'Red.'

'What you did for me. You saved me from –'

'You've already thanked me.'

'Who knows what might have happened if you hadn't come.'

Will struggled with himself. 'I don't think you'd have bled to death. I don't think he was quite that bad. He wouldn't have left you there.'

'Maybe not, but you couldn't have known that.' She broke the seal on an unopened bottle, unscrewed the cap, and filled two glasses.

'He was sorry afterwards,' said Will. 'When the police came, he was crying.'

'In his own strange way I think he loved me.'

She handed him his glass. The wine was his favourite, a rich Burgundy. He took a sip, wondering if she had bought it specially. 'Nevertheless, I'm glad I came.'

He had expected that they would sit at the kitchen table, but Josie led him into the sitting room. This was more formal, more restrained. She sat down on the sofa and motioned him to a chair.

'I've been meaning to ask,' she said. 'What made you turn up then, at exactly the right time, in the middle of the night?'

'I don't know.'

'There must have been something.'

'I woke up. I think it might have been the noises that alerted me, thumps and bumps from down the corridor. But I felt worried. What Esme had told me was in my head. It was somehow insistent.' He shrugged his shoulders. 'I couldn't sleep. So I got up and just came over. To check, you know, to make sure.'

Josie looked at him curiously, as if about to press him for a fuller explanation, then thought better of it. 'Well, thanks anyway.' She took a mouthful of wine and put down her glass. 'So what now?'

Will wondered how much it had cost her emotionally to come to the point. Neither of them had yet mentioned the child. His child.

'Josie, I never planned …' he began.

'Didn't you?'

'No.'

He had to be careful. He realised he didn't want to betray Katy. He had to stand by her now. At the same time he wanted to spare Josie further pain.

'I didn't mean to hurt you.' He knew how pathetic that sounded.

'No.' Josie's voice was expressionless. He wondered if she believed him.

'I got caught up.'

Josie inclined her head.

Why was she being so damned understanding, he asked himself. It was making his job harder.

'You appreciate I have to put her first now,' he said. 'Because of the child.'

'I understand.'

Josie looked down at the floor. Then Will did too. Together they followed the parallel lines drawn by the floorboards across the room.

'Are you planning to come back here?' Realising what she'd said, she added quickly, 'I mean with her.'

'I don't want to turn you out.'

'No. But you'll have to, won't you?'

How was she managing to be so brave? This was her house. She'd put so much into it. Everything here reflected her care, her artistry.

'No,' he said. 'But we'll have to sell it, I'm afraid.'

She nodded. 'I see that.'

'Divide the money.'

'Could you …?' She stopped. 'Could you afford to keep it, buy me out, if you sold her flat?'

He shook his head. 'It wouldn't fetch enough. But we can stay on in the flat for a while,' he said, offering her a little hope. 'You don't have to go just yet.'

'Perhaps I do. It would be difficult to sell in the depths of winter and, besides, I'd have to keep an eye on the garden, prepare it for next spr ...' She stopped. He thought she was going to cry. 'I don't think I could bear that.'

Will thought he had never admired her so much. He'd never seen her so calm, so accepting. He wanted to take her in his arms. Instead, he put his glass down, leant back in his chair and sighed. 'Oh, Josie, I'm so sorry.'

Just then the house phone rang. Josie made no move to get up. They sat looking at each other as the answerphone clicked on. Then they heard Esme's voice, loud and excited:

'Great news, Josie. I've just sold another painting!'

Josie

I draw up outside Esme's house. She made me promise to come over as soon as Will had gone. So here I am.

'How did it go?' Esme leads me into the kitchen. She sits me on a metal stool at the breakfast bar. Everything is white and uncluttered around us, low-lighting skittering across the shiny surfaces.

'It went OK,' I say, blankly. 'Now that I know the score, I suppose I can start making proper plans.'

Esme hands me a glass of wine.

'Except that I do have to sell the house.'

'Ah!' She pushes a bowl of cashew nuts over to me. 'That will be quite a wrench.'

'At least it's not going to that woman!' I take a few nuts.

'So, she wasn't casing the joint?'

'It seems not.'

'Then I wonder what she was doing?'

I shrug. 'Idle curiosity, I suppose. Wondering what Will's place looked like. What he was leaving behind ...'

'Maybe.'

'Did you talk about money at all?'

'Not really. He just said I'd have half the proceeds of the house.'

Esme dips her head. 'That seems fair.'

'And there's no hurry to sell.'

'That too.'

'Actually, it's more than fair. Despite what Katy might imagine, he hasn't got the money to go on paying his half of the mortgage.'

'Then he's doing it for you.'

'So it seems. But I can't go on living there knowing I have to give it all up. I'd rather cut my losses and go now.'

'Did you tell him that?'

'Yes.'

'What did he say?'

'He looked sad. And then the phone rang and it was you telling me I'd sold another painting.'

'I don't expect you to be able to appreciate that right now.'

In answer I look away and study a small cartoon hanging on the wall. Esme changes the subject.

'By the way, I had something to eat earlier with Nathan, before he went out, but if you're hungry I can easily rustle something up.'

'Thanks, but I don't really want anything. These are fine.' I help myself to more cashews.

'Well, if you change your mind ...'

'I'd rather talk.'

'Sure. How are you feeling about it all?'

'Not as bad as I thought. But then, I've been expecting this for a while.'

'Have you?'

'Of course. It had to happen. It was the inevitable outcome.'

'Even so.'

'Well, it's a strange thing, but I think I've turned a corner. It's only just happened.' I force animation into my voice. 'I feel strong, poised. That's why I was able to ring him and arrange to see him. And now that I've seen him, now I've heard it all from his own lips instead of through other people, I feel peaceful somehow. As though I can cope.'

I look across and catch an expression of disbelief on Esme's face.

'But maybe I'm just kidding myself that I can cope with all this,' I add quickly. I realise I haven't cried for a while now. Seeing Will today should have dredged up the pain again. Instead I feel nothing.

Esme rises from her stool and fetches the bottle of Pinot Grigio from the fridge. She refills our glasses and brings over another packet of cashews. Handing them to me, she says: 'I think from what you're describing, what's happening to you at the moment is you're entering a frozen state: you're in denial.'

I look up, my head propped on one hand.

'It's such a huge thing, splitting up with someone,' Esme says carefully. 'I think you'll need quite a long time to process it all.' She pauses as if waiting for a response. I sit, unmoving. 'And you'll go backwards and forwards between pain and denial.'

'Is this your therapist's hat you're wearing?'

'That's the one I've been trying not to wear. But, actually, yes. With or without that hat as you call it, the signs are pretty obvious.'

'You mean because I'm not crying anymore.'

'I mean because you've locked off your feelings.'

'But I've done a lot of crying. And resting. All that time my mother was with me. All that time I was processing Will leaving me.'

'You were recovering from Tom's assault. You've hardly begun with this.' She changes tone, speaking more softly. 'Josie, you've had a lot to contend with. More than you realise. More than most people have to cope with in one go. And you need time to find out who you are, who the new Josie is.'

'The Josie without Will.'

Esme nods sagely. I feel like a client who has said the right thing. I want to impress her further.

'And', I begin, looking meaningfully at her across the table at her, 'the Josie without the child.'

Esme leaves the remark hanging. Which child does she think I mean?

At last she says quietly: 'It's no bad thing to tend the inner child – your creativity, if you like. But you need to be in a stable place to do it. Which is why I think this idea of change, of selling up, might be harder than you imagine.'

'Well, what do you think I should do about it?'

'Now you've told me that Will isn't pushing you to sell the house, it seems to me, if you delayed the move for a while, you could press on with your paintings. I mean, I know they're important in themselves, but painting them must surely be therapeutic too.' She looks at me encouragingly. 'And, just think: if you did some more and sold really well, you'd have more money for the move.'

'I can see what you're saying, but it would help Will if I moved.'

'I know, and that's really good of you. But I still think it would be a huge emotional wrench. What with all the packing up and everything.'

'Of course, there's the question of the garden,' I begin.

'Exactly. And you use that for your inspiration. What would happen if you …'

'I know.'

'Look, I'm only trying to help you with all this. Leaving the counsellor part out of it, there's still the fact that I'm not only your friend but also your agent. And, speaking in both capacities, it seems to me the garden's important.'

'But maybe I need to move away from that, too. Maybe I need a different setting – something more urban?'

Esme frowns. 'I'm not sure. Your garden seems to be such a part of it.'

'I use the shapes as a backdrop.'

'Whatever. The point is it works. So promise me you'll consider putting off the move. It could be really important that you stay on there while you're in the flow.'

'That painting you just sold. Was it Paul who bought it?'

'I thought you'd never ask. Yes, it was.'

I know I should be pleased – more than pleased, elated. Esme has been showing my work to a dealer, Paul Redmond.

'And he likes the new direction you're going in. If you want to keep him interested, I think you should keep your new approach just as it is.'

'Is that what he said?'

Her eyes are glowing with pleasure. 'It's a good explanation but, actually, I don't think he knows why he likes them. I think he's just got a nose for these things. He's even talked of giving you an exhibition. So you need to get on with them.'

'Oh, so now my agent wants to browbeat me into action!'

'He's the only one who's interested at the moment. But he's a good bet. And he wants to get you noticed.'

'I know. And I'm really grateful. But I don't know where I'm going with them.'

Esme smiles. 'It doesn't matter. As long as you have some idea of what informs them, that's enough. There's no need to spell it out.'

'You're right again. I suppose it's not my job to explain.'

Esme fills our glasses once more. She climbs back onto her stool and leans an elbow on the breakfast bar. 'Actually, Josie,' she says, 'talking of your paintings …'

'Yes?'

'There is one in particular – a painting that your mother and I came across when we were clearing up. I think it's the one you were working on when ...'

'I haven't been able to finish that one,' I say, almost savagely.

'I understand. But, perhaps you should. It's your most powerful piece to date. In fact, I'm taking a risk here, but I think it might help you to work through some of what's happened.'

Josie

Esme was right. After living in the denial, the emptiness, I feel the thaw slowly begin, the pain return. And now it spasms across my chest continually, restricting my breathing, slowing everything I do. I still paint every day. Burying myself in a canvas is my only solace. As I look out from my studio I sometimes see people in my garden. I even hear little delighted exclamations and, for a split second, think they are late visitors enjoying its dying beauties. Then I see them stand and peer up at the house, assessing it, and realise they are potential buyers, usurpers of my little paradise.

For a while now, the 'For Sale' sign has brooded at the gate like a gallows, a final judgement on my relationship with Will. Ours has been a brave attempt to merge two hearts and minds of such disparate material that the attempt was bound to fail. This is the conclusion I cling to now. So, despite what Esme urged, there's no point delaying the sale for selfish reasons, especially if it compromises Will's ability to look after his new child.

But there is one thing I've determined to do while I'm still here. And today I'm doing it. I'm tackling the painting I've been dreading – the one Esme challenged me to finish, insisting it might help. I need help. I'll resort to anything, even that painting, if there is the faintest chance of finding some relief, some resolution. But this is my darkest painting. Finishing it will take me to the brink.

The large canvas lies across my easel. Already I have murky pools of Prussian blue on my palette, a wet splatter of dead crows on the bones. Dipping my brush into the blue, I reach up to the eagles flying across and start touching up their wings. As I do so, I imagine I hear the sounds again – the sighing of my name, the moving door handle. I put my brush down, select another and make a pale mix of Cremnitz white and Naples yellow. I begin filling the gaps in the blue with yellow-white bones.

As I engage with the painting, I try to empty my mind, concentrate on each stroke, hoping I can somehow find a turning point. But instead the questions come again, the arguments I've been hiding. Why did I defy Will, my mother, all of them? Why did I ignore the obvious way forward, and follow a beckoning phantasm? No wonder none of them supported me. And where am I now? Where has the witchy child led me? Inside the canvas, with bones all around me. Death is all I can see. Death of hope, death of relationship, death of love.

Will

Will sat in his car, shaking. He'd thought she was using the cards to manipulate him. He'd thought that all along she was in control, and part of him had hated her for it. There was no doubt she *had* manipulated him. But now he saw for the first time that she was their victim too. She said she had done it in obedience to their message. She said she believed in them implicitly. And wasn't it all proving true anyway? He could see there was a kind of ridiculous nobility in her foolishness, a martyrish impulse in her service to the cards, and to what she regarded as her fate. But what an appalling price to pay! Unless she somehow knew there was no other real option.

After she and her mother had sat him down and told him everything, after he'd absorbed the initial shock, there were so many questions he had wanted to ask. It made sense, of course. Finally, it made sense of all the mysteries, all the revelations that had happened, one after the other. Especially Katy's so-called greatest magic. Withholding that had taken the most ingenuity. He had been angry then, angry at being duped so cleverly by the two of them. It was a cheap trick they'd pulled on him. Now he didn't know what to feel about Katy. Whether to admire her or hate her. Mostly he felt pity. He feared for her now and, yes, he felt responsible. It was his child she had chosen, after all. Above everything. 'It was there in the cards all along,' she said. 'The shining child.'

She'd shown him the picture on her card and he'd seen for himself how the child blazed in the sunlight like a divine thing: his child, his light, his little beacon. But how much had that innocent-seeming child extracted in payment for its gift of itself? There seemed to be no end to its demands – from him, from her. Especially from her. And how was he to cope? Tears started and he didn't know who they were for – Katy, himself, or even Josie.

He thought of Josie now. Bravely working in her studio, looking out over the garden she'd created, watching it die in reds and golds. Something in him yearned to stop all this happening. But fate was pitiless, and there was no glorious last blaze in human death unless, as Katy said, it brought about new life. It was brave and it was an explanation, but it wasn't good enough. He banged his hands on the steering wheel. His palms were stinging as he opened the glove compartment, took out a packet of cigarettes and lit one. Smoke filled the car and hurt his eyes. He was glad. He deserved it. He'd never taken her seriously. To him, she'd been nothing more than mistress material. He hadn't really known her at all. Until now, he had no idea she could be so stupidly unselfish. The realisation almost made him love her.

Josie

Pulled by the child, I know I have to go through this. I have to enter the painting, die among the bones and wait to be delivered. There is white paint on my brush. One moment I'm painting and the next I'm inside – the smear of white on my face, the smell of turpentine, the bones heaped over me. *Caput Mortuum*. Death's Head. Two holes in a white skull. The bones shift as I breathe.

Then I hear the wings. Whirring, coming close, hammering in my ears. Huge birds alighting on the bones, their wing beats on setting off as loud as an earthquake. A dark wing takes me and I soar into the sky. Blinded by stars I can see nothing.

And now I am falling from the painting, tumbling onto the pale straw matting in my studio. I pull myself up, stumble to the window, steady myself on the sill. As I struggle to catch my breath I'm searching for a quote, a scrap of wisdom – anything to pin me to the light. The words of a psalm come to me, remembered from schooldays: 'I will lift up mine eyes unto the hills, from whence cometh my help.'

I gaze at the horizon. The Sugar Loaf is rising behind the holy mountain, its crown splintering into ash-white smoke.

My mobile rings, the jerky tune snatching me from my visionary world.

'Mrs Jones?'

'Yes.'

'It's Sue from Marchant Properties. You'll be pleased to hear we may have found you a buyer.'

'Oh!'

'They're a very nice couple. I think you'll be glad to know they not only loved the house, they completely fell in love with the garden. The wife's a keen gardener and she wants to keep it up. So, anyway, they've asked to have another look round this afternoon, when they're hoping to measure up –'

'Measure up?'

'For their furniture.'

'Oh, yes, of course.'

'Obviously, I told them there was no chain. That you could move out anytime. I think that made the whole thing even more attractive. The market's so slow these days, and so many sales fall through.'

'Do they have a house to sell themselves?'

'No. That's the beauty of it. They're first-time buyers – a young couple, about to get married, and this would be their first house. They've got a mortgage provisionally agreed, so I think they can move quickly. They're a lovely couple. I think you'd like them.'

As I put down my mobile, I notice I'm shaking slightly. Selling the dream, that's what it feels like. Selling the dream to another pair of young hopefuls bravely conjuring their own little Eden.

I press the speed dial button for Will's number and hear his voice speaking the familiar recorded message. I try to make my voice sound light, happy for him.

'Will,' I say, 'it's me. We may already have a buyer.'

Will

Will had asked his mother to meet him at the pub. When he told her the news, she seemed unmoved. But he noticed she had the grace to leave her ploughman's lunch untouched. Returning from the bar, he heard the bleep of his phone on the table and glanced down. He saw it was a voicemail from Josie. His mother was sitting opposite him. She watched his face while he listened. As he put the phone down, he struggled to keep his face impassive.

'It's Josie. She thinks she's got a buyer for the house.'

Frieda let out a fast breath. 'Oh, but!' she began.

'But what?'

'Surely you're not thinking of going ahead with all that, now?'

'I've got to. What else can I do?'

'But the child needs a house, a garden to run around in.'

'Mother, you're forgetting about Josie.'

'Well, she hardly contributed to it financially, did she? It should be yours by right.'

'The law doesn't work like that, Mother. We're married. The house is in joint names, I can't just throw her out. Besides –'

'Besides what? That woman hasn't cared for you – she's just pursued her own interests. Wouldn't even consent to have a child with you.'

'Well, I'm not in need of children now, am I?' His voice had a tinge of bitterness. 'In any case, it wasn't like that with Josie and you know it!'

'If she'd gone along with that treatment in the first place, you wouldn't be in this mess now.' Casting a venomous look towards a young couple sitting on adjacent stools at the bar, their arms about each other, she added, muttering, 'And goodness knows what the child will be like with a mother like that!'

Will was outraged. 'But you know it won't have a mother like that!'

'Well, you know what I mean!' Frieda snapped, then looked away and sipped her drink. Falling silent was the nearest she ever came to an apology.

Josie

I'm still in my studio when I hear a car coming down the drive. It must be the potential buyers. Until now the agent has taken care of all the viewings. Today, although the agent is with them, I will have to meet the 'lovely couple'. There's nowhere for me to hide. So far I've managed to keep the studio out-of-bounds, but serious buyers will obviously want to see inside. I know they'll go round the house first, then the garden, and finally the studio. What will they use my studio for? A workshop, a garden store? Or might they convert it into a holiday let? I begin preparing myself to meet them. It should be half an hour or so before they appear – time enough for me to view them first in the garden. A car door slams and footsteps approach the studio. So there is only one person. It must be the agent arriving in advance. Hearing a tap on the door, I put down my brush and go to open it.

To my astonishment I discover Frieda standing outside swathed in her dreadful bismuth yellow raincoat, her pink face thrust forward, inches from my own.

'May I come in?' she says.

It seems anyone can invade my territory now. It's my *Holy-of-holies* no longer. I swing back the door and motion Frieda to a chair.

'Coffee?'

'No thank you, dear.'

Frieda is looking round the room, evidently feeling far from her comfort zone. 'Josie,' she begins, then stops.

I've rarely seen her stuck for words, but evidently what she's come to say is difficult to express.

'I'm sorry,' she says.

I'm still standing. I look down at her enquiringly.

'I'm sorry I haven't been back to see you. You see ...'

'I know,' I say.

'So, although, of course, I didn't want to, I had to go along with ...'

'I understand.'

'But you must see, dear, how difficult it is for me now.'

She looks down to where her fingers are fidgeting with her rings. I wonder what she's summoning the strength to say.

'Now that the situation's changed, I wondered whether you'd reconsider.'

Reconsider what? Splitting with Will? Having him back?

Frieda looks up at me. 'Selling the house.'

'Selling the house? But I thought he wanted that.'

'He did. But now everything's different. He needs it.'

'Why? What's different now?' As she speaks, a wild thought enters my head. 'Has there been a miscarriage?' I ask.

'No.' Frieda looks surprised. 'I thought you knew.'

'Knew what?'

'I thought Will had been in touch with you – that you'd talked. About the house and everything.'

'We've talked about the house,' I say, 'but nothing else. What is it you think I should know?'

'You mean you *really* don't know.' Frieda sounds genuinely astonished.

'Know what?'

'That she's dying.'

'What!' I need several seconds to understand what she's saying. Questions form in my mind, one foremost.

'But what about the baby?'

'They think it will survive.'

'Then how? Why?'

'She never told him. He never had any choice in the matter. And now he's going to be lumbered with a family. On his own. With no house, no garden, no one to ...' Frieda takes out a linen handkerchief and blows her nose.

'What do you mean she never told him?'

'She knew. Weeks ago she discovered she had cancer. But she never said. And then, after it was too late to do anything about it, she told him.'

I stare at her. I'm still trying to take in the information.

'She refused treatment. She said she'd done it for the baby. She said she had to – she said it was in the cards.' Frieda starts to cry noisily.

My mind is spinning with the implications of the news, my image of Katy dissolving and reforming into something new, totally unsuspected.

'But suppose she didn't know before,' I say. 'Suppose she only found out after she got pregnant? That would be a difficult choice.'

'Then why didn't she tell him before it was too late? Why didn't she let him in on the decision? Surely he had a right to know? The manipulative bitch!' Frieda's face is fierce with condemnation.

It is in this moment that I see Katy clearly – as a glow of rose madder. And Esme was right. The crescent moons and stars are a blind; the cards are what she lives by. They're what give her life meaning.

'The reason she didn't tell him', I say, 'was because he didn't believe in the cards.'

'Well, of course not. Why should he?' Frieda says angrily. 'But that wasn't the only thing! There was never any genuine feeling there; she was just using my son. What she really wanted was his support and his money to help care for –'

At that moment there's a tap on the door. It opens and the agent peers in.

'Just to let you know the couple have arrived,' she says cheerily. 'Can I show them into the house?'

Frieda looks at me, an unspoken plea in her eyes.

'I'm afraid', I say, 'there's been a sudden change of plan. I've just heard some bad news. A serious illness in the – in the family. I'm sure you understand. This is not the time to be selling up.'

Will

'I'm so sorry, Will.'

They were sitting at a table in Artco. Tom no longer worked there. The young woman who'd replaced him brought over a couple of soft drinks.

Will's face was drawn.

'Why didn't you tell me?' asked Josie.

Will shook his head. 'How could I? It was bad enough your finding out about the ...'

'Baby?'

He nodded.

'But the baby's going to be OK?'

'That's what they say.'

'How is she?'

'Who? Katy? Not at all good, but bearing up.'

'She's quite strong then.'

'In a way, yes.'

'Are you angry with her?' Josie immediately regretted the question. Will's face closed. 'I'm sorry,' she said. 'It's just that when she came to see me your mother said –'

'Oh, God!' Will put his head in his hands. 'Listen, Josie, I didn't know. You must believe me. I had no idea my mother would do that. I thought I'd put her in her place at last. I thought ...' He looked up. 'I swear I didn't know she'd try to stop ...'

'Stop what? Stop me selling the house?'

'Yes.'

He was struggling with himself.

'But, Josie, it's not too late to get the buyers back, is it? I mean, I know I'm in a mess but we can still sell the place, can't we? That *is* what you want, isn't it?'

Josie glanced towards the counter, where a middle-aged couple were paying their bill.

'I don't know.'

The waitress arrived and placed two plates of warm chicken salad in front of them. As they ate, Josie looked at Will. He ate mechanically, overwhelmed by events.

'How will you manage?' Josie said at last. 'With the baby. After she's gone.'

'Her mother's offered to help. She's very good, you know. She's very good with Katy. In fact Katy's already taken her in to help look after ...' Will stopped, leaving the sentence hanging. Looking at Josie's face, it occurred to him that his mother hadn't told her everything. If Josie didn't yet know, he didn't want to be the one to tell her – at least not now. For the time being, the news of the new baby and Katy's dying were more than enough. He looked away.

'I've seen *her*, too,' Josie said quietly.

'What?' Will's head shot round. 'Who?'

'Her mother. She was with Katy when she came to the garden. They came together.'

Will's face conveyed both pain and relief.

'I'm so sorry, Josie. That was a most extraordinary thing. I've never understood.' He paused, lost for words, and looked round at the walls as if seeking inspiration. His glance fell on one of Josie's new works.

'I'm beginning to wonder if it wasn't a kind of test.'

'But – what?'

'I think they were scoping out the place, and for some reason they were scoping me out at the same time.'

'But why, in God's name?'

Josie shrugged. 'I expect for the same reason Frieda came round.'

Will was increasingly confused.

'Frieda told me I was being selfish, selling the house.'

'She said that?'

'Yes. That now you had a family, you'd need the place yourself, and the child would need the garden to run around in. She said that if I had any feelings left for you or any sense of gratitude for what you'd provided for me in the past few years, then the least I could do was move out and hand it all over to you.'

'Oh, my God, Josie. I had no idea, I swear!'

'So you really didn't put Frieda up to it?'

'Absolutely not!' Will looked at her anxiously but saw Josie was laughing at him. The sound of her laughter was wonderful. He'd never expected to hear it again.

'Oh, Josie, what a mess we've made ...' he began. His voice was wistful. 'If only ...'

'It's too late for "if onlys",' Josie said briskly. 'And in any case, we've both moved on now.'

'Well you certainly have,' said Will, pulling himself together. He indicated the canvases on the walls around them. 'All this new work of yours. Quite remarkable.'

Josie laughed. 'Do you like it?'

He thought there was a touch of mischief in her voice. 'I think it's very accomplished,' he said carefully.

'But do you like it?'

'All right. Yes, I do. I think it's odd but it has something, even for a philistine like me – though I can't say I understand it.'

'That's all right. Neither do I.'

Will looked at her incredulously. 'What do you mean?' he said.

'I mean just that.'

After she'd gone, Will lingered in the restaurant, looking at Josie's paintings, reluctant to go back to the office. She had certainly changed her style. It was now semi-abstract and she'd used a lot of subtle shades with bright colours leaping out incongruously – yellow and white and red. But in each strange, surreal canvas, there were shapes he thought he recognised woven into the patterns: bits of the garden and, here and there, unexpectedly, aspects of himself – the line of his nose, the tail of his eye. Then, of course, there were some paintings he didn't like. There were ones with huge black orbs with spindly white lines inside them. But others were more playful – suns and moons and fantastical creatures bowing violins and blowing horns. These were images he thought he could make out, but then he'd look again and notice only random shapes and colours. It was all a weird puzzle to him, yet in a way it affected him and made him glad.

He left the coffee house, deep in thought. It was clear to him, Josie had moved to a new space in her art, and in her head. But the house was another thing. She was trying to be generous. But could he really expect her to give that up? More particularly, could he expect her to give up her precious garden for another woman's family to run around in? He kicked at a stone on the pavement. None of it was right. She should stay on. He'd find somewhere else. That was the answer.

But where would he go? There was Katy's flat, of course. The thought of it pained him. It smelled of sickness. The ruins of her spells were everywhere. He tried not to resent her but it was difficult. After all, it wasn't any magic that had produced the child – it was her cunning and duplicity that had brought it into being. He found himself thinking bitterly that if it was just a case of his child, he might have had a chance. Josie might, in time, have come to love it. But the complete legacy she'd left him was too much.

Josie

The year is turning slowly and painfully. Life is withdrawing from the garden and I am trying to capture its embers in my paintings. Visions of death still haunt me, but now they are tangled with thoughts of Katy. In her the balance of death and birth will come together, the one yielding to the other. I still don't know whether Katy had any choice in the matter. Did she really choose to sacrifice herself for the sake of the child? Of course, I know what Esme would say. Esme would ask how much freedom of choice Katy had outside the cards anyway. Then I think of my own vision, my belief in the painted child. That child is less real than any child in Katy's womb. And yet I've thrown my life at it.

Though preoccupied by these thoughts, my work is going well. Already I have quite a collection of new pieces. More and more canvases appear on the walls of Artco and a smattering of red stickers announce some sales. Paul, the 'discerning dealer', as Esme has dubbed him, is agitating for an exhibition. To date, Esme has kept him from meeting me. Cultivating me as a reclusive genius is her way of increasing the mystery surrounding my paintings.

The eagle painting, the one I feared so much, is now finished and hanging on my wall. I know the dark place it has come from only too well. The illustration I used showed only the bones and the eagles above them. The bones in their twisted, sinewy heap seemed to me morbid, abhorrent. But after I'd been inside the canvas, I felt an unexpected liberation. I discovered the bones were just bones, the vestiges of flesh that clung to them merely remnants of the lives they'd once supported. Death is still part of life. It has its own truths. And as for the eagles flying above the bones, I understand now they symbolise the work itself, the endless process of death and renewal.

And I've added something new. Between the winged confusion of the blue eagles, titanium yellow and white stars leap out, spilling light over the heap of bones below. I added the stars, not only in a bright blaze, but in a bold pattern which interacts with the birds, making the whole thing like a dance.

'It's a true inspiration,' Esme said, her eyes shining when I showed it to her. 'It's everything I imagined it could be. In fact, I think it's your greatest painting.'

Josie

It's the last Saturday in October and I am driving down the dual carriageway. As the road makes its final long swing towards the town, the familiar cone of the Sugar Loaf fails to appear. Blotted out by mist and drizzle, it is indistinguishable from the sky. I turn into the car park on the edge of town, and get out, battling the wind with my umbrella. The Blorenge is still visible, its blurred grey bulk bounding the horizon. Despite the fact that I am meeting Esme, I feel depressed.

At a metal table in Artco, and with my paintings hanging on the walls around her, Esme beckons me over. She seems more excited than usual.

'This isn't just a social,' she says, after we've kissed briefly. 'It's a business meeting, too.' She pauses to order our coffees then comes straight to the point. 'As you know, Paul was planning to give you an exhibition next year, but now it seems he can offer you space earlier than expected. Someone's dropped out and he wants to bring your exhibition forward. He thinks it'll be good to have it in mid-December, in time for Christmas.'

'That's great.'

'I know,' Esme agrees, ignoring my lack of enthusiasm. 'And you'll have enough work ready by then. Paul's saying he wants to meet you as soon as possible. He's been asking for a while and I've held him off long enough. It's time you got to know each other, so I'll arrange a meeting.'

'That's fine by me.'

'The only thing is, you'll have to go prepared.'

'What do you mean?'

'I mean, we've got to stage it right. I've built you up as this mysterious artist and you've got to act the part. For a start you need to be able to spout convincingly about your paintings. I don't mean explain them, I mean talk about their inspiration, their symbolism ... that kind of thing.'

'Or not,' I say.

'What do you mean?'

'I haven't a clue what they're about and I'm not about to start bullshitting to please anybody.'

'Oh!' Esme's face registers momentary dismay. Quickly recovering, she says: 'Well, perhaps that's the way to go after all. Say nothing. Refuse to be drawn. That could be just what would put you on the map.'

'I don't know about any map,' I say, 'but as for meeting Paul Redmond, I think it's high time I did.'

'So do I. But when you do, don't be too quick to judge him. He might seem a bit flamboyant, but there's more to him than meets the eye.'

Next day Esme drives us both to Bath. Paul's flat is in the middle of the grand sweep of the Royal Crescent, commanding an uninterrupted view of the lawn below. He plans to hold my exhibition in his honey-stoned gallery in the centre of town, near the Abbey. As we ascend the wide stairway, I look up at the high ceiling where a chandelier hangs. The proportions of eighteenth-century buildings never fail to elate me. We reach the second floor and Esme taps on a door painted a discreet shade of pebble grey.

When Paul swings the door open, he regards me, I think, with some surprise. I wonder if he expected someone older. Paul himself, I'm guessing, is in his mid forties. He is dressed in a pearl-white shirt and Venetian red trousers. The shirt is slightly ruffled at the sleeves. He wears a silk waistcoat decorated like an abstract painting, which curves over his slight paunch. His auburn hair flows to the top of his shoulders, completing the Regency image.

'This is Josie,' Esme announces, with a mixture of pride and respect in her voice.

'I've long awaited this meeting.' Paul takes my extended hand and kisses it with old-fashioned courtesy. 'This is a wonderful moment. Wonderful! Come inside!'

We enter the drawing room. A careful juxtaposition of antique furniture and modern art reveals a keen eye for the aesthetic. He waves us towards two Georgian armchairs and lifts a gold-necked bottle from a bucket of ice-cubes.

'High time for this, I think.' He pops the cork and fills the champagne flutes to overflowing.

'To success in your exhibition, Josie!' He raises his glass.

'Hear, hear!' echoes Esme, raising hers too.

'This is such good news – my gallery being able to accommodate you so soon. But, of course, it means we'll have to hurry the publicity in time for the preview. It's not how I normally like to do things – I like more of a run-up, but in the circumstances I thought why not just surrender to fortune?'

'Why not, indeed?' Esme laughs.

Paul turns his gaze in my direction.

I raise my glass, angling it towards him. 'I'm very happy to be in your hands. Both of you,' I add, throwing an inclusive glance at Esme.

'Well, we have great hopes,' says Paul. 'I've been in touch with various collectors, and already there seems to be considerable interest.'

'There's nothing like it,' Esme says. 'It's an extraordinary vision. Unique.'

'May one enquire what ignites this spark of genius?' Paul asks.

I study the polished floorboards while considering my reply. The others wait patiently, as if for the words of a genius.

'It's not unique,' I say. 'Because, actually, there is nothing unique. There's nothing new under the sun. It's all been done before.'

Paul chokes on his champagne. Esme swings round and gapes at me. I remain unfazed.

'The only new vision that can possibly be achieved', I say, 'comes through trying to see things in a different light.'

I can tell from their faces that this isn't enough.

Esme drains her champagne and puts down the glass.

'OK, if you want something more definite,' I say at last, 'then I can quote my mentor, the Russian mystic Ouspensky: "In art we find the first experiments in a language of the future."'

There is an audible release of tension in the room. Paul is squirreling away the sound bite. He asks me no more questions about my art, and I am grateful for that.

'My God!' Esme says as we drive home. 'I thought for a moment you were going to blow it!'

'I won't be compromised by anything,' I say decisively. 'I refuse to cultivate a fake personal image. Paul's doing enough of that by himself.'

'But you have to ...' Esme begins. 'Everyone has to nowadays. It's what ...' She breaks off and remains in thought as we drive up the seemingly endless hill towards the motorway. 'OK,' she concedes at last. 'If you're determined, that's it! You're uncompromising. You say it like it is. That'll be your image.'

'No,' I say. 'That'll be me.'

Josie

Despite my reservations about him, I can't help being encouraged by the faith Paul has shown in me. I spend the next weeks furiously finishing my last few canvases before the Bath exhibition. I am carried by the energy of it, the drive towards the deadline. But this time my energy is of a different sort. I've left behind the nervousness that drove me. Now it's the thrill of the work itself, the creative excitement that keeps me to it.

When I have leisure to think of the house at all, I find myself wondering what I'll feel when the time comes to give it over to Will. I don't have to worry yet about the practicalities of the move. Will's going to sell Katy's flat first and use that money to buy me out. If I do well at the exhibition, I can add more money to the fund, possibly enough to buy a small cottage – something a bit tumble-down with a wild garden I can tame. Also, if I want, I can rent a studio elsewhere. But I doubt I'll do that. Living on my own I'll probably use the dining room as my studio and crowd the cottage walls with my canvases.

Will rings me from time to time. I know things are hard for him. He needs my support and that's fine. We aren't divorced yet, after all. I wonder if I'll go on seeing him after the child is born and he's moved back into our house. What will I feel, I wonder, seeing my precious garden with his child in it – Katy's child? Will it even belong there? From time to time I glance at the corner of my studio where my own child once was. I told Will to destroy her portrait, and in its absence the pain is easing. I've almost made peace with her, with her strange beckoning and then her sudden abandonment of me. Now she represents the only child I might ever have – a wish, a dream, a wraith of a thing whose pale face will haunt me for ever. But why she came to me in the first place I'll never know.

Josie

Esme drives me into Bath in good time for the preview. I'm wearing a long indigo skirt slit up the side to reveal a length of leg, and my high vermilion heels. Over the skirt flows a tangerine blouse splattered with abstract motifs. I want to look as if I've just climbed out of one of my own paintings.

Before we open the doors to the guests, I place a red sticker beside a large canvas.

'That one's already spoken for,' I tell Esme firmly.

'I'm not surprised,' Esme says.

As soon as the first guests arrive, Paul, resplendent in a turquoise silk jacket, takes them in hand. 'It's a new vision,' he tells them, 'and the artist has selected a series of quotes which you can read as you go round. They help illumine her work. Her vision is extremely daring and uncompromising – much of it inspired by the workings of the unconscious, as you'll see for yourselves.'

As the guests go round looking at the paintings, they are given only short quotes by way of explanation. Paul has taken the quotes from Ouspensky that I gave him and broken them into aphorisms, then used them to intersperse the canvases:

Art is based on emotional understanding.

Art is based on the feeling of the Unknown.

Art expresses a certain fugitive sensation.

The final quote is:

In art we find the first experiments in a language of the future.

This is the one Paul used in all the publicity.

It isn't long before the gallery begins filling up. To my surprise a clutch of red stickers rapidly appears beside some of the canvases.

'Is there a smaller one that I can actually afford!' enquires a familiar hearty voice.

Dominic is advancing across the space towards me.

'My dear,' he says, enveloping me in his capacious arms, 'what a triumph!'

Close behind him is Isobel, with Nathan following behind. Paul advances graciously towards them. He takes Isobel's hand and kisses it with his usual flourish.

'Oh, Josie,' says Isobel, 'you've already sold some!' She looks round the room. 'Even that one ...' she points towards the large painting hanging on the end wall with angular yellow-white shapes splashed across the top of it.

'Yes,' I say. 'That was actually the first to go!'

'Well, in a way, I'm not surprised. It's very fine.'

I turn away quickly and go to fetch her a glass of wine. By the time I return, Isobel is deep in conversation with Esme.

True to his word, after a lot of deliberation, and with much tactful help from Paul, Dominic finally selects a small canvas. It is strongly patterned like the rest and, viewed in a certain light, could be seen as the outline of two people fused together, but looking in different directions.

'A splendid work. Splendid!' he says, squeezing my arm as Paul places the red sticker over the price beside it.

I overhear Nathan holding forth to a group of younger art-lovers. 'Yes, one can see the influence there – various mystical elements derived from the Metaphysical school. Of course, they've been given quite a new treatment but still, to the academic eye ...'

I smile and turn away. I had determined to keep quiet but, after a couple more glasses of champagne, I start to comment on my art. I speak of the mute promptings of an unspoken language, the rich legacy of symbolism and imagery. My words receive several murmurs of approval and appreciation. Enough for me to feel I've at last made a small beginning in realising my vision.

After the exhibition ends and most of the paintings have been either taken down or taken away to grace new walls, and new homes, the large canvas still hangs there. The one against which I placed the first red sticker.

Paul puts his hands either side of the canvas and lifts it down carefully. It is heavy, the largest one on display.

'I see you held this one back,' he says. 'So where's it to go? In the van with the rest?'

'Would you do me a special favour?'

'You know you only have to ask!'

'Will you deliver it to Esme?'

'Oh, my dear, what a splendid gesture!'

Paul props it carefully against the wall, before coming over and embracing me.

Josie

Winter deepens and the mountains blend once more into the horizon. But on rare fine mornings the Sugar Loaf reappears, its familiar cone sparkling as if frosted in sugar crystals. In the garden below there are only silhouettes of dead things to paint, branches and twigs, bare bones. Yet I press them into service, using the twisted outlines as backbones to a series of new paintings.

Snow arrives at the end of December, smothering the lawn and strewing white webs across the trees. I make several sketches and take photographs before packing up and going to my parents' house, where I've planned to spend Christmas.

Immediately on arrival I can tell they've tried hard to conjure an atmosphere of festivity. They've festooned the house with holly branches, teasels and pine cones from the garden. My father has bought a large fir tree, and the scent of pine mingles with the smell of baked biscuits. On the sideboard in the dining-room, my mother has placed painted candles and tinselled baubles nestled in ivy. All this has been done for my benefit. It reminds me of the efforts made when I was a child. I feel grateful and am even glad when my parents ask me to stay on for a few more days.

As New Year struggles into life, I return home to begin cottage-hunting in earnest. It's then I get Will's phone call saying the baby has been born prematurely. A little boy. They aren't sure whether it will survive. I wait a few days, then ring him to ask about the child. He's hanging on, he says.

Three weeks later Will rings again. He tells me that Katy and the baby are coming out of hospital. They are going to Katy's mother's house, where she can help care for Katy and the new .... He breaks down. He cries a long time, while I wait.

'Will you come with me?' he says at last, his voice pleading. 'Will you come with me to see him? I – I'll be able to hold him for the first time. He's been too delicate up to now. I don't know if I can do it. And – I know it's a lot to ask, but if you came ...'

We drive in silence to the terraced house on the outskirts of town. Will parks the car, but as I open the door to get out, he stops me.

'Before we go in, there's something I've got for you. I know you said you didn't want it, but it's in the boot. Wait there!'

He scrambles out and lifts the boot-lid. He brings out the canvas, swathed in a cloth and climbs back into the car with it.

'Don't do this to me. I don't want to see it!'

'No, wait, Josie. You don't understand. It was too late to stop it. I mean it was already restored – as well as possible, and I've just got it back. Josie you must look at it, you must! He's unwrapping the painting, holding it up. I'm turning away, reaching for the door handle.

'Josie, look!'

The child's face is inches from my own. I see again the shape of the head, the yellow hair that defines it. The child's skin is even more ghostly, bleached by the chemicals. But the eyes staring starkly from the washed out canvas are, if anything, more compelling.

'Josie, there's something else. Something I haven't told you. Something I only recently discovered, and I didn't know how to ... Yet you knew about it. You knew all along. You must have done to have painted her! But how on earth could you? They were both so extraordinarily clever. Keeping this one secret, fearing that if I found out, I'd think it was too much to take on, I'd disappear, leave her in the lurch, just like her ex ....'

'Her ex? Was she married? Did she have ...?' I force my gaze away from the painting, my mind tumbling with speculations. Without saying anything more, Will climbs out of the car, slides the painting onto the back seat and hurries me towards the house. He's shaking. I've never seen him like this before – his nervousness so extreme that it makes me feel almost calm as I walk beside him. But, as we approach the front door, I feel a sudden rush of excitement.

The door is opened by Katy's mother, who gives us a tired smile and waves us towards the living room.

Katy is lying on the sofa covered by a blanket, a weak arm hanging towards the floor. Will bends and kisses her. Katy's eyes are fixed on me, filled with a huge and desperate plea. Behind her, asleep in a cot, lies a small lemon-wrapped bundle, its face turned towards the wall. At sight of it Will begins to tremble again. This is his flesh and blood, his son. He moves towards him.

'Mummy?' a voice calls. I freeze. 'Mummy?' it calls again, uncertainly.

Then I see, cowering behind the cot and fingering the curtain edge as if it were the skirt of a gigantic deity, a child. She is about three years old. Waves of dishevelled blonde hair lie on her shoulders. She lifts her eyes and gives me a blue stare, bold yet wary.

I stare back. Is it? Could it ...? The child lets go of the curtain and comes towards me. I stand, uncertain. The child hesitates, then advances again. I drop down, my knees biting the worn carpet. The child comes near, so near, umber pupils fixed on me, eyes cobalt blue muted with olive green.

Could I, should I open my arms?

Acknowledgements

Thanks to Debbie Johnson, Catherine Kirwin, Vanessa Dodd, Pam Moolman and Deborah Gregory for listening, and for ideas, and to Ann Hulme for her artistic expertise and tuition.

About the Author

Claire Hamilton was brought up in the Temple, London, and lived in Herefordshire, Bath and Bristol, where she raised her two daughters. She finally settled in Llandogo, in Monmouthshire's Wye Valley, where she lived for eighteen years. She published books on King Arthur and the Holy Grail, and, with her partner Steve Eddy, on the Celts, and on Greek and Celtic mythology. Her popular *Maiden, Mother, Crone* and *Tales of the Celtic Bards* are fictional and poetic retellings of the Celtic myths.

Claire was a captivating harpist and storyteller, and for several years she performed in a theatrical storytelling group, the Company of Strangers. She continued to play the harp on moving to the Wye Valley, but became increasingly devoted to writing, and to her creative writing students. She was an inspiration, and many of her students came back to her year after year. She was also a keen narrowboater, finding relaxation and inspiration on the Warwickshire Avon and much of the canal network.In later years, Claire became an accomplished amateur painter, and her passion for this pastime informed her portrayal of her main character in *I, A Child*.